From da Big Island

New York defined her – Hawaii changed her

Screenplay and Novel

BILL HUTCHINSON

Published by Bill Hutchinson
Web Site: FromDaBigIsland.com

Screenplay and Novel ISBN-13: 978-0-9996268-7-0

10 9 8 7 6 5 4 3 2 1

REVIEWS:

"Great tale, well told." – Ian, Signal Hill, CA

"Living on da Big Island for two years in the early 2000's I learned very quickly about the differences from the mainland. The main character's move from New York celebrity to kama'ina is a delightful tale of transitions with plenty of local color included! What a refreshing look at many of the people who make Hawaii Island my favorite place!" – An Amazon Customer

"Fun from beginning to the end. Very light hearted read about a hardcore New Yorker who really begins to grow on you as her life takes her to "da Big Island". Her escapades turn the island into a warm, friendly, home but not without some bumps and bruises along the way. Very enjoyable and not easy to put down. Leaves me wanting more." – Bud on Amazon.com

"*From Da Big Island* is a delightful debut novel. I'm simply in love with Ruth, the protagonist. Once Ruth hits the island, I find myself smiling for the rest of the book. Talk about a fish out of water. Hope there's a sequel." – Sergio on Amazon.com

"Fantastic combination of characters and family values. The novel should be turned into a television series." – Sonja (84), Palmdale, CA

"The book *From da Big Island* by author Bill Hutchinson is a delightful and entertaining little book that I read through in almost one sitting while I had a long wait. He captures the beauty of Hawaii and the friendliness of its people so well that I had the strong urge to pack my suitcase and head of to the islands. It warmed my heart on a cold January day in Colorado, and I hope it will do the same for other readers." – Erika (82), Colorado Springs, CO

"My favorite characters in the book were Auntie and William... The world definitely needs more positive and uplifting literature... I truly enjoyed exploring the Hawaiian culture through the eyes of each character. After years of reading [John] Grisham, [Joseph] Finder and [Jack] Higgins, I was very pleased to refresh my mind with such meaningful content. Thank you for your creativity." – Melissa (39), Long Beach, CA

"Loved it all. How a high powered New York reporter can become a laid back regular person, finally able to enjoy her life? Much better. Great story. We can all learn from it! A good read!!" – V. K. Kristoffersen, Hagerstown, MD

"The education of the uptight, successful New Yorker in the life and culture of Hawaii. Lovingly and thoughtfully written. It's da bomb!" – Rick Lacy on Amazon.com

ABOUT THE STORY:

From da Big Island is a baby boomer coming of age, fish out of water, woman-centric comedy about Ruth, a famous New York syndicated television personality. Following a horrific accident, Ruth wants to be alone and have peace that she cannot find in New York City. The allure of Hawaii and the need for change beckons her. She accepts the change, moves to the Big Island of Hawaii, and soon discovers life is vastly different than she expected and gets what she wishes, to be alone. Will Ruth accept change and adjust to her new life on the Big Island, or will she reject it and return to the Big Apple?

AUTHOR:

Bill Hutchinson was born in Pennsylvania and lived in Germany, Italy, Japan, and the Netherlands. He attended Universität Heidelberg in Germany, and holds degrees from California Institute of the Arts, Pepperdine University, and Chapman University. Professor Hutchinson taught Business Management, Information Technology, Student Success Strategies, and Critical Thinking courses. His articles and photographs have appeared on social media, in annual reports, newspapers, magazines, and other publications. He is the author of *From da Big Island*.

FROM DA BIG ISLAND SCREENPLAY AND NOVEL

CONTENTS

BILL HUTCHINSON

INTRODUCTION

The primary purpose of this book is to assist students and others in understanding the differences between a novel and a screenplay. Also, to help as an instructional aid on what a screenplay and a novel look like, how story elements are slightly changed, albeit marginally, based upon the medium.

This book is not an instructional tool for writing a novel or a screenplay. Other books cover that subject in detail. Very few cover or assist in understanding conversion from one medium to the other, in this case, between a screenplay and a novel.

SPOILER ALERT

This introduction contains information from novels and movies that could be considered spoilers; meaning a potential crucial story element may be revealed.

LAYOUT

This book is laid out in three major sections; the introduction, the screenplay, and the novel. If you look in the footer at the bottom of this page, you will note the black box with INTRODUCTION in it. Each section, including the introduction, contains a black box with the name of that section. Turn the book on its side, and look at the lower edge (bottom) of the book. Note the black area for each section can be seen. This will help quickly identify where the Introduction, Screenplay, and Novel are located.

Page numbers for each work are in the top margin, while the bottom margin contains the actual page numbering of the book, encased in dashes (e.g., -1-, -2-, -3-, etc.). This will make it easier when referring between the screenplay, novel, and this book. All novel or screenplay references in the Introduction will be to their respective page numbers located in the top margin. However, references within the Introduction will be to the page numbers in the bottom margin.

The film industry standard for screenplays is single-sided. The first page of a script does not contain a page number. Page numbers start on the second page in the upper right margin, followed by a period. This book adheres to that numbering schema. Scene numbers are generally added to each scene *after* the screenplay has been optioned and is in pre-production.

Film industry standards are a 12-point Courier font size, a 1.5-inch margin on the left, and a 1-inch margin on the page's right, top, and bottom. Character names must be uppercase and start at 3.7 inches from the left side, with the dialogue block 2.5 inches from the left side of the page. Due to the book size, the book's screenplay is double-sided and proportionally smaller.

In a novel, page numbering is generally in the footer section aligned relative to the margin on the fore-edge (the side opposite of the book's spine), meaning odd-numbered pages are on the right, even on the left.

To avoid confusing the reader, this book varied from that normality by moving the novel page number from the footer to the header since the footer contains this book's actual page numbers.

Generally, the novel's title is in the header on odd pages and the author's name on even pages, except for a new chapter, where the novel title is always in the header.

In the introduction, examples of each area of focus are from well-known novels, novellas, or movies, which help the reader better understand that specific section's application to the work. The actor or actress who plays the screen role is in parentheses.

At the end of each section are suggested exercises representative of that specific section. These exercises help understand that section and, hopefully, help with the creative writing process. Being imaginative is necessary; each of these sections applies to all genres.

AUDIENCE

Before writing their first words, one of the primary considerations a writer needs to define is who they are writing the story for, also known as a target audience. This applies to any work, whether fiction, non-fiction, advertising, product release, podcast, or creative work. Without first defining the audience, the work is bound to flounder.

Millennials and Zoomers (Generation Z) appear to prefer movies heavily leaden in computer-generated imagery (CGI), watching a glorified animated film portrayed by live-action people with animated action, and, perhaps most of all, the enjoyment of in-your-face conflict. Whereas seniors generally prefer subtle intellectual conflict, family values, and action that does not require CGI for entertainment.

Luminaries like Carl Reiner, Mel Brooks, Norm Lear, and others have difficulty getting their material sold and made into motion media due to the refusal of the powers that be to believe seniors would like the material targeted to them and the baby-boomer generation. This unwillingness to think outside the accepted norm also applies to print media. The executives genuinely need to understand they are missing a mass target market.

Audience – *A Christmas Carol*

Dickens, a master storyteller, wanted to write a story that would help people appreciate the true meaning of Christmas and create a heartwarming and memorable tale that would bring joy to them during the holiday season.

Audience – *The Color Purple*

Who is the intended audience in Alice Walker's *The Color Purple*? The following are Alice Walker quotes about her target audience.

"I wrote The Color Purple for black women ... that would give voice to the experiences of black women, but I also wanted to write a book that would be read by everyone."

Audience – *From da Big Island*

The film's primary target audience is a woman-centric, senior coming-of-age story for senior citizens, including the current baby boomer generation, retirees, and others who continue to undergo significant life changes. Being one myself, I knew what that target audience generally prefers regarding entertainment.

Audience – Exercise

Every time you watch a movie, read a book, a show on TV, or a commercial, list the work, who the target audience is, and what elements helped make that decision.

BACKGROUND

This section includes the background of four works appearing in the introduction.

Background – *A Christmas Carol*

Charles Dickens was 12 years old when his father was imprisoned for debt, and the family was forced to live in a debtors' prison. This experience left a lasting impression on Dickens, and he often wrote about the social and economic inequalities prevalent in Victorian England, particularly the harsh conditions faced by the poor and the exploitation of the working classes in his novels.

In six weeks, he finished *A Christmas Carol* releasing it on December 19th, 1843. It was an immediate success, with the initial print run of 6,000 copies selling out within days. Since then, the novella has been translated into over 100 languages and adapted into countless films, television shows, and stage productions. It is still one of the most popular and beloved Christmas stories ever.

Background – *The Color Purple*

Alice Walker wrote the novel to explore African American women's lives in the early 20th century and was inspired by the stories of her own family and friends, as well as by the work of other African American writers. The best background is to quote Alice Walker, "I wrote *The Color Purple* because I thought it was time for us black women to tell our own stories. I wanted to speak about the things we go through that are not commonly talked about. We're not just mammies and Sapphire women. We're complex and interesting, too ... I wanted to create a story that would challenge and disrupt the traditional narratives about race, gender, and power. I wanted to create characters who were complex and flawed, who defied stereotypes and demanded to be seen and heard."

Background – *Star Wars: Episode IV - A New Hope*

George Lucas was a fan of classic science fiction and fantasy works. He drew inspiration from the *Flash Gordon* and *Buck Rogers* serials of the 1930s along with Joseph Campbell's book *The Hero with a Thousand Faces*, which explores the common elements found in myths and legends. He incorporated these archetypal elements into the story, particularly the hero's journey of Luke Skywalker, the protagonist. Lucas studied aerial footage of dogfights and incorporated their thrilling nature into the film's space battles. These influences resulted in its unique blend of science fiction, fantasy, mythology, and adventure storytelling.

Background – *From da Big Island*

During my Master of Fine Arts screenwriting program, I had to write short three to five-page vignettes based on various screenwriting techniques. Eventually, these vignettes were incorporated and became my thesis screenplay. Some of those vignettes had to be cut or significantly reduced from the final screenplay to keep the final length of the screenplay under 120 pages. Later, most of the vignettes that did not make the final cut were incorporated into the novel.

I sent copies of the screenplay to family and ohana to review, specifically to ensure I captured the Big Island culture and language, and because they wanted to read it. They liked the story. However, their primary issue was how it varied syntactically from a novel and how difficult the screenplay was to read. The most common suggestion was to convert the screenplay into a novel. Which, in time following my early retirement, I did. Thus, the ten-plus-year gap between the screenplay and the novel's release.

BACKSTORY

A backstory helps support understanding the events leading up to the story. Which can include important, relevant information about the story itself or its characters; in short, it is a history that may be interesting how something or someone came to be. It is best to keep the backstory short and to the point and only be used with the protagonist, antagonist, and in rare cases, the facile; for definitions, see page 13, Character Roles.

FROM DA BIG ISLAND SCREENPLAY AND NOVEL

Backstory – *A Christmas Carol*

The Ghost of Christmas Past reveals to the reader and Scrooge that he had a challenging childhood, lacking love and support, while enjoying time with his school and work relationships. Scrooge focuses not on Bell, his fiancé, but on making money, leading him to prioritize wealth and become bitter and miserly.

Backstory – *Star Wars: Episode IV – A New Hope*

Luke Skywalker (Mark Hamill) is the protagonist, a farm boy from the desert planet of Tatooine who lives with his aunt and uncle. However, Luke is unaware of his true parentage. His life changes when droids R2-D2 (Kenny Baker) and C-3PO (Anthony Daniels) reveal a message from Princess Leia Organa (Carrie Fisher), being held captive by the Empire and needing help from Obi-Wan Kenobi (Alec Guinness), a wise old Jedi Knight. When Luke meets "Old Ben" Kenobi, he learns Ben knew his father, about the Force, and trains Luke to become a Jedi. Luke's journey from a young farm boy to a Jedi Knight is a classic hero's journey, filled with adventure, danger, and self-discovery.

Through Obi-Wan Kenobi, the audience discovers Darth Vader's (David Prowse, voice by James Earl Jones) backstory, that he was a talented Jedi Knight who fought for the Republic, later turning to the dark side of the Force. Vader is feared and respected by his subordinates, known for his ruthless tactics, iconic breathing mask, and black armor. Together, Luke and Vader represent the light and dark sides of the Force.

Backstory – *From da Big Island*

Ruth's backstory starts at the very beginning of both the screenplay and the novel with the 21 Club shooting flashback. Then later, during the From the Big Apple post-show argument and Charley Chan movie night between Ruth and Sarah.

Backstory – Exercise

When you finish reading a book, watching a movie, or a show on TV, make a list of the protagonist, antagonist, and, when applicable, the facile. List their name, the backstory, and what elements helped make that decision.

CATHARSIS

Also known as the *aha moment!* a point in time when the protagonist has the sudden insight, realization, or comprehension of the resolution to the primary issue or problem.

Catharsis – *A Christmas Carol*

Towards the end of "Stave Four – The Last of the Spirits," Scrooge experiences his catharsis. All versions of the film and stage productions will have some semblance of his aha moment, using a variation of the following from the novel:

> Following the finger, read upon the stone of the neglected grave his own name, EBENEZER SCROOGE.
>
> "Am *I* that man who lay upon the bed?" he cried, upon his knees.
>
> The finger pointed from the grave to him, and back again.
>
> "No, Spirit! Oh no, no!"
>
> The finger still was there.
>
> "Spirit!" he cried, tight clutching at its robe, "hear me! I am not the man I was. I will not be the man I must have been but for this inter- course. Why show me this, if I am past all hope ?"
>
> For the first time the hand appeared to shake.

> "Good Spirit," he pursued, as down upon the ground he fell before it: " Your nature intercedes for me, and pities me. Assure me that I yet may- change these shadows you have shown me, by an altered life!"
>
> The kind hand trembled.
>
> "I will honour Christmas in my heart, and try to keep it all the year. I will live in the Past, the Present, and the Future. The Spirits of all Three shall strive within me. I will not shut out the lessons that they teach."

This is where Scrooge and the audience know his journey and why the story has been retold over and over for almost two centuries.

Catharsis – *The Color Purple*

The protagonist, Celie (Whoopi Goldberg), has her aha at the Easter gathering when an argument escalates at the dinner table. Celie asks her husband, Albert (Danny Glover), often referred to as Mr.___, if any more letters from her sister in Africa. Albert responds, "Could be, could be not. Who's to say?" Celie grabs her steak knife and leaps from her chair towards Albert, plunging it into the table before him. Then she pulls the knife out, waving inches from his nose, "Until you do right by me, everything thing you think about will crumble."

In the next scene, Celie gets into the convertible. Albert comes out the front door yelling, "I'm going to knock you up!" He reaches out to slap Celie, who raises her hand, making the victory symbol, pointing at Albert, who stops in his tracks as Celie calmly states, "Everything you done to me, I already done to you." then climbs into the car. As the car pulls away, Celie declares, "I'm poor, I'm black, I may even be ugly, but dear

God, I'm here!" affirming her freedom from Mr.___. Thus ending Act II, if *The Color Purple* were a three act play.

Catharsis – *From da Big Island*

Ruth experiences her aha moment following Mrs. Wiggin's death on page 72 of the screenplay, and page 89, in the "Be Careful What You Wish For" chapter. This aha moment comes earlier than one would expect. If *From da Big Island* were a stage production, Act I is Ruth's ordinary world turned upside down and her deciding to leave the Big Apple. Act II starts with Ruth's arrival in Hawaii and ends with the death of Mrs. Wiggins, just like Celie gaining her freedom in *The Color Purple*, Act III begins with Ruth's catharsis and decision to embrace the Big Island, ending with the joy of William graduating high school, which would not have happened without her intervention.

Catharsis – Exercise

When you finish reading a book, watching a movie, or a show on TV, make a list with the name of the work, what the catharsis is, and what elements helped make that decision.

CHARACTER ARC

In basic terms, a character arc is the transformation or change of the protagonist from the beginning to the end of the story. There are numerous books and courses on this subject alone. In a screenplay or novel, the development of a character's arc does not change much in its execution. How it is relayed may be slightly different.

Character Arc – *A Christmas Carol*

Many adaptations have left out non-critical information, which some scholars feel is essential to the story or the character arc of Scrooge, such as his relationship with Dick Wilkins, his fellow apprentice at Fezziwigs. Dickens writes:

> 'Dick Wilkins, to be sure!' said
> Scrooge to the Ghost. 'Bless me, yes.
> There he is. He was very much attached
> to me, was Dick. Poor Dick! Dear,
> dear!'
>
> . . .
>
> His heart and soul were in the scene,
> and with his former self. He
> corroborated everything, remembered
> everything, enjoyed everything, and
> underwent the strangest agitation. It
> was not until now, when the bright
> faces of his former self and Dick were
> turned from them, that he remembered
> the Ghost.

Most adaptations do, however, cover the failed relationship with Belle:

> "It matters little," she [Belle] said,
> softly. "To you, very little. Another
> idol has displaced me; and if it can
> cheer and comfort you in time to come,
> as I would have tried to do, I have no
> just cause to grieve."
>
> "What Idol has displaced you?" he
> rejoined.
>
> "A golden one."

All adaptations cover "Stave One – Marley's Ghost," which starts with the death of Jacob Marley, Scrooge's former partner. Through the first few pages, the reader discovers several years have passed since Marley's death and how the event affected and embittered Scrooge. It isn't until several pages later reader learns:

INTRODUCTION

'Mr. Marley has been dead these seven
years,' Scrooge replied. 'He died seven
years ago, this very night.'

Later, during Scrooge and the Ghost of Christmas Present's visit to Fred's, Scrooge's nephew, Christmas Party, the statement involving Topper, "a bachelor [who] was a wretched outcast." One could argue that Dickens went into detail about the above to help develop Scrooge's character arc and negative demeanor over relationships and Christmas.

One of my students mentioned they assumed Scrooge was gay, a thought which, until that moment, never crossed my mind nor any Dickens scholar I communicated with. We all agreed with the student who supported the claim, using the Ghost of Christmas Past and how Scrooge's only female relationship was with Belle; albeit happy, it ended sourly. Further supporting the student's claim Scrooge was gay. All his fond memories were with his male companions while at school and work, again ending on a sour note with Marley's death which was no fault of his own.

Character Arc – *From da Big Island*

The first few pages of the screenplay will give the actress who will portray Ruth a rough idea of Ruth's demeanor. However, the first chapter of the novel, "Ruth," starting on page 3, delves into greater detail about Ruth's character, which is not much different than Dickens did regarding Scrooge in *A Christmas Carol*. One could argue the novel goes into more detail than the screenplay to assist the actress who plays Ruth with a better idea of her character portrayal.

In both the screenplay and novel, Ruth has a significant character arc from being a quintessential New York high society socialite to a more accepting, relaxed person. On a more subtle side, in the beginning, Ruth uses the word

"Darling" so excessively that she doesn't realize she is doing so. Eventually, while in Hawaii, she realizes how offensive using darling is to people and stops using the word altogether.

Later, upon her return to New York, Ruth chastises her sister for excessively using darling because she can't remember the names of Ruth's Hawaiian ohana. Little things like the use of darling help build Ruth's character arc.

Character Arc – Exercise

When reading a book, watching a movie, or an episode on TV, make a list; what is the character arc? This exercise will be more challenging for a TV episode since the character's arch has already been established. In this case, note any changes, no matter how subtle.

CHARACTER ROLES

The protagonist and antagonist are two of the most important characters in any story. The protagonist is the main character whose story is being told. The antagonist is the character who opposes the protagonist, creating conflict and driving the plot forward.

Protagonist: The protagonist is the central character the story revolves around and the audience identifies with. They are usually the main character or one of the main characters trying to achieve a goal. The story follows their journey as they try to overcome obstacles and achieve their goal, and their actions and decisions drive the narrative forward. The protagonist is typically portrayed as the hero or character the reader is meant to sympathize with and root for.

Antagonist: Conversely, the antagonist is the character or force that opposes or creates conflict for the protagonist. They serve as the primary source of opposition or resistance the protagonist must overcome to reach their goals. The antagonist can be a person, an entity, a group, a villain, a force of nature, or even the protagonist's inner demons, and they are often villainous or morally evil. The antagonist's goal is to prevent the protagonist from achieving their goal, and create tension, obstacles, and challenges for the protagonist, driving the conflict and the plot forward. While the antagonist is often portrayed as the villain or the character with negative intentions, they can also be complex and multi-dimensional, with their own motivations and perspectives.

Facile: A facile in literature can vary depending on the context. Sometimes, a facile may provide comic relief or add a touch of humor to a story. In other cases, a facile may explore complex ideas or emotions in a more accessible way. They could be easygoing, content to go with the flow, and not challenge themselves or others, and may be perceived as lazy or apathetic. A facile character may be someone who can think quickly and come up with clever or witty remarks and may be seen as charming or entertaining. They also help drive the story forward through interactions with the protagonist and antagonist.

The Relationship Between the Protagonist and Antagonist: This is one of the most important aspects of any story. The conflict between the two characters drives the plot forward and keeps the audience engaged. The protagonist and antagonist can be evenly matched, or the antagonist can be more powerful than the protagonist. The relationship between the two characters can also be complex, with the protagonist and antagonist sometimes working together or even becoming friends.

In summary, the protagonist is the central character around whom the story revolves and whose actions drive the plot

INTRODUCTION

forward. In contrast, the antagonist is the character or force that opposes the protagonist and creates conflict and obstacles for them to overcome.

Examples of Protagonists and Antagonists:
- *Dracula* by Bram Stoker – Protagonist: Jonathan Harker, Antagonist: Count Dracula. This is based on the novel and not the movie versions of the novel.
- *Harry Potter* series by J.K. Rowling – Protagonist: Harry Potter (Daniel Radcliffe), Antagonist: Lord Voldemort (Ralph Fiennes) is mentioned in the films. However, his first on-screen appearance is in the fourth film, *Harry Potter and the Goblet of Fire* (2005).
- *Lord of the Rings* by J.R.R. Tolkien – Protagonist: Frodo Baggins (Elijah Wood), Antagonist: Sauron (Sala Baker)
- *One Flew Over the Cuckoo's Nest* by Ken Kesey – Protagonist: Randle Patrick McMurphy (Nicholson), Antagonist: Nurse Ratched (Louise Fletcher)

Character Roles – *A Christmas Carol*

Protagonist – Ebenezer Scrooge is an enigma, as he could be both the protagonist and the antagonist. He is the force driving himself as the protagonist and the central character around whom the story revolves, and his actions move the plot forward. In contrast, the antagonist is the character or force that opposes the protagonist and creates conflict and obstacles. Therefore, Scrooge could also be the antagonist, the protagonist's inner demon being the ghosts of Christmas past, present, and future.

Antagonist – It has been argued that Marley and the three ghosts as a collective group are the antagonists. However, Jacob Marley is generally accepted as the primary antagonist. He is Scrooge's deceased business partner, who died seven years before the story and played a vital role as a ghost. In his own words, his backstory reveals that he was as greedy and unkind as Scrooge during his life. After his death, Marley is condemned to wander the afterlife, burdened with chains forged in life from his selfish actions.

Facile – The Cratchit Family: Bob Cratchit (Scrooge's clerk), his wife, and their children have a backstory highlighting their poverty and struggles. Despite their meager means, they maintain a strong sense of happiness, togetherness, and love, which contrasts Scrooge's materialistic view.

Character Roles – *The Color Purple*

Protagonist – Celie (Whoopi Goldberg), a young black woman whose father abused her, is forced into an unhappy marriage with Mr.___. She is illiterate and has no control over her own life. Through her letters to God, we learn about her past and how she has come to be where she is.

Antagonist – Mr.___ (Danny Glover), also known as Albert Johnson, is Celie's abusive husband. Mr.___ is a wealthy landowner who believes he has the right to do whatever he wants to his wife. We learn he was raised in a household where violence was commonplace and never learned to express his emotions in a healthy way. As a result, he takes his anger out on Celie.

Facile – Shug (Margaret Avery) is a blues singer and a former lover of Mr. Albert, also known as Mr.___. Shug catalyzes Celie's transformation and self-discovery. When Shug arrives at Celie's home, she forms a close bond with and later becomes her close friend and love interest, which helps Celie discover her capacity for love, pleasure, and intimacy. Shug enables her to break free from the confines of her oppressive environment and embark on a journey of self-discovery, empowerment, and liberation.

Character Roles – *Star Wars: Episode IV – A New Hope*

Protagonist – Luke (Mark Hamill) is a young farm boy from the desert planet of Tatooine who becomes entangled in the Rebel Alliance's fight against the Galactic Empire and eventually discovers his connection to the Force. Luke undergoes a hero's journey, discovering his true identity and setting him on the path to becoming a Jedi Knight.

Antagonist – Darth Vadar (David Prowse, voice by James Earl Jones), also known as Anakin Skywalker, is a Sith Lord and enforcer of the Galactic Empire. Vader is a powerful and menacing figure, serving as the right-hand man to Emperor Palpatine and tasked with hunting down the Rebel Alliance and suppressing any opposition to the Empire's rule. His imposing presence, mastery of the dark side of the Force, and connection to Luke Skywalker create a central conflict in the story.

Facile – C-3PO (Anthony Daniels) is a protocol droid fluent in various forms of communication and etiquette. His primary function is to assist with etiquette, translation, and diplomatic protocol. He often provides comic relief; his anxious and sometimes fussy nature and tendency to worry and overanalyze situations create humorous moments.

Character Roles – *From da Big Island*

Protagonist – Ruth is the central character the story revolves around. The story follows her journey as she tries to overcome obstacles and achieve her goals, and her decisions drive the narrative forward.

Ruth is a famous New York syndicated television personality. Following a horrific accident, she wants to be alone and have the peace she cannot find in New York City. Ruth moves to the Big Island of Hawaii and soon discovers life is vastly different than she expected. Through the help of her Hawaiian neighbors, Ruth learns what ohana is all about.

Antagonist – Auntie is the classic antagonist. However, she does not appear until the second act, in the screenplay on page 38 and the novel on "The Neighbors" chapter on page 52. Before Auntie's appearance, multiple minor antagonists ranging from Sarah to Gloria La Fong, George Epstein, Mrs. Strong, and Hawaii all help create conflict for Ruth, driving the story forward.

Auntie is Ruth's uphill neighbor who grows marijuana plants. Most people think she was born and raised in Oahu and only speaks pidgin. She speaks perfect English, has a Ph.D. in horticulture, and works for the government, something not revealed except to a few individuals.

Facile – Although, in the novel, the story is told from William's perspective, writing the prologue and epilogue, which bookends the story. However, William is not the protagonist; he falls into the traditional role of the facile. William, Ruth's downhill neighbor, is an at-risk high school student who would rather surf than be in class. Ruth helps William become more literate through reading.

Character Roles – Exercise

Make a list of the protagonist and antagonist from a book, movie, or episode on TV and your thoughts on why you chose them.

CONFLICT

Conflict is a competition, rivalry, or obstacle between two opposing forces. Put differently, a character has a want. To get that want, there is some obstacle that causes conflict. It is often used to help move the storyline or scene forward.

To level set and use as a baseline in this discussion, there are two distinct types of conflict; internal and external. Each has similar subcategories.

An internal conflict is a character versus themselves. The character is in conflict with a decision, be it moral, desire, belief, or otherwise. Internal conflict is a necessity for good character development. Generally, internal conflict will generate external conflict.

As the name implies, the external conflict is external to the character, such as another person, society, nature, technology, fate, the supernatural, or the unknown.

The most common external conflict in the early twenty-first century is the in-your-face conflict, which one could say occurred during the pre and post-COVID-19 riots or a plethora of video games where the player is encouraged to be in aggressive combat to win the game.

On the opposite end is subtle conflict which means the conflict is there. However, on a much more intellectual level, where the audience uses their mind, such as commonly used in mystery, crime, romance, and other genres.

Conflict – *A Christmas Carol*

The story utilizes internal, external, in-your-face, and subtitle conflict. Internally, Scrooge dislikes Christmas because of his memories of being abandoned as a schoolboy, the loss of Belle, and the death of his business partner, Jacob Marley, who died seven Christmas' ago.

Externally, Scrooge is reminded every Christmas of Marley's death. This becomes external when on Christmas Eve, the carolers, charitable solicitors, and his nephew Fred call on

Scrooge in his office and, later, with the visitation of the four ghosts.

Conflict – *The Color Purple*

The story is primarily told through Celie's (Whoopi Goldberg) perspective, a strong, resilient woman and the protagonist because she is the story's main character. She endures physical, emotional, and sexual abuse from her stepfather and later from her husband, Mr. ___. Despite her hardships, Celie displays remarkable resilience and inner strength. We follow her journey from a young woman to a strong, independent woman who finds her voice and place in the world.

Mr.___ (Danny Glover) is a cruel and abusive man who perpetuates the patriarchal system and mistreats women and is the antagonist because he is the primary source of conflict in Celie's life. He is a brutal and abusive husband who treats Celie like property. He keeps her from seeing her family, forces her to work long hours, and beats her regularly.

Conflict – *From da Big Island*

The story also utilizes internal, external, in-your-face, and subtitle conflict. Ruth and Sarah are arguing about a guest who canceled at the last minute on page 7 of the screenplay and page 9 of the novel, which escalates when Ruth notices the "Come to Hawaii" advertisement running again, sarcastically stating, "Sarah, I could have said, 'Tomorrow we will be coming to you from Hawaii!'" This is an in-your-face conflict causing an exchange that helps propel the story forward, paying off numerous times throughout the story.

Conflict – Exercise

An easy way to remember the difference between in-your-face and subtle conflict is to think about a scenario where a person cheats on their spouse, and the spouse finds out about the cheating episode. We will call the couple Abe and Bob, where Bob is seeing Charlie. All grew up and graduated from high school together. This scenario can be portrayed in several ways. In the interest of keeping it simple, Abe and Bob attend their fifth high school reunion. They are seated at a table for ten, having an enjoyable time together. Other people are at the same table with several empty seats, all reminiscing about their fun during high school. Charlie walks up and takes the empty seat next to Abe, starting a conversation with Abe, then quickly changes focus to Bob, talking over Abe to Bob. What transpires next is Abe realizes Charlie and Bob are carrying on a relationship without his knowledge.

Write a scenario based on the above parameters using in-your-face, and then, still using the same setup, write another scenario using subtitle conflict. After you do this exercise, give yourself a day or two, come back, and re-read both scenarios. You will probably find significant differences and perspectives of utilizing both in-your-face and subtitle conflict.

DRAMATIC IRONY

Dramatic irony involves the audience knowing something the protagonist or a character does not know.

Dramatic Irony – *The Birds*

A classic example of dramatic irony is in Alfred Hitchcock's film *The Birds* (1963). Melanie (Tippi Hedren) goes to the school to pick up Cathy (Veronica Cartwright). The teacher, Ms. Hayworth (Suzanne Pleschette), informs Melanie to wait for recess to pick up Cathy. Hitchcock masterfully builds suspense for the next two and a half minutes using dramatic irony through visual and aural cues.

As Melanie exits the school, in the background is the empty playground, she and we, the audience, hear the students singing

Risselty Rosselty now now now. Melanie sits on a bench to wait for the students to finish the song and come out to play. The tempo and melody of the song are equivalent to a ticking clock, along with the words *now now now* add to the suspense.

Behind Melanie, crows land on a jungle gym one by one. While reaching for a cigarette in her purse, she turns slightly towards the playground, yet not enough to notice the crows. The audience wants Melanie to turn and see the gathering crows. She turns, facing the street, and starts smoking the cigarette. The song continues as crows silently gather on the jungle gym, swing sets, and in the playground, all unnoticed by Melanie. The entire time, the audience wants her to notice the impending danger. This is dramatic irony in its finest moment.

Finally, Melanie notices a solo crow flying overhead towards the playground. She turns to see the murder of crows also waiting for the children. Realizing the children in the school are in danger and could be attacked and killed by gathering crows, just like what happened the night before. The song ends before she reaches the school's steps as Ms. Hayworth tells the students to prepare for recess.

Dramatic Irony – *A Christmas Carol*

In novel form, a similar approach is used for dramatic irony and, generally, may take pages. "Stave Four – The Last of the Spirits" provides the audience and Scrooge clues about the identity of the dead man everyone is talking about. However, the audience picks up clues, which Scrooge does not, that Scrooge is the dead man being discussed. Examples are the nickname of the dead man, "Old Scratch," "wicked old screw," the dead man's cheapness, and perhaps most of all, the following:

> He looked about in that very place for
> his own image; but another man stood in

```
his accustomed corner, and though the
clock pointed to his usual time of day
for being there, he saw no likeness of
himself among the multitudes that
poured in through the Porch.
```

Only when Scrooge is guided to the churchyard standing amongst the gravestones does he realize the man is himself.

```
The Spirit was immovable as ever.
```

```
Scrooge crept towards it [the grave],
trembling as he went; and following the
finger, read upon the stone of the
neglected grave his own name, Ebenezer
Scrooge.
```

```
"Am I that man who lay upon the bed?"
he cried, upon his knees.
```

```
The finger pointed from the grave to
him, and back again.
```

```
"No, Spirit! Oh no, no!"
```

Dramatic Irony – *From da Big Island*

Soon after Ruth arrives in Hawaii, the audience discovers keiki's are maturing marijuana plants occurring in the screenplay on page 40 and the novel on page 53. Later, Ruth asks Ben, "Darling, what are those keiki things that lady is always talking about? Why are they so important?" Ben replies, "Keiki, it Hawaiian for little ones or children." In Auntie and everyone's case, keiki's are little plants. The definition occurs in the screenplay on page 49 and the novel, "Doesn't Anybody Knock" chapter, page 65. Later, Ruth discovers what keiki's are in the screenplay on page 69 and the novel "No More Keiki's" chapter, page 86. This is a key dramatic irony episode initially set up in New York, where the audience finds out Ruth's stance on marijuana and then pays off towards the end of Act II.

Dramatic Irony – Exercise

Think of other examples of dramatic irony in film and literature. List the work, the item or issue, and its payoff to the protagonist.

FLASHBACK & FLASHFORWARD

A flashback is an event or scene before the current scene in a story or film, while a flashforward occurs in the future. A writer must identify flashbacks and flashforwards to avoid confusing their audience.

Flashback & Flashforward – *A Christmas Carol*

"Stave One – Marley's Ghost" starts with the following statement or preamble, which lasts for three pages and is a flashback, setting the tone for the rest of the story.

```
Marley was dead, to begin with. There
is no doubt whatever about that.  The
register of his burial was signed by
the clergyman, the clerk, the
undertaker, and the chief mourner.
Scrooge signed it.  And Scrooge's name
was good upon 'Change, for anything he
chose to put his hand to.  Old Marley
was as dead as a door-nail.
```

The actual current time of the story, if you will, places the present time frame with:

```
Once upon a time — of all the good days
in the year, upon a Christmas eve — old
Scrooge sat busy in his counting-house.
It was cold, bleak, biting, foggy
weather ; and the city clocks had only
just gone three, but it was quite dark
already.
```

The above "Once Upon a Time" sets the current timeframe of the story. Dickens masterfully identifies the point of the flashback and each flashforward.

In "Stave Two – The First of the Three Spirits," the Ghost of Christmas Past visits Scrooge. The ghost takes Scrooge into the past to scenes from his childhood, his early years in business, and his misplaced love for money over Belle.

In "Stave Three – The Second of Three Spirits," Scrooge is visited by the Ghost of Christmas Present, which is in the future, albeit in the morning. The ghost takes Scrooge to scenes of joyous celebrations of Christmas with love, joy, and generosity. They visit Bob Cratchit's family, where Scrooge sees how his accounting clerk and family are happy, despite struggling to make ends meet. Scrooge focuses on Tiny Tim, the Cratchit's youngest crippled son.

In "Stave Four – The Last of the Spirits," the Ghost of Christmas Yet to Come visits Scrooge. The spirit takes Scrooge into the future, where he sees a series of grim scenes from the future Christmas', including the death of Tiny Tim and Scrooge's lonely death.

Flashback & Flashforward – *From da Big Island*

The screenplay starts with a title card stating, "June 17, 1965." The audience knows the timeframe at the very beginning of the story. By page 4, the flashes forward from 1965, with the title card stating, "Christmastime, 40 years later."

Like Dickens, the novel *From da Big Island* has a prolog and an epilogue in the contemporary timeframe. The story itself takes place in the early 21st century post 9/11. Once Upon a Time is not used since the novel has a prologue and epilogue.

The novel's timeframe is established in the first paragraph of the story on page 3:

> "Ruth, Ruth Newcomb, is that you?" an
> elderly woman yelled, running after
> Ruth, a red-haired lady, who continued
> her brisk walk down New York's post
> 9/11 Fifth Avenue totally oblivious of
> the Christmas shoppers and the woman
> calling her name.

The flashback occurs on page 4 and is identified as a flashback:

> A man accidentally bumped into Ruth and
> in a thick Italian accent said, "Excusa
> me." For some reason, perhaps the
> combination of seeing The 21 Club and
> the Italian accent caused Ruth to
> flashback to that one unusual evening,
> many years ago, when Mario Manzoni, the
> head of one of New York's key crime
> families, was assassinated in front of
> the restaurant.
>
> It was the evening of June 17th, 1965.

The return to the present time on page 7 is also identified as not to confuse the reader:

> "Andiamo, we go, light change!" Ruth
> was knocked back into the present day
> as the light at 52nd Street changed and
> the man with the Italian accent pushed
> his way past her.

Flashback & Flashforward – Exercise

List other books or movies you can identify using flashback and flashforward sequences. Were they easy to identify or not? If not, what could have been done to identify the flashback and flashforward sequence more clearly?

FORESHADOWING

Foreshadowing is giving hints or clues of future events that occur later in the story through dialogue, events, imagery, or symbolism. It is a way of creating anticipation and building suspense for the reader or audience. Foreshadowing should be used sparingly to strike a balance between providing hints and preserving the element of surprise.

Foreshadowing – *A Christmas Carol*

The first foreshadowing occurs in "Stave One – Marley's Ghost," when two portly men are in the counting-house, appealing to Scrooge to donate.

> "At this festive season of the year, Mr. Scrooge," said the gentleman, taking up a pen, "it is more than usually desirable that we should make some slight provision for the poor and destitute, who suffer greatly at the present time."
>
> "Are there no prisons?" asked Scrooge.
>
> "Plenty of prisons," said the gentleman.
>
> "And the Union workhouses?" demanded Scrooge. "Are they still in operation?"
>
> "They are." returned the gentleman.

The above foreshadowing pays off numerous times throughout the story. Perhaps the most valuable payoff is at the conclusion of Stave III when the Ghost of Christmas Present lifts his robe revealing a malnourished boy and a girl both in tattered clothing.

> "Spirit! Are they yours?" Scrooge could say no more.

INTRODUCTION

```
"They are Man's," said the Spirit,
looking down upon them.  "And they
cling to me, appealing from their
fathers.  This boy is Ignorance.  This
girl is Want.  Beware them both ..."

"Have they no refuge or resource?"
cried Scrooge.

"Are there no prisons?" said the
spirit, turning on him for the last
time with his own words.  "Are there no
workhouses?"
```

Foreshadowing – *From da Big Island*

Hawaii is first foreshadowed during the opening credits through the music, in the screenplay, on page 5. If the director decides to utilize something other than the song, the next occurrence of Hawaii is during the *From the Big Apple* post-show argument between Ruth and Sarah, page 7, the same place as the novel, page 9. The Hawaii payoff is throughout the story.

Marijuana is foreshadowed, again occurring early on page 11 of the screenplay and in the novel "Number 3 Beekman Place", page 15. As with Hawaii, the marijuana payoff is throughout the story.

Ruth's support for reading is foreshadowed before she meets William. The first is during *From the Big Apple* broadcast where she tells her audience, "Darlings, I adore the New York Public Library Reading is Fundamental program" on page 6 of the screenplay and "Ruth" chapter page 8 of the novel. In Ruth's office description "On the wall was a framed 'Reading Is Fun' poster from the New York Metropolitan Library with Ruth holding *The Adventures of Huckleberry Finn* in the center" on page 14 of the screenplay and "Ruth" chapter page 17 of the novel. Later in Hawaii, William sees the novel in Ruth's bookcase on page 47 of the screenplay and "Doesn't Anybody

Knock?" chapter page 63 of the novel subtly foreshadows Mark Twain's novel. The payoff occurs when Ruth gives William *The Adventures of Huckleberry Finn* to read on page 66 of the screenplay and "Reading is an Adventure" chapter page 83 of the novel.

Foreshadowing – Exercise

List novels or movies where foreshadowing was used, and list the item being foreshadowed, followed by the payoff and how well it worked or did not work.

HOOK

A hook comes from the fishing world, where one who fishes uses a hook to obtain their catch. An author will use a hook to catch or grab their audience to keep them reading or watching their film. The ordinary world generally follows a hook.

Hook – *A Christmas Carol*

Earlier, we discussed the opening sentence in "Stave One – Marley's Ghost," where Dickens skillfully hooked the reader with six words, "Marley was dead, to begin with." It is similar to the headlines in a newspaper, the evening news, or a social media post. Later, smaller hooks drive the reader forward, wanting to discover what happens next. Primarily, Marley's ghost in Stave One when Marley says, "'You will be haunted,' resumed the ghost, " by Three Spirits.'" The reader wants to find out more about these three spirits.

Hook – *From da Big Island*

The screenplay starts with the 21 Club shooting sequence, immediately grabbing one's attention and hooking them to discover more. While in the novel, the shoot occurs immediately after the reader gets an idea of Ruth's stature. The payoff occurs throughout the story, primarily with marijuana and secondarily with The Mob.

Hook – Exercise

List hooks from any novel, movie, news report, or newspaper article where a hook draws your attention, driving you to continue reading or waiting to discover more. Define the hook and explain the reasoning for your decision.

INCITING INCIDENT

An inciting incident is a literary device describing a specific event or happening that kicks off the story and sets the plot in motion. The inciting incident generally follows the protagonist's ordinary world and is often unexpected or surprising to both the protagonist and the reader or audience. The inciting incident gets the story moving and prepares readers for future events. A well-written inciting incident will hook the reader's attention and make them want to keep reading.

Tips for writing an inciting incident:
- Make it unexpected or surprising. The reader should not see it coming.
- Make it significant. The inciting incident should have a major impact on the protagonist's life.
- Make it clear what the stakes are. The reader should understand what the protagonist can lose if they don't act.

Inciting Incident – *A Christmas Carol*

In "Stave One – Marley's Ghost," the first inciting incident is very subtle, the door knocker changing to Marley's image, followed more succinctly by the visit of Marley's ghost.

FROM DA BIG ISLAND SCREENPLAY AND NOVEL

Inciting Incident – *From da Big Island*

The inciting incident occurs in the screenplay on page 20, and in the novel, "The Nutcracker," chapter, page 22, riding in the limousine at the time of the accident.

Depiction in the screenplay:

> From Ruth's point of view, over Sarah's
> shoulder and through the window, we see
> a large truck plowing toward the
> limousine.
>
>   RUTH
>
> Brace yourselves!
>
>   CUT TO BLACK:

Depiction in the novel:

> Over Sarah's shoulder, through the
> limousine window, Ruth watched in
> horror as a large truck skidding
> sideways was headed directly towards
> the side of the limousine where Sarah
> was seated. Ruth stiffened and yelled,
> "Brace yourselves!"

Inciting Incident – Exercise

List any movie or novel you read where the inciting incident occurs and why you think so.

MacGUFFIN

MacGuffin is an object or device in a film or a book that serves merely as a trigger for the plot and is insignificant, irrelevant, or unimportant. The term was originated by Angus MacPhail, who worked on numerous films with Alfred Hitchcock. MacPhail may have based the term on the Scottish word "mawguffin," which means "a useful object."

Hitchcock himself used both spellings of MacGuffin and McGuffin interchangeably. The term has since become a standard part of film jargon.

At Columbia University in New York City, on March 30, 1939, Hitchcock gave a lecture followed by a question and answer session with his audience. He explained a MacGuffin is "something that the characters worry about, but the audience does not ... it is the thing the hero chases, the thing the picture is all about ... it is very necessary ... the MacGuffin is not important. It is only there to set the machinery in motion."

A MacGuffin is often used in thrillers and mystery films to create suspense and mystery. The audience is not privy to the true nature of the MacGuffin, and this can lead to speculation and guessing about what it could be. This can help keep the audience engaged and guessing until the film's end.

Here are a few high-level examples of films that have used the MacGuffin:

- *The Bourne Identity* (2002) is the list of secret CIA agents Jason Bourne is trying to find.
- *Goldfinger* (1964) is Fort Knox, the United States Bullion Depository, where Goldfinger plans to irradiate with a nuclear bomb and steal all of the gold inside.
- *Jurassic Park* (1993) is the park's security system, which the characters try to unravel to escape.
- *The Maltese Falcon* (1941) is the statuette of the falcon everyone is fighting over and serves as a motivating factor for the characters, driving the plot forward.
- *The Omen* (1976) is after the anti-Christ, Damien Thorn, who is a mysterious and powerful force that keeps the audience engaged and drives the plot forward.
- *Raiders of the Lost Ark* (1981) is the Ark of the Covenant. It is of little intrinsic value to the story but motivates the characters and drives the plot forward.

FROM DA BIG ISLAND SCREENPLAY AND NOVEL

MacGuffin – *The Birds*

The generally accepted MacGuffin is the birds themselves, and the characters are trying to figure out why the birds are attacking. While others have argued there is no MacGuffin because the birds are the story's driving force, and their motivations are never explained. In contrast, others have argued that the romance between Melanie (Tippi Hedren), the protagonist, and Mitch (Rod Taylor) is the MacGuffin. While romance is integral to the story and helps develop the characters and their motivations, it cannot be classified as the MacGuffin.

It is worth noting Hitchcock himself did not refer to any MacGuffin in *The Birds* and instead focused on the horror and suspense elements created by the bird attacks. The film remains open to interpretation and could be considered the MacGuffin.

MacGuffin – *North by Northwest*

The MacGuffin is the microfilm containing government secrets that Roger Thornhill (Cary Grant) is mistaken for having and is the object of a nationwide search. Thornhill is forced to go on the run, and he must use all of his wits to remain one step ahead of the law and the people trying to kill him.

The microfilm is a MacGuffin because it is unimportant in and by itself. It is simply a plot device used to drive the story forward. The film focuses on Thornhill's journey, and the microfilm is merely a way to put him in danger and force him to grow as a character.

MacGuffin – *A Christmas Carol*

The ghost of Jacob Marley is the MacGuffin. Marley is the ghost of Scrooge's former business partner, who has been condemned to wander the Earth for eternity for his sins of greed and selfishness.

> Let it also be borne in mind that Scrooge had not bestowed one thought on Marley, since his last mention of his seven-years' dead partner that afternoon. And then let any man explain to me, if he can, how it happened that Scrooge, having his key in the lock of the door, saw in the knocker, without its undergoing any intermediate process of change : not a knocker, but Marley 's face.

> Marley's face. It was not in impenetrable shadow as the other objects in the yard were, but had a dismal light about it, like a bad lobster in a dark cellar. It was not angry or ferocious, but looked at Scrooge as Marley used to look: with ghostly spectacles turned up upon its ghostly forehead. The hair was curiously stirred, as if by breath or hot-air; and though the eyes were wide open, they were perfectly motionless. That, and its livid colour, made it horrible; but its horror seemed to be, in spite of the face and beyond its control, rather than a part of its own expression.

> As Scrooge looked fixedly at this phenomenon, it was a knocker again.

Later that Christmas Eve, Marley returns to warn Scrooge of the same fate as he if Scooge does not change his ways. Marley's ghost is the catalyst for Scrooge's transformation, and his message of redemption ultimately saves Scrooge's soul.

MacGuffin – *From da Big Island*

The MacGuffin is marijuana, which drives the story forward.

MacGuffin – Exercise

List movies or novels you believe use a MacGuffin and what the MacGuffin is.

ORDINARY WORLD

Most movies and novels start with the protagonist's world, known as the ordinary world, meaning the world before the inciting incident or change. In other words, when the ordinary world changes, that event is known as the inciting incident.

Ordinary World – *A Christmas Carol*

In "Stave One – Marley's Ghost," Scrooge's ordinary world is exposed to the reader that he is a bitter miser, loves money, and hates Christmas; the audience doesn't know what made Scrooge so. His ordinary world changes with the transformation of the door knocker to Marley's face then is solidified with Marley's appearance in the bedroom chamber.

Ordinary World – *From da Big Island*

Ruth's ordinary world of being a well-known television celebrity is established before the limousine accident.

Ordinary World – Exercise

List movies or novels and identify the protagonist, their ordinary world, and the inciting incident.

STORY LENGTH

Viewers who read the book version of a film often complain the film version of the book left out essential elements or changed what the novel conveyed. This is because these are two different mediums; novels primarily are verbal, where readers utilize their imagination, while movies use both verbal and visual, leaving little to one's imagination, feeding the moviegoer a specific filmic interpretation of the novel which may or may not have been the same as the novels author or its reader's imagination.

Generally, a novel or novella will contain much more story than what can be transformed into a motion media adaption. The general rule for a screenplay is that one page equals one minute of screen time. Theater owners prefer to show films under two hours, which gives the theatre more showing times per day than one over two hours. Thus, the desire that screenplays be under 120 pages or 2 hours of screen time.

The one-page, one-minute rule is not steadfast, depending on the type of story it is. If it is an action screenplay, one paragraph of action may equal more than a minute on the screen.

Story Length – *A Christmas Carol*

The novel has been adapted into radio, stage, and film versions well over two hundred times since its initial release almost two centuries ago in 1843. Many adaptations left out non-critical information in the interest of getting the running time down for maximum profit and turnover, such as Scrooge's melancholy dinner scene, Fezziwig's, his relationship with Belle, his nephew Fred, the scene between Mrs. Dilber and Joe, the counting-house, and other settings Dickens included in the novella.

Story Length – *Where the Crawdads Sing*

When the novel was made into a movie, many people complained the film did not do the 2018 novel justice because, in their opine, the movie left out critical information and action required to develop Kya, the protagonist. The novel was 368 pages, whereas the script was only 120 pages long, making the final movie 125 minutes, including credits. The screenplay is significantly shorter than the novel. To accommodate critical parts of the storyline being removed, the screenplay needed to be condensed and modified to include dialogue and action not in the novel, hoping it would help reduce confusion to the audience who had not read the novel.

Story Length – *From da Big Island*

The screenplay is 110 pages; using the above formula would mean the film should be about 110 minutes or 1 hour, 50 minutes long, within the 2-hour limit (120 pages). All of the screenplay's primary elements are expounded on in the novel.

When the novel was written, a few scenes were added, or the order of events occurred to help the reader better enjoy the story or understand Ruth's decisions. Specifically, in the novel, the "More Time, Please" chapter, page 29, the reader meets Jim, the Chief Executive Officer of Ruth's network. However, in the screenplay, that scene does not appear. We first meet Jim when Ruth returns to New York for the Emmys.

Story Length – Exercise

Think of novels made into movies, even Pulitzer Prize or *New York Times Best Seller's List* books. What critical items, if any, are left out of the movie version that are in the novel? What would you have done differently, if anything, to help reduce confusion to the audience?

STRUCTURE

Generally, screenplays and novels follow the three-act scenario, with acts one and three usually having two segments, while the second act has multiple segments or challenges for the protagonist.

Since structure is an essential element of any form of writing, a little more detail is needed.

Two great must-read books on this subject are Paul Joseph Gulino's *Screenwriting: The Sequence Approach*, which best documents the sequence approach, and Christopher Vogler's *The Writer's Journey: Mythic Structure for Writers*. Both books detail the writing structure supported by examples and utilize the three-act approach. Below are very high-level summaries of each work.

Screenwriting: The Sequence Approach – Paul Gulino

Act I

Sequence 1 – Ordinary world (Exposition): First fifteen minutes, answer the questions of who, what, when, where, and under what conditions the movie will take place.

Most successful films begin by posing a mystery to the audience, raising questions in their minds, and promising a solution. The audience is introduced to the protagonist in the first sequence. The end of the sequence is the point of attack or inciting incident: The ordinary world has changed, forcing the protagonist to respond in some way.

Sequence 2 – Setting up main tension: Second fifteen minutes, setting up the main tension by posing the dramatic question that will shape the rest of the picture. Whatever solutions the protagonist attempts during this sequence will lead to more significant issues or predicaments, making it the end of the first act.

Act II

Sequence 3 – First attempt at Resolution: First attempt to resolve the issue introduced in the first act.

Characters tend to choose the easiest solution to the issue; however, the resolution can lead to bigger and deeper issues.

Sequence 4 – First Culmination: The protagonist tries desperate measures to return their life to stability. The hope is that the protagonist will succeed at resolving their issue only to see the circumstances turn the story the other way. The sequence ends with the first or midpoint culmination, a revelation or reversal of fortune that makes the Protagonist's tasks more difficult.

Sequence 5 – Impact from the First Culmination: The protagonist works on whatever new complication arose in the first culmination. New characters are introduced, and new opportunities present themselves. The resolution of the tension in this sequence does not resolve the main tension; it merely creates new complications, usually more complicated and higher stakes.

Sequence 6 – Second Culmination: Having eliminated the easy potential solutions and finding the most challenging works towards resolving the main tension. At the end of this sequence is the Second Culmination. It is a moment in the story concerning the main tension in some profound way – either by completely resolving it or reframing it significantly.

Act III

Sequence 7 – Unexpected consequences: The main tension is not entirely resolved. Unexpected consequences of that resolution can occur, and other storylines force the protagonist to work against their previous objective: higher states and a more frantic pace.

Sequence 8 – Resolution: The instability of the point of attack is settled. The tension is fully and ultimately resolved. It contains the epilogue or coda, a brief series of scenes tying up loose ends.

The Writer's Journey – Christopher Vogler

Vogler also refers to *The Hero's Journey*, a twelve-stage narrative structure found in many stories, myths, and legends. The stages are also linked to the three-act approach.

Act I

Stage 1 – The Ordinary World: The hero is introduced to their everyday life before the adventure begins.

Stage 2 – The Call to Adventure: The hero is presented with a challenge or opportunity that will change their life.

Stage 3 – Refusal of the Call: The hero is hesitant to accept the call, often out of fear or a sense of duty.

Stage 4 – Meeting with the Mentor: The hero meets a mentor who helps them to prepare for the journey.

Stage 5 – Crossing the First Threshold: The hero commits to the adventure and crosses into the unknown.

Act II

Stage 6 – Tests, Allies, and Enemies: The hero faces challenges and makes friends and enemies along the way.

Stage 7 – Approach to the Inmost Cave: The hero approaches the center of the story, where they will face their greatest challenge.

Stage 8 – The Ordeal: The hero faces their most significant challenge and experiences death and rebirth.

Stage 9 – Reward: The hero is rewarded for their efforts, often with a new understanding or power.

Act III

Stage 10 – The Road Back: The hero begins the journey home, changed by their experiences.

Stage 11 – The Resurrection: The hero faces a final challenge, which they overcome, and is reborn.

Stage 12 – Return with the Elixir: The hero returns home with the knowledge or power they gained during their journey and shares it with others.

Structure – Exercise

After reading both the screenplay and novel:
- Map out the sequence approach and the hero's journey to each work.
- Compare them to see how similar yet dissimilar each is.
- Do the same with *A Christmas Carol* and any film adaptation, including the year of the film production, the director, and the *screenplay by* credits.

You can apply this exercise to other works. Examples could be The Birds, The Color Purple, The Fellowship of the Rings, North by Northwest, Star Wars, Them!, Where the Crawdads Sing, The Wizard of OZ, and the like.

SUSPENSION OF DISBELIEF

Suspension of disbelief is the willingness of the viewer or reader to overlook and accept certain implausible or fantastical elements to maintain the illusion of and accept the basic premise of a story, even if it is unrealistic or impossible. Suspension of disbelief allows the reader or audience to enjoy the story without constantly questioning its believability.

Not all screenplays, novels, or other written works use suspension of disbelief, which is typically found in the following genres:

- Fairy tales: such as Cinderella, Little Mermaid, Snow White.
- Fantasies include C. S. Lewis's *The Chronicles of Narnia* series, J. K. Rowling's *Harry Potter* series, and J. R. R. Tolkien's *The Lord of the Rings* trilogy.
- Horror/Thriller: *The Birds* (1963), the *Halloween* series, *Psycho* (1960), *The Shining* (1980), and *The Silence of the Lambs* (1991).
- Mythology: Clash of the Titans (1981), Jason and the Argonauts (1963), and Troy (2004).
- Sci-Fi: 2001: A Space Odyssey (1968), Blade Runner (1982), Star Wars (1977).
- Superhero: the *Avengers*, *Batman*, and *Superman* series.

Suspension of Disbelief – *Them!*

A classic example of the suspension of disbelief can be found in *Them!* (1954), a Sci-Fi movie revolving around a series of deaths in a small New Mexico desert town. The local authorities have nothing to go on except for an unidentifiable footprint from which they made a plaster cast. Unable to identify the strange plaster print, the government is contacted. When the military aircraft arrives, Dr. Harold Medford (Edmund Gwenn) and his daughter, Dr. Patricia Medford (Joan Weldon), from the Department of Agriculture disembark. They review all the known facts, including the 1945 atomic testing that occurred nearby. Harold thought aloud, "1945, that's nine years ago. Yes, genetically, it's certainly possible."

Both doctors, FBI agent Bob Graham (James Arness), and local authorities visit the murder scenes, one being a torn-apart trailer. A brewing dust storm is increasing. While inspecting the kitchen area, Pat remarks, "Rather slim pickings for food, Dad. They'd turn carnivorous for lack of a habitual diet." Her father agrees. Bob asks what they are talking about. Pat responds that they are expert myrmecologists (the study of ants) and want to wait until they are sure before informing them of their theory.

Now outside the trailer, the dust storm has cut visibility to a few feet. Pat's father finds a series of footprints, measures them, and determines what made them to be over eight feet long.

Meanwhile, Pat follows the tracks and hears a chirping sound. She soon discovers the sound is coming from a giant ant approaching her. She screams, backing away. The others arrive, shooting the ant to no avail. Harold yells, "Shoot the antennae." When they do, the giant ant stops. They finish killing it with a machine gun.

This is the first time the audience knows about the giant ants. Later, the team finds the massive ant hill, killing the ants with poisonous cyanide gas. They enter the nest to ensure all ants are dead and discover two hatched eggs in the queen's chamber. Pat takes photographs and orders the chamber burned.

What follows next is the classic payoff on a suspension of disbelief sequence.

While in Washington, D.C., briefing a panel of military and government personnel on their discoveries. Harold explains that the ants are a byproduct of nuclear testing and shows them a film about everyday black ants to give them some idea of what they face in combating the giant ants. He warns if the ants cannot be stopped, "Man, as the dominant species of life on Earth, will probably be extinct within a year."

Them! successfully confirms the suspension of disbelief, allowing viewers to temporarily accept the existence of giant ants and fully engage with the thrilling sci-fi story being presented.

Suspension of Disbelief – *A Christmas Carol*

Suspension of disbelief is the willingness of the viewer or reader to accept the belief in the four ghosts, that Scrooge can fly, be invisible, and time travel. Scrooge is believable, as are the ghosts and other characters we meet.

Dickens uses vivid imagery to describe the scenes in the story. For example, before the ghost of Jacob Marley enters Scrooge's chamber, Dickens describes the sounds of chains, "as if some person were dragging a heavy chain over the casks in the wine-merchant's cellar." This imagery helps the reader visualize the scene and believe it is real. Without the suspension of disbelief, the story would not be compelling.

Suspension of Disbelief – *The Birds*

Hitchcock skillfully uses suspension of disbelief following the birds attacking the school. At the town diner, Melanie calls her father to report the phenomenon of the recent bird attacks. Everyone hears her call, which attracts the diners' attention; most people are skeptical, including Mrs. Bundy (Ethel Griffie), a highly respected older Bodega Bay resident and experienced birdwatcher who is an expert in ornithology.

Mrs. Bundy's expertise helps to lend credibility to the unusual occurrences surrounding the birds by presenting knowledgeable insights into bird behavior, migration patterns, and dismisses Melanie's account as impossible and contends that birds could never launch a mass attack on humanity because they lack the intelligence which contributes to the film's atmosphere and tension by providing a plausible explanation for the unnatural behavior of the birds.

Suspension of Disbelief – Exercise

Why is the suspension of disbelief not applicable to *From da Big Island*? List examples of other works where suspension of disbelief can be found, and what is the belief being suspended?

TELESCOPING

Telescoping condenses a series of events into a shorter span, skipping over unimportant details and focusing on the most important events to keep the story moving forward and not getting bogged down in minor details. This technique allows authors to streamline the plot, maintain a steady pace, and focus on the most significant or impactful moments. It's essential to use telescoping judiciously and strengthen coherence in the narrative. Too much compression or distortion of time can lead to confusion or a disjointed storyline. This typically happens when the writer skips back and forth between chronological and telescoping time.

Telescoping – *A Christmas Carol*

The story occurs in one night. Dickens telescopes the time it takes Scrooge with each visit of three ghosts. In the real world, covering the locations and events the ghosts present would take several hours, even days. However, in the story, each spirit takes under an hour to focus on the most critical events in Ebenezer Scrooge's transformation from a miserly older man to a kind and generous one.

Telescoping – *The Lord of the Rings*

The novel and movie telescope the time it takes for Frodo and his companions to travel from the Shire to Rivendell. This allows the story to focus on the most important events of their journey, such as their meeting with Elrond and encounters with the Nazgûl.

BILL HUTCHINSON

Telescoping – *From da Big Island*

Telescoping is used several times to compress events. The first is the months between the limousine accident and Ruth's decision to leave the Big Apple for the Big Island. Another example would be when Ben drives Ruth from Kona Airport across the island to her house, usually taking ninety minutes. In the screenplay, the episode starts on page 32 ending two pages later, or two minutes of screen time. In the novel, the journey begins on page 43 ending three pages later.

Telescoping – Exercise

What books or movies can you identify where time seems to be compressed? Read or watch them paying attention to the dialogue and the visuals to see how they create a sense of urgency or suspense.

VERB TENSE

English has three verb tenses: past, present, and future. The *past* is an event that has already happened, is not currently happening, nor will occur in the future; something that happened a second, hours, days, years, or millennia ago. As you read these words, the *present* is occurring at this very moment and continuing to happen. The *future* has yet to transpire, something that could occur in seconds, hours, days, years, or millennia ahead of the here and now. For example:

Past: He read the book.
Present: He is reading the book.
Future: He will read the book.

The significant difference in tense between the two mediums is in a novel, action is written in the *past* tense. In contrast, in a screenplay, action is written in the *present* tense, also known in the industry as scene descriptions.

Furthermore, in a novel, action is generally reflected in one or several paragraphs, whereas in a screenplay, *scene descriptions* are split into multiple segments; each offering broad strokes of individual action in one or two sentences to help the actor, director, editor, Foley (sound), artists, and the film crew identify specific items to focus on during filming and editing the scene.

Verb Tense – *From da Big Island*

On page 25 of the novel, the following sequence is in past tense:

```
Ruth walked to the Emmy photograph and
picked it up.  She took it with her to
a plush chair next to the fireplace.
Studying the photograph for a moment,
she gently stoked it and smiled.   A
purring Mrs. Wiggins nudged her leg,
letting out a short meow.   Ruth put the
photograph on the side table, reached
down, and stroked the black cat, who
took the stroking as an invite and
leaped up on Ruth's lap, nudging her
little black head against Ruth's arm
and purring.
```

The exact sequence in the screenplay is present tense on page 20, INT. RUTH'S LIVING ROOM – DAY. Notice how each sentence conveys the action and can be shot in one overall master shot, then each sentence could be shot in different angles, close-ups, or cut-a-ways. A sound or key element is *capitalized* to identify and call attention to the film crew of action required on their part: In this case, both the purring and meow are capitalized to let the sound editor know to add the sounds at that point in the scene.

Ruth moves to the Emmy photograph and picks it up.

She takes it with her to the chair near the fireplace and sits.

Studying it for a moment before gently stroking it and smiling.

Mrs. Wiggins PURRS, nudges her leg, and lets out a curt MEOW.

Ruth reaches down, picks up the cat placing it on her lap.

Mrs. Wiggins PURRS.

Verb Tense – Exercise

Write a paragraph or two in past tense, and then take what you wrote and write it again in present tense. Review what you just wrote, compare and make any corrections. Then put what you wrote aside. Then reread what you wrote the day before in a day or so. You will probably find at least one or two syntactical grammar errors. Putting time between each revision of any work will hone your writing skills.

BIBLIOGRAPHY

Campbell, J. C. (1949). *The Hero with a Thousand Faces*. Fontana Press.

Dickens, Charles (1843). *A Christmas Carol: In Prose. Being a Ghost Story of Christmas*. London, England: Chapman & Hall.

Dickens, Charles (1877). Charles Dickens Dramatic Readings as Read in America – A Christmas Carol. Boston: Lee and Shepard.

Gulino, P. (2004). Screenwriting: The Sequence Approach. A&C Black.

Hitchcock, Alfred (1939). *Hitchcock on Hitchcock Lecture*. Columbia University, New York, New York, 30 Mar. 1939

Vogler, C. (1998). The Writer's Journey: Mythic Structure for Writers. Michael Wiese Productions.

FILMOGRAPHY

2001: A Space Odyssey (1968), novel by Arthur C. Clarke, directed by Stanley Kubrick, screenplay by Stanley Kubrick

The Birds (1963), story by Daphne Du Maurier, directed by Alfred Hitchcock, screenplay by Daphne Du Maurier and Evan Hunter

Blade Runner (1982), novel by Philip K. Dick, directed by Ridley Scott, screenplay by Hampton Fancher and David Webb Peoples

BILL HUTCHINSON

The Bourne Identity (2002), novel by Robert Ludlum, directed by Doug Liman, screenplay by Tony Gilroy and William Blake Herron

The Chronicles of Narnia series, novels by C. S. Lewis, (2005) directed by Andrew Adamson, screenplay by Ann Peacock, Andrew Adamson, Christopher Markus, and Stephen McFeely

Clash of the Titans (1981), story by Beverley Cross, directed by Desmond Davis, screenplay by Beverley Cross

The Color Purple (1985), novel by Alice Walker, directed by Steven Spielberg, screenplay by Menno Meyjes

Dracula, novel by Bram Stoker, (1931) directed by Tod Browning, play by Hamilton Deane and John L. Balderston, screenplay by Garrett Fort, (1992) directed by Francis Ford Coppola, screenplay by James V. Hart

Goldfinger (1964), novel by Ian Fleming, directed by Guy Hamilton, screenplay by Richard Maibaum and Paul Dehn

Harry Potter series, novels by J.K. Rowling, (2002) directed by Chris Columbus, screenplay by Steve Kloves

Jason and the Argonauts (1963), poem "The Argonautica" by Apollonios Rhodios, directed by Don Chaffey, screenplay by Jan Read and Beverley Cross

Jurassic Park (1993), novel by Michael Crichton, directed by Steven Spielberg, screenplay by Michael Crichton and David Koepp

Lord of the Rings: The Fellowship of the Ring (2001), novel by J.R.R. Tolkien, directed by Peter Jackson, screenplay by Fran Walsh, Philippa Boyens, and Peter Jackson

INTRODUCTION

FROM DA BIG ISLAND SCREENPLAY AND NOVEL

The Maltese Falcon, novel by Dashiell Hammett, (1931) directed by Roy Del Ruth, screenplay by Maude Fulton and Brown Holmes, (1941) directed by John Huston, screenplay by John Huston

North by Northwest (1959), story by Ernest Lehman, directed by Alfred Hitchcock, screenplay by Ernest Lehman

The Omen (1976), story by David Seltzer, directed by Richard Donner, screenplay by David Seltzer

One Flew Over the Cuckoo's Nest (1975), novel by Ken Kesey, directed by Milos Forman, screenplay by Lawrence Hauben and Bo Goldman

Psycho (1960), novel by Robert Bloch, directed by Alfred Hitchcock, screenplay by Joseph Stefano

Raiders of the Lost Ark (1981), story by George Lucas and Philip Kaufman, screenplay by Lawrence Kasdan

The Shining (1980), novel by Stephen King, directed by Stanley Kubrick, directed by Stanley Kubrick

The Silence of the Lambs (1991), novel by Thomas Harris, directed by Jonathan Demme, screenplay by Ted Tally

Star Wars: Episode IV – A New Hope (1977), story by George Lucas, directed by George Lucas, screenplay by George Lucas

Them! (1954), story by George Worthing Yates, directed by Gordon Douglas, adapted by Russell S. Hughes, screenplay by Ted Sherdeman

Troy (2004), poem "The Iliad" by Homer, directed by Wolfgang Petersen, screenplay by David Benioff

BILL HUTCHINSON

Where the Crawdads Sing (2022), novel by Delia Owens, directed by Olivia Newman, screenplay by Delia Owens, Lucy Alibar

The Wizard of OZ (1939), novel by L. Frank Baum, directed by Victor Fleming, screenplay by Noel Langley, Florence Ryerson, and Edgar Allan Woolf

FROM DA BIG ISLAND SCREENPLAY AND NOVEL

NOTES

BILL HUTCHINSON

NOTES

INTRODUCTION

The Screenplay

From da Big Island

New York defined her
Hawaii changed her

by

Bill Hutchinson

FADE IN:

EXT. 21 CLUB - NIGHT

Title card "June 17, 1965"

A crowd of spectators surrounds the red carpet and chrome stanchions from the entrance.

PAT, a local New York television commentator, wears a blue blazer with a large number 3 on his lapel and microphone. He stands near a waiting limousine.

BOB, the cameraman, has his camera focused on Pat.

>   PAT
>   This is Pat Patterson in front of The
>   21 Club, where in a few moments, along
>   with their wives, mob boss Mario
>   Manzoni, his lieutenant Joe Baccio, and
>   attorney Zach Newcomb will be exiting.
>   It is rumored they have been discussing
>   the turf wars between the Manzoni and
>   Sarducci crime families here in New
>   York.

In the crowd, next to Pat is an Italian ASSASSIN (mid-20s with slicked-back black hair) in one hand in his heavy long black raincoat, holding a concealed 45 AUTOMATIC.

No one notices the Assassin nor his concealed gun.

>   PAT (CONT'D)
>   Manzoni prefers using the legal system
>   to resolve a conflict over the use of
>   force, as some of the other crime
>   families do.

A DOORMAN opens the door.

BODYGUARD #1 and BODYGUARD #2 (their early twenties) dressed in black with slicked-back black hair, exit.

>   PAT (CONT'D)
>   It looks like they are starting to exit
>   the 21 Club.

Bob, the cameraman, turns the camera from Pat to the door.

Bodyguard #1 and #2 make their way to the limousine, scanning the crowd, not noticing the Assassin next to Pat.

The doorman opens the door again, this time MARIO MANZONI (mid 60's) and a BLONDE BOMBSHELL (early 40's) exit, followed by JOE and EILEEN Baccio (early 20's), the guys dressed in white tuxedos and the women in colorful gowns.

> PAT (CONT'D)
> Here comes Mario Manzoni, Joe Baccio, and their wives.

Copper red-haired RUTH NEWCOMB (23), wearing a shimmering green skin-tight evening gown, and her husband, ZACH (23), in a white tuxedo exit.

> PAT (CONT'D)
> Here's Zach Newcomb and his wife, Ruth Newcomb, our very own junior reporter.

Ruth throws Pat a loving kiss.

> RUTH
> (mouths)
> I love you, darling.

Pat smiles and focuses his attention back on the unfolding events.

> PAT
> (calling)
> Mario!

Mario acknowledges Pat by nodding.
Pat extends the microphone in his direction.

Mario and his wife move towards Pat.

Joe holds the limo door open as his wife enters, he follows her.

The Assassin moves between Pat and the limo and now has an unobstructed view of Mario.

> PAT (CONT'D)
> Mario, do you have anything you are willing to tell us?

The crowd moves forward in anticipation of getting the news firsthand.

Bodyguards #1 and #2 have focused on the onslaught of people rushing forward.

Zach holds open the limo door for Ruth.

Mario is at point-blank range from the Assassin.

The Assassin pulls out the gun, pointing it at Mario.

BANG! The gun goes off.

Bob, holding the camera, follows Mario dropping.

The crowd SCREAMS.

Bombshell Wife falls to the ground grabbing Mario. Blood covers his white tuxedo and starts blending into her dress.

The surrounding crowd drops to their knees.

Bodyguard #2, with his gun out, points it at the Assassin.

The Assassin turns, bumping Pat.

A crowd member bumps Bodyguard #2 the instant he fires.

The shot misses the Assassin, hitting Pat.

Pat falls to the ground dead.

Bodyguard #1 fires, killing the Assassin.

Zach holding the limo door sticks his head into the limo.
                    ZACH
          I think we're safe now that the
          assassin is dead. Joe, Get out of here!
          I'll handle it.

As the limo speeds away, Zach embraces Ruth kissing her.
                    ZACH (CONT'D)
          I'm glad you're alright. I love you.

Ruth observes the carnage.

                    RUTH
          Pat's dead!
               (shaking her head in
               disbelief)
          I need to get this news story to the
          newsroom now!

Ruth seeing Bob, the cameraman, rushes towards him.

Bob is filming the body of Mario being held by his wife, much like the Pieta, with Pat lying to the side in a pool of blood.

                    RUTH (CONT'D)
          Darling, get some cut-a-ways.

Bob films the bodies and faces in the crowd as they get up, taking in the carnage.

Shaken, Ruth searches the ground, spotting spots the bloodstained mic Pat was holding.

Trembling, Ruth bends down and picks the mic up by the wire mesh, wiping the blood off on Pat's news jacket.

Ruth stands, holding the mic in front of her.

> RUTH (CONT'D)
> Bob!

Bob engrossed, films the carnage.

> RUTH (CONT'D)
> (louder)
> Bob!

Bob acknowledges Ruth.

> RUTH (CONT'D)
> Focus on me.

Bob swings the camera around, focusing on Ruth, giving her the thumbs up.

Ruth takes a deep breath.

> RUTH (CONT'D)
> This is Ruth Newcomb, coming to you
> from The 21 Club, where a few moments
> ago, we witnessed the brutal murder of
> Mario Manzoni, the reputed mob boss,
> and television commentator, Pat
> Patterson, by a lone assassin ...

                                        DISSOLVE TO:

EXT. NEW YORK SKYLINE - DUSK - HELICOPTER SHOTS

Title card "Christmastime, 40 years later"

The screen glows an eerie reddish orange. We fly through fluffy clouds, emerging to see the golden light of the setting sun shimmering through a layer of clouds.

Descending through more clouds, the lights of New York Harbor materialize. In the distant background, the lights of the Brooklyn Bridge come into view.

The sound of a sole UKULELE strumming the tune of Holly and the Ivy sneaks in.

The lights of cars crossing the Brooklyn Bridge reflect the falling snow, making glistening diamonds appear.

MAIN TITLES OVER:

The wind blows snow across the rooftops of New York City.

The red and green lights of the Empire State Building illuminate snow as if rubies and emeralds fall from the sky. There's no doubt it's Christmastime in the big city.

EXT. CENTRAL PARK - DUSK

Bundled up, PEOPLE skate on the lit frozen lake in
Central Park.

A cold, bitter wind blows the falling flakes around
the snow-covered Alice In Wonderland statue.

Near the statue, illuminated by a street lamp, sits
MICHAEL (late 40s, a portly Hawaiian) wearing an
Aloha shirt over his parka, seated on a park bench,
strumming his ukulele to Holly and the Ivy. His
breath can be seen as he starts singing in thick
Hawaiian pidgin.

> MICHAEL
> (sings)
> From da Big Ap-ple she come
> to my Big Is-land home
> A-lone, she be-lieves she wants to be
> Not on da Big Is-land
>
> Da grow-ing of da Kai-ke's
> Da kil-ling of da pig
> Da hang-ing of da cars in da trees
> All from da Big Is-land
> All from da Big Is-land
>
> Ben, da lay-back care-ta-ker,
> Aunt-ie grows da Kai-ke's
> Ah, da driv-ing of the lawn-mow-er
> Ka-ku-a Will-iam needs
>
> Da grow-ing of da Kai-ke's
> Da kil-ling of da pig
> Da hang-ing of da cars in da trees
> All from da Big Is-land
> All from da Big Is-land

PEOPLE, some carrying skates, while others carrying
gift- wrapped packages, stop to listen, dropping
loose change in the ukulele case, while others
hurry to pass by.

EXT. TIMES SQUARE - DUSK

The SINGING continues.

Cars whizz by. PEOPLE carrying holiday packages
scurry about.

EXT. ROCKEFELLER PLAZA - DUSK

The SKATERS, young and old alike, make their way
around the lit rink as people watch.

A FATHER and MOTHER hold the arms of their four-
year-old BOY, teaching him how to maneuver the ice.

On the Jumbotron television screen, the Rockettes
perform their Christmas Spectacular. Their routine

SCREENPLAY

ends, and the Jumbotron dissolves to a much older
copper-haired RUTH (now 63) wearing a red dress.

                                    DISSOLVE TO:

INT. TELEVISION STUDIO – DUSK

Ruth is seated at the anchor desk; behind her, the
logo of a LARGE RED APPLE with FROM THE BIG APPLE
written in white, at a thirty-degree angle.

                    RUTH
          So don't miss the Rockettes Christmas
          Spectacular at Radio City Music Hall
          through January second.

          Darlings, I adore the New York Public
          Library Reading is Fundamental program.
          I love it so much that I will read
          Charles Dickens, A Christmas Carol, at
          the New York Public Library mid-town
          branch this Saturday at two PM.

Next to the camera stands the FLOOR MANAGER holding
up both hands, indicating twenty seconds to go.

                    RUTH (CONT'D)
          So don't forget to be there because
          reading is fundamental.
               (beat)
          This wraps up another edition of From
          the Big Apple.

Ruth is reading from the Teleprompter.

The Teleprompter displays "TOMORROW WE WILL HAVE
???? UNTIL NEXT TIME..."

                    RUTH (CONT'D)
          Tomorrow we will have...

Ruth pauses, gives a curious look, and takes a deep
breath.
                    RUTH (CONT'D)
          We will have a wonderful show for you.
          Until next time, this is Ruth Newcomb,
          From the Big Apple.

Ruth looks at the camera smiling. The tally light
goes out.

                    FLOOR MANAGER
          We're clear.

Ruth no longer smiles.

                    RUTH
               (directed at the camera)
          What the heck was that?

SCREENPLAY

                    FLOOR MANAGER
          What was what?

                         RUTH
          Darling, you know what I mean.   The
          question marks!

SARAH MARTIN, 64, the producer and Ruth's childhood
friend, runs up.

                         RUTH (CONT'D)
                    (addressing Sarah)
          I thought we had the next show planned.

PAULINE, 30's, Ruth's niece, production assistant,
and wanna-be producer, carries a clipboard, loyally
following Sarah. Her ponytail bobs up and down as
she struts.

                         PAULINE
          We don't!

Ruth scowls.

                         RUTH
                    (pleasantly)
          Pauline, darling, would you be a doll
          and get Auntie some water?

Pauline stops, making an about-turn, causing her
ponytail to slap her face as she leaves.

Ruth glances at the MONITOR next to the camera.

On the MONITOR is a montage of palm trees, sandy
beaches, Diamond Head, Waikiki Beach, and other
Hawaiian images.

                         SARAH
          In any event, George called during the
          segment and canceled.

                         RUTH
          So what if he canceled, Sarah. You
          could have had Teleprompter Bob put
          something on the Teleprompter other
          than those damn question marks in the
          Teleprompter. Darling, you know how I
          hate that.

Ruth glances back at the monitor.

                         SARAH
          You did a good job faking it.

The promo on the monitor ends with "COME TO
HAWAII."

                    RUTH
            (sarcastically)
        Sarah, I could have said, "Tomorrow, we
        will be coming to you from Hawaii!"

                    SARAH
        Coming from Hawaii?

Ruth points to the monitor.

                    RUTH
        Yes, Hawaii. Ever since Thanksgiving,
        that <u>Come to Hawaii</u> ad has aired. We
        might as well do the show from Hawaii!
            (beat)
        What's going on here?

                    SARAH
        It's cold; people want to escape to a
        warm climate like Hawaii. You know,
        warm, friendly, happy people, tropical
        drinks, ukuleles, luaus, hukilaus, and
        Hula dancing.

                    RUTH
        Not everyone has a little grass shack
        like you and Paul do in Hawaii. Some
        people like to ski, go to a cozy
        mountain cabin, and enjoy the snow.

                    SARAH
        And then there are those like you who
        never leave New York.

                    SARAH
        And then there are those like you who
        never step foot out of New York.

Pauline returns with Ruth's water, handing it to
Ruth.

                    RUTH
            (to Pauline)
        Thank you, darling.

Ruth takes a sip.

                    SARAH
        We need to think of something for the
        next show.

                    RUTH
        Maybe we could do <u>The Nutcracker</u>?

Sarah and Pauline grimace.

                    SARAH AND PAULINE
            (in unison)
        Not again!

                    PAULINE
          We've never done an inside tour of
          Tiffany's. We can tie into the re-
          release of <u>Breakfast at Tiffany's</u>.
          Or maybe we can cover the medicinal
          marijuana trial Uncle Zach is working
          on. Sparks are flying, and I'm sure we
          can do an interview with Uncle Zach
          about why the Baccio trail is so
          important.

                    VOICE (O.S.)
          Pauline, telephone.

Pauline leaves.

                    SARAH
          We did The Nutcracker last year. Think
          of something else. We'll talk about it
          first thing tomorrow, before the
          production meeting.

                    RUTH
          Darling, I was thinking of an easy way
          out.

                    SARAH
          I'm with you. We're still on for
          Charlie Chan tonight, aren't we?

                    RUTH
          Starts at seven. I have the
          chopsticks, so don't forget the sushi.

                    SARAH
          Big Apple or Mr. Okomoto's Sushi?

INT. RUTH'S NEW YORK PENTHOUSE SCREENING ROOM -
NIGHT

CLOSE ON - OKOMOTO'S SUSHI BOXES

Pull back to reveal a personal thirties-style
theater with red curtains flanking the large
projection screen.

Ruth, Sarah, ZACH (60's), and PAUL (60's) in plush,
overly-stuffed, red velvet love seats. Manhattan's
and an entire bowl of popcorn are on the low table
in front of them.

MRS. WIGGINS, a rather portly BLACK CAT, curled up
on Ruth's lap, PURRING.

                    ZACH
          Manhattan's, sushi, and popcorn.
          Cheers!

They all toast. The glasses CLINK.

Zach grabs the remote from the table and presses the play button.

Everyone turns their attention to the screen.

Following the opening credits of <u>The Black Camel</u> are surfers surfing in the foreground and Diamond Head in the background. A few moments later, a shot of 1930's Waikiki Beach from the surfer's point of view with the only two multistory hotels; the Royal Hawaiian and the Halekulani.

                    PAUL
               (to Zach)
          That reminds me...

                    RUTH
          Shhh...

                    PAUL
               (whispering to Zach)
          That reminds me, Charlie liked to have
          his Manhattan's at the Halekulani House
          Without a Key Bar under the kiawe tree.

                    ZACH
          Hal-le-ku-lani? kiawe tree?

                    RUTH
          Can't you guys let us enjoy the movie?

Zach grabs the remote and pauses the movie.

                    RUTH (CONT'D)
          What are you doing?

                    ZACH
          Paul was saying something about Charlie
          and the Hall-le-ku-lani House Without a
          Key Bar ...

                    SARAH
          Oh, that!
               (to Ruth)
          It's nothing. The real Charlie Chan
          hung out at the Halekulani Hotel and
          its House Without a Key Bar. It is as
          simple as that.

                    PAUL
          Honey, I thought you liked your
          tropical drinks and listening to the
          live Hawaiian music under the kiawe
          tree at sunset.

                    SARAH
          I do, darling, it's a fantastic hotel,
          but we're here to watch a movie, not
          talk about Hawaii.

Zach presses the button on the remote and places the remote on the table.

The girls smile.

Zach and Paul's eyes wander around the room.

> ZACH
> (whispering to Paul)
> I thought you liked the remoteness of your vacation home on the Big Island.

> PAUL
> (whispering to Zach)
> We do, eccentric neighbors and all; it's like something straight out of a Ma and Pa Kettle movie or The Beverly Hillbillies.

Ruth glares at the two of them, grabs the remote, and presses the pause button.

> RUTH
> So you want to watch Ma and Pa Kettle?

> PAUL
> No, we're talking about our house on the Big Island.

> SARAH
> Darling, they already told us they don't want to go to Hawaii. Why push it?
> (Looking at Zach)
> Zach always has an excuse for being tied up on this or that trial. And...
> (Looking at Ruth)
> Ruth doesn't want to leave the comfort of the Big Apple.
> (Looking at the screen)
> Now that we have everything cleared up let's watch the movie.

INT. RUTH'S NEW YORK PENTHOUSE TERRACE - DAWN

Ruth takes a sip of coffee from her Tiffany coffee cup.

Zach finishes his half-eaten bagel while reading the New York Times.

INSERT: NEW YORK TIMES headline DEFENSE ATTY. NEWCOMB DROPS BOMBSHELL AT BACCIO TRIAL.

> ZACH
> A Bombshell! It's only the beginning! The medicinal marijuana issue came to a head yesterday.

                    RUTH
          Darling, you know marijuana is bad. I
          don't understand why you are for it.

                    PAUL
          I'm not. Joe thinks since states have
          started to allow medicinal marijuana,
          it's another way to make money.

                    RUTH
          Darling, I don't understand it at all.
          People are using the medicinal excuse
          to get high.

                    PAUL
          We have documentation that it does help
          some people.

The sun rises over the East River, illuminating the
covered terrace with a golden glow that further
enhances the Christmas decorations and lights.

Mrs. Wiggins plays with one of the ornament balls
hanging nearby.

Ruth, having finished her breakfast, gets up.

                    RUTH
          Got to run.

Ruth kisses Zach.

Zach smiles, watching her leave.

EXT. NUMBER 3 BEEKMAN PLACE - DAY

The DOORMAN opens the door.

Ruth exits wearing a long black woolen COAT, a RED
WOOLEN SCARF, and DESIGNER HIGH HEEL SHOES exits.

The snow-covered black canopy covering the entrance
states #3 Beekman Place.

The doorman hurries over to the waiting cab at the
end of the canopy, opening the door for her.

INT. TELEVISION STATION HALLWAY - DAY

The office hallway is filled with business PEOPLE
dressed in holiday clothing, all scurrying around.

Pauline stands by the elevators, staring at her
watch, and then sips her coconut water bottle.

DING, the elevator door opens, PEOPLE exit, while
others enter, the door closes. Another look at the
watch followed by a sip. Ding, another elevator
door opens, PEOPLE exit, and the door closes. Ding,
another elevator door opens.

Ruth steps out of the elevator, dressed in her woolen coat and scarf..

> PAULINE
> Aunt Ruth, great show yesterday. Nothing like the Rockettes.

> RUTH
> (nodding)
> You said it, Pauline. Ruth strides toward her office. Pauline runs to catch up with Ruth.

> PAULINE
> So we're doing another segment on The Nutcracker?

> RUTH
> Haven't decided yet.

> PAULINE
> When are you and Uncle Zach seeing it?

> RUTH
> Tomorrow.

Sarah struts up.

> SARAH
> I was able to get Alex Baldwin for today's show.

> PAULINE AND RUTH
> (in unison)
> Great!

Pauline takes a sip from her coconut water.

> RUTH
> Pauline, why are you drinking that stuff?

> PAULINE
> Coconut water is an excellent alternative to other drinks as it is all-natural, healthy, and potassium-rich. Some call it 'Mother Nature's sports drink.'

> RUTH
> It sounds like you're an advertisement.

They reach Ruth's office.

INT. RUTH'S OFFICE - DAY

Ruth, Sarah, and Pauline enter.

Ruth puts her COAT and the RED WOOLEN SCARF on the COAT STAND.

The clean office has a feminine air: flowers on the desk, a plant in the corner, a goldfish bowl on the credenza next to a few Emmys, needlepoint "I Love New York" pillow on the sofa.

Pictures of Ruth with the Clintons, Donald Trump, Jackie Onassis, Princess Diana, and other celebrities adorn the walls, along with diplomas from New York and Columbia Universities next to a plaque for the Nobel Prize in Journalism. On another wall is a framed New York Metropolitan Library READING IS FUN poster with Ruth in the center, holding a bound edition of The Adventures of Huckleberry Finn.

Behind her desk, floor-to-ceiling windows provide a spectacular view of the New York skyline.

Ruth moves behind her desk, placing her purse in the drawer.

                    SARAH
          We need to work on the show. We cannot
          do another year of The Nutcracker.

                    RUTH
          Darling, I was trying to make things
          easy, and we're seeing it tomorrow
          night.

                    SARAH
          We will need a different angle than
          what we've done. Any suggestions?

                    RUTH
          I see, making me do all the work! Hmm.

                    SARAH
          We might as well run last year's show.

                    RUTH
               (laughs)
          You're so funny, Sarah. How about the
          fight scene between the soldiers and
          the mice or the costumes and make-up?

Sarah starts taking notes.

                    SARAH
          That's a thought.

                    RUTH
          Sure, the conflict, the intrigue, the
          combat. Finally, the soldiers all
          dead...
               (smiling)
          Not unlike living in New York.

They all laugh.

SCREENPLAY

                    SARAH
          This is Christmas! And fights don't
          mix, Ruth. The Sugar Plum Fairy and the
          Nutcracker dance sequence is more
          Christmassy.

                    RUTH
          Do we always have to sugarcoat it?

They laugh again.

                    SARAH
          You know what I'm talking about. You're
          the one who mentioned The Nutcracker.

                    RUTH
          I was trying to keep things simple.

Pauline glances at the framed READING IS FUN
poster.

                    PAULINE
          Aunt Ruth, you did a great job reading
          A Christmas Carol last night. Maybe we
          could do a segment on that instead of
          The Nutcracker.

                    SARAH
          That's an idea. Let's keep our options
          open. Best of all, we are going to see
          The Nutcracker tomorrow.

INT. RUTH'S BATHROOM VANITY AREA - DAY

Zach attempts to put on his black onyx cuff links
without a jacket.

Ruth notices his difficulty and helps him put them
on. Ruth reaches for her pearl necklace.

Zach takes the necklace and finishes placing it on
her neck. He romantically gives Ruth a whack on the
derriere.

Ruth smiles.

Zach takes hold of her; they embrace and kiss.

EXT. LINCOLN CENTER - NIGHT

Light snow continues to fall. Limousines and taxis
pull up.

Ruth, Zach, Sarah, and Paul exit one limousine,
dressed formally. Ruth is wearing her RED WOOLEN
SCARF.

We see the activities of the arrivals for the
performance.

SCREENPLAY

The foursome stroll with other people dressed formally, passing the illuminated fountain towards the golden-lit Lincoln Center entrance.

A large poster announces <u>The Nutcracker</u>.

INT. LINCOLN CENTER - NIGHT

The Nutcracker and the mice battle sequence starts.

Ruth and Sarah look at each other, smiling. They return their attention to the stage.

We see the mouse go for the Nutcracker.

Ruth reaches into her purse, pulling out a notepad and paper.

> SARAH
> (whispering)
> Enjoy it! Don't take notes.

> RUTH
> Darling, you know me. I need to.

Sarah places her hand on Ruth's notepad and shakes her head.

Ruth pays attention to the ballet.

The mouse takes another swipe with the sword at the Nutcracker.

INT. LINCOLN CENTER MEZZANINE - NIGHT

It's intermission. People dressed in black ties and Christmas evening gowns sip Champagne and wine.

Ruth, Zach, Sarah, and Paul sip Champagne.

> RUTH
> The fight sequence was better than in past years. However, I don't think we have enough to do an entire eight-minute segment on this version being different.

> PAUL
> Wait until the third act.

> ZACH
> During the Sugar Plum Fairy and the Nutcracker dance.

> PAUL
> (leans into the group
> whispering)
> We heard a rumor that they are seeing each other.

                    SARAH
          Who's seeing whom?

                    ZACH
          The Sugar Plum Fairy and the
          Nutcracker, who else?

                    RUTH
          Oh, stop it, you two.

                    PAUL
          We're not kidding. In real life,
          Rudolph and Natasha are seeing each
          other. I heard that scene makes the
          show.

EILEEN and JOE BACCIO (now in their 60's) walk up
to the foursome.

                    ZACH
          Joe, I didn't know you were going to be
          here tonight. Are you enjoying the
          show?

                    JOE
          Fantastic. The tension between the
          Sugar Plum Fairy and the Nutcracker is
          unbelievable! I don't recall that from
          prior performances.

                    SARAH
          Zach put you up to this, didn't he,
          Joe?

                    JOE
          Up to what?

                    SARAH
          Oh, never mind. How's the trial going?

MILLIE, a rather tall woman carrying a Playbill
program and pen, makes her way to the group with
BILLY, her meek short, balding husband in tow,
interrupts the conversation.

                    MILLIE
          You're Ruth Newcomb of From the Big
          Apple, aren't you?

                    RUTH
          Darling, who else could I be?

                    MILLIE
          I ADORE your show. May I have your
          autograph?

Millie pushes the Playbill program and pen at Ruth.

                    RUTH
          Darling, what's your name?

                  MILLIE
    Millie ... Millie Greenwald.

Ruth looks at Billy, who looks down, avoiding eye
contact.

                  RUTH
    Do you want me to add your husband's
    name, too?

Millie smiles, clasping her hands together.

                  MILLIE
    Oh, would you, please?

Billy looks up at Ruth, smiling.

                  MILLIE (CONT'D)
    His name is Billy.

                  RUTH
    Ah, Millie and Billy, what a pair!

Ruth laughs, followed by everyone else as Ruth
signs the front of the Playbill program.

INSERT: TO MILLIE AND BILLY, MY FAVORITE FANS, RUTH
NEWCOMB. Around her signature, she draws her
stylized From the Big Apple logo.

Ruth hands the program back to Millie.

Millie looks at the signature on the Playbill
program.

                  MILLIE
    Oh, thank you so much, Mrs. Newcomb.
    Thank you, and Merry Christmas.

Millie and Billy both bow as if they are in the
presence of royalty and turn to leave the group.

                  EILEEN
    Ruth, every time we get together, your
    fans interrupt. Don't you ever get
    tired of it?

                  RUTH
    Not in the least, Eileen. It's
    expected. Now, where were we?

                  JOE
    Sarah asked me how things were going
    with the trial. I think it's going
    better than expected. We're dealing
    with medicinal marijuana; it is enough
    to cause significant issues.

The FIRST CHIME is heard.

The audience starts to head into the theater. A few look at Ruth and smile, giving her a nod as they pass the foursome.

Ruth nodded back.

> JOE (CONT'D)
> I believe medicinal marijuana is the way to go, legalize it, not only here but nationwide, and tax it. The government and I make money, and everyone will be happy.

The SECOND CHIME is heard.

> JOE (CONT'D)
> We better get back to our seats. I hope you all have a wonderful evening. See you later. Merry Christmas!

Joe and Eileen turn, leaving the group and joining the crowd as they return to their seats.

EXT. LINCOLN CENTER STREET SIDE - NIGHT

The snow continues to fall. Snow covers the ground. Ruth, Zach, Sarah, and Paul enter the limousine.

The limo pulls away.

EXT. COLUMBUS CIRCLE - NIGHT

Trucks, cars, and limousines whiz around the circle.

We follow the exact limousine we saw leaving Lincoln Center.

INT. LIMOUSINE - NIGHT

Ruth seated across from Ruth.

> RUTH
> Let's focus the next show on the Rudolph and Natasha romance.

> SARAH
> We can't.

> RUTH
> Why not, darling? I think it's what made the show so good.

> SARAH
> We need to verify if it is true.

> RUTH
> Pshaw!

From Ruth's point of view, over Sarah's shoulder and through the window, we see a large truck plowing toward the limousine.

                    RUTH (CONT'D)
          Bracc yourselves!

                                        CUT TO BLACK:

EXT. CEMETERY - DAY

Hundreds of cars, limousines, flower cars, and news trucks line the road through the Brooklyn cemetery. A television film crew is filming Zach's funeral.

The HEADSTONE reads ZACHARIAH NEWCOMB. Mourners surround the bouquet-laden coffin, weeping with grave expressions. Next to Ruth is LINDA (60's), her look-alike sister, Pauline, Madam GLORIA La Fong (60's), Ruth's born-again hippy therapist.

Nearby are Joe and Eileen Baccio beside GEORGE Epstein (60's), a short, stocky, balding man and Zach's business partner.

INT. RUTH'S BATHROOM VANITY AREA - DAY

Ruth, in her designer woolen bathrobe, brings Zach's bathrobe to her nose, smelling and holding it to the side of her face.

Ruth smiles and stares as if remembering a moment she had with Zach. Shaking her head and sighing, she places the robe on its hook.

INT. RUTH'S LIVING ROOM - DAY

Ruth meanders in, pensively moving around.

A fire rages in the fireplace.

On the mantle contains Emmy's and photographs; a picture of Ruth holding an Emmy with Zach and the Martins, Ruth and Zach with Jackie Onassis at the Tavern On The Green entrance, and Ruth and Zach with Bill and Hillary Clinton all in golf attire.

Ruth moves to the Emmy photograph and picks it up.

She takes it with her to the chair near the fireplace and sits.

Studying it for a moment before gently stroking it and smiling.

Mrs. Wiggins PURRS, nudges her leg, and lets out a curt MEOW.

Ruth reaches down, picks up the cat placing it on her lap.

Mrs. Wiggins PURRS.

EXT. NEWCOMB AND EPSTEIN BUILDING AND LAW OFFICES - DAY

Ruth wearing her long black woolen coat, and the red woolen scarf, stops at a modern Upper East Side marble facade, staring at the lavish NEWCOMB AND EPSTEIN sign.

She reaches sliding her finger over the N in Newcomb before entering the building.

INT. GEORGE EPSTEIN'S OFFICE - DAY

Ruth sits in a chair.

George is behind his desk. In front of him a stack of legal-sized papers. He puts his reading glasses on.

> GEORGE
> Do you like Hawaii?

> RUTH
> George, you know I've never been.

> GEORGE
> Now's your chance.

> RUTH
> Darling, what do you mean?

> GEORGE
> You now own the Martin's house in Honokaa on the Big Island of Hawaii.

Ruth's mouth drops.

> GEORGE (CONT'D)
> What's also great is the Martins had entered into a ten-year contract with the caretaker, Ben Kokua, who lives on the property. He takes care of the six acres, including the macadamia nut orchard.

Ruth shakes her head in disbelief.

> GEORGE (CONT'D)
> The perfect vacation home. You don't have to worry about anything.

> RUTH
> If everything has been taken care of, why didn't they will it to ... what's his name?

                    GEORGE
          Ben has a heart of gold, is a great
          caretaker, and is, how should I put it,
          a little inept.

                    RUTH
          Darling, what would I do with a place
          in Hawaii?

                    GEORGE
          At the funeral, you told me you wanted
          to get away from it all, right?

Ruth nods.

                    GEORGE (CONT'D)
          What better place than Hawaii?

                    RUTH
          It's so far away.

                    GEORGE
          You're right; that's what makes it
          perfect for a vacation home.

                    RUTH
          I don't want it.

                    GEORGE
          It's prime real estate, in a
          rainforest, with a great view.

                    RUTH
          Then make arrangements to sell it.

EXT. CENTRAL PARK - DAY

Ruth strolls through the park, bundled up in her
long black woolen coat and the red woolen scarf.

Some of the passersby smile and nod to her, while
others stop and point in her direction.

We hear the sounds of a ukulele and a man singing
My Little Grass Shack.

Ruth follows the music to find MICHAEL (40's), a
Hawaiian Man, wearing his Ray Bans and an Aloha
shirt over his parka.

Ruth stops listening, reaches into her purse, takes
out a twenty-dollar bill, and drops it in his
ukulele case.

Michael continues strumming the song My Little
Grass Shack on the ukulele.

                    MICHAEL
               (thick Hawaiian accent)
          Ma-ha-lo! Dat mean thank you in
          Hawaiian.

Ruth starts to leave.

>   MICHAEL (CONT'D)
>   Aaa-loooo-haa! Dat mean hello and
>   farewell. Da boss goin do plenny good
>   stuff fo you.

Ruth pauses and looks over her shoulder at Michael.

Michael smiles and winks.

>   MICHAEL (CONT'D)
>   Change, she come soon.

Ruth turns, continuing her stroll.

>   MICHAEL (CONT'D)
>   "I'm just a little Hawaiian A homesick
>   island boy,
>   I want to go back to my fish and poi,
>   I want to go back
>   to my little grass shack."

INT. 21 CLUB - NIGHT

Ruth sits alone at a cleared table. She stirs her
coffee. The candle illuminates her pensive face.

The MAÎTRE D' escorts a 20's something couple to
their table.

As they pass Ruth, the Wife recognizes her, nudging
her Husband, who notices Ruth.

They stop at Ruth's table.

The Maître d' continues walking, not realizing the
couple has stopped.

>   WIFE
>   It must be a terrible loss.

Ruth stops stirring but doesn't look up.

Upon hearing the Wife, the Maître d' turns around
to break the conversation up.

>   HUSBAND
>   Terrible.

>   WIFE
>   We miss your show.

Ruth looks up. Generating a slight but noticeable
smile. The Maître d' arrives at the table.

>   MAÎTRE D'
>   (to the couple)
>   Please follow me.

SCREENPLAY

INT. MADAM LA FONG'S THERAPIST OFFICE - DAY

MADAM GLORIA LA FONG (60's), Ruth's Earth Mother
therapist, wearing an Indian tunic and long tie-
died dress, giving the appearance of a born-again
hippy, lounging in an over-stuffed padded chair
holding a notepad and pen. 1960's and 70's rock
posters adorn the walls.

                    RUTH
          I hate it here. I hate my job. I hate
          that people stare at me. Everywhere I
          look, I remember things Zach and I did.
          I can't get him out of my mind.

                    GLORIA
          You two were together for over forty
          years.

Gloria puts down her notepad, thinking for a
moment.

                    GLORIA (CONT'D)
          Ruth, what happened to you is
          monumental. There's been a significant
          change in your life; your world has
          been turned upside down. You not only
          lost Zach, but you also lost Sarah,
          your childhood friend as well.

                    RUTH
          Gloria, that's why I'm here. I'm
          looking to you for guidance.

                    GLORIA
          It takes people years to get over
          similar circumstances. Your entire life
          is changing; you are at the crossroads
          of life with many paths to take. Over
          the years, you've been given crumbs to
          help you find your way through changes
          such as this, and when you reach the
          crossroads, you can make a more
          informed decision.

                    RUTH
          Oh, stop it, Gloria. Everything and
          everyone I love is gone.

                    GLORIA
          Are they?

                    RUTH
          Yes!

                    GLORIA
          What would make you happy?

                    RUTH
          I don't know.

SCREENPLAY

                    GLORIA
          You do.

Ruth became more uncomfortable, adjusting her body
in the bean bag.

                    GLORIA (CONT'D)
          You must discover what you want for
          yourself. No one can make your choices.
          You have more money than you know what
          to do with. Think of people who would
          give anything to be in your situation,
          given the opportunity to change their
          life and direction. You have to let
          loose, let go of the old, and think of
          something you've always wanted to do
          and never had time to do it. Open up,
          Ruth; you can do it! What is it that
          you want or need?

                    RUTH
          I spent my entire life here in New York
          or the Hamptons. I'm a New Yorker.
          And now, I hate it!

                    GLORIA
          Now, we're getting somewhere! What is
          it that will make you happy?

                    RUTH
          I want to be alone and write my
          memoirs.

                    GLORIA
          Well, you are not going to be alone
          here in New York. You said so yourself;
          you're too well known; everywhere you
          go, people know you. Privacy and
          solitude cannot be found here. It would
          help if you had a place somewhere you
          can go. Do you?

Ruth shakes her head no.

                    GLORIA (CONT'D)
          Think of those breadcrumbs that have
          been laid before you. The answer is
          right before you, and you choose not to
          see it. Think. Think about a place
          where you will have peace and solitude.

Ruth looks around the room at the posters, then
focuses on the 1966 Elvis Presley Blue Hawaii
poster with his hands stretched with Diamond Head
in the background, the palm trees, the beach, Hula
girls, the outrigger canoe, and other elements of
that vintage poster. Ruth grins, becoming giddy and
nodding in agreement.

                         -81-

                    RUTH
          The breadcrumbs have been there all
          along, haven't they? The allure of
          Hawaii beckons me. The change will be
          wonderful, won't it?

EXT. MADAM LA FONG'S THERAPIST'S OFFICE - DAY

Ruth exits Madam La Fong's smiling, wearing her
long black woolen coat, designer shoes, and the red
woolen scarf. Takes her cell phone out of her
purse. As she starts to dial, the phone RINGS.

                    RUTH
          Hello?

                    GEORGE (O.S.)
          It's George. Good news.

                    RUTH
          Me, too. I'm moving to Hawaii.

                    GEORGE
          What? Joe Baccio just made an offer for
          the property in Hawaii.

                    RUTH
          Darling, tell him no, and I'll explain
          it later.

                    GEORGE
          But, Ruth!

                    RUTH
          Darling, a new door has opened for me,
          and I refuse to let it close. This is
          an opportunity of a lifetime that will
          provide me many new challenges and
          adventures. There is nothing here for
          me anymore. I want to be alone and
          want a place to go where no one knows
          me. Hawaii is the place. Sell Beekman
          place.

The SOUND OF A JET creeps in.

                                        DISSOLVE TO:

EXT. AIR-TO-AIR AIRPLANE FLYING - DAY

In the foreground, an airplane travels westbound
toward Honolulu International Airport. In the
background, Diamond Head and Waikiki Beach.

EXT. AIRPLANE LANDING - DAY

The airplane lands at Honolulu International. In
the distant background, we see Diamond Head.

SCREENPLAY

INT. GLOBAL AIRWAYS FIRST CLASS SECTION - DAY

Ruth, at a window seat, dressed more for attending
the opera than for flying, wearing a designer
dress, Tiffany jewelry, and her designer high heel
shoes, stares out the window.

>   FLIGHT ATTENDANT (V.O.)
>   We ask that you remain seated until the
>   captain turns off the seat belt sign.
>   Mahalo.

The flight attendant approaches Ruth.

>   FLIGHT ATTENDANT
>   Mrs. Newcomb, can you gather your
>   belongings, please?

Ruth nods and smiles.

>   RUTH
>   The captain hasn't turned off the seat
>   belt sign.

>   FLIGHT ATTENDANT
>   It's okay. We need to deplane you
>   first.

Ruth beams. She leans forward, reaching under the
seat before her, pulling out her purse and a nylon
pet carrier.

Mrs. Wiggins yellow eyes peer out.

Another FLIGHT ATTENDANT opens the front left door.

Ruth gets up and follows the flight attendant to
the front door.

An OFFICER wearing a Hawaii Department of
Agriculture uniform enters the aircraft, waiting at
the door for Ruth.

Other passengers watch the "special treatment" Ruth
receives. Some get up from their seats.

>   FLIGHT ATTENDANT (V.O.)
>   Please remain seated until the captain
>   has turned off the seat belt sign.
>   Mahalo.

>   OFFICER
>   Mrs. Newcomb, can you come with me,
>   please?

The Officer turns and exits the aircraft.

INT. JETWAY - DAY

>   OFFICER
>   Can I have your pet carrier, please?

-83-

Ruth hands the Officer the pet carrier.

>   RUTH
> You're wearing a funny uniform for a
> limo driver.

>   OFFICER
> I'm not a limo driver. I'm here to
> quarantine your cat. Hawaii is rabies-
> free.

Ruth's eyes widen.

>   RUTH
> Mrs. Wiggins doesn't have rabies!

>   OFFICER
> I'm sure she doesn't.

>   RUTH
> You can't quarantine her; she's all
> I've got!

>   OFFICER
> She must be quarantined for five days.
> It's not a long time to wait.

INT. HONOLULU INTERNATIONAL AIRPORT BAGGAGE CLAIM -
DAY

A few passengers mill about wearing leis, claiming
their bags. A set of Louis Vuitton bags continue
their ride around the baggage carousel.

A lone LIMO DRIVER, holding a printed cardboard
sign, MRS. NEWCOMB studies every person in the
baggage claim area.

Next to where the bags come out, a door opens. The
Officer holds the door for Ruth, who exits, holding
only her purse.

Ruth spots the Limo Driver and smiles.

The Limo Driver spots Ruth and heads for her.

EXT. DOWNTOWN HONOLULU - DAY

The limo makes its way down King Street.

INT. LIMOUSINE - DAY

Ruth, transfixed, absorbed with the century-old
buildings next to modern-day ones.

EXT. HALEKULANI HOTEL - DAY

The limo pulls up to the Halekulani Hotel. The
PORTER opens the limo door for Ruth.

SCREENPLAY

Ruth gets out, looking at the Halekulani hibiscus logo.

Another PORTER takes her baggage from the limo, placing them on a waiting cart.

Ruth smiles at all the attention the porters and limo driver give her.

She sees people wearing muumuus and Aloha shirts strolling and enjoying the sights. Some stare at her.

EXT. HOTEL LANAI - DAY

Ruth opens the floor-to-ceiling sliding glass door to her lanai (Hawaiian for verandah) and goes to the handrail.

She takes in the panoramic view of Diamond Head, Waikiki Beach, the hotel pool ten stories below her corner room suite, and the palm trees with coconuts. She smiles, nodding.

She turns to the ocean and sees the SURFERS catching their waves in the distance. Smiling, she takes a deep sigh of relief.

EXT. "HOUSE WITHOUT A KEY" BAR - DUSK

The sun sets on the horizon. A TRIO dressed in blue and white hibiscus shirts play a Hawaiian song as another member, a WOMAN dressed in an eloquent blue and white hibiscus muumuu, does the hula.

Ruth, dressed in a designer evening dress, seated at a table, sips her Manhattan watching the activity.

INT. HOTEL SUITE - NIGHT

Tropical flowers and a basket of fresh Hawaiian fruit are on the coffee table. There's a fully stocked bar with glasses of all kinds. A slight breeze blows the lace curtains.

Ruth on the phone, no answer. She hangs up.

EXT. KALAKAUA BOULEVARD - DAY

Women in muumuus and missionary dresses and men in shorts, aloha shirts, and T-shirts meander the boulevard—all wear zoris (Hawaiian for flip-flops) or sandals.

Ruth stands out as being the only one in a designer silk dress and high heel shoes.

People stare at her and smile while others nod.

INT. HOTEL SUITE - DAY

Ruth on the phone, no answer. She hangs up.

                                    DISSOLVE TO:

INT. HOTEL SUITE - NIGHT

Ruth, in an evening dress, is on the phone.

                    RUTH
          Hello, are you Ben?
               (listens)
          Darling, I'm Ruth Newcomb, the new
          owner.
               (listens)
          Yes, that's right, I'm in Waikiki.
          I'll be arriving tomorrow on the noon
          flight.
               (listens)
          Yes, it ARRIVES in Kona at noon.
          You'll be there, right?
               (listens)
          Good! I want a limo with a full bar
          and sushi.
               (listens)
          Darling, do what you can do.
               (listens)
          I'm looking forward to meeting you.
          You'll have a sign so I know who you
          are, won't you?
               (listens) ·
          Good! See you then. Goodbye.

Ruth hangs up.

She goes over to the lanai.

EXT. HOTEL LANAI - NIGHT

We see the shimmering lights emanating from the
city. A full moon rises over Diamond Head. HAWAIIAN
MUSIC filters up from The House Without a Key bar.

Ruth smiles.

EXT. AIRPLANE LANDING AT KONA - DAY

The black lava flow surrounds the Kona Airport as a
Hawaiian Airlines MD-80 lands.

EXT. KONA AIRPORT BAGGAGE CLAIM - DAY

Ruth, wearing a fashionable designer dress and her
high heel designer shoes, carrying her purse and
the pet carrier, heads to the baggage claim area.

She has trouble maintaining her balance as she
walks due to her shoes and the rough surface.

Lei greeters place leis on a few arriving passengers.

EXT. KONA AIRPORT BAGGAGE CLAIM - LATER

Ruth, the sole person, sits on a bench, Louis Vuitton next to her, as she reads a throwaway magazine entitled "The Big Island."

She glances at her gold Rolex watch.

ONE O'CLOCK

Ruth tries her cell phone, it doesn't work.

She spots a pay phone.

Leaving her luggage, she goes to the phone.

She reaches into her purse and pulls out a paper and a quarter. She puts the quarter in and dials the number on the paper. She shakes her head and hangs up.

She goes back to her luggage and sits on the bench.

BEN KOKUA (45), a Hawaiian man wearing Ray Ban sunshades, an Aloha shirt, and blue jeans, meanders in from the street. He holds a sheet of notebook paper upside down with LUKA NEWCOMB hand-printed.

Ruth sees Ben and goes over to him.

                    RUTH
          Darling, it's about time! I've been
          waiting for over an hour. I did say
          noon, didn't I?

Ruth notices the sign.

                    RUTH (CONT'D)
          Darling, I'm Ruth Newcomb, not Luka
          Newcomb.

                    BEN
          Aaa-loooo-haa!
                    BEN (CONT'D)
               (beat)
          You, Mrs. Newcomb?

                    RUTH
          Darling, I just told you who I am.

                    BEN
          You go, shishi. We have long drive.

                    RUTH
          Shishi, what's shishi?

                    BEN
          You go baf-room.

-87-

SCREENPLAY

Ruth shoots Ben a look of surprise.

                    BEN (CONT'D)
          I watch your bags. You go!

Ruth stands up and leaves her luggage and the pet
carrier taking her purse.

EXT. KONA AIRPORT PARKING LOT - DAY

Ruth, carrying the pet carrier and her purse,
follows Ben, who has her bags.

They approach a stretch limousine parked to the
left of a rusty mud incrusted blue pickup truck.

Ben heads for the passenger side of the limo.

Ruth follows Ben.

Ben heaves the bags into the back of the pickup
truck.

Ruth looks at the truck, dumbfounded.

                    RUTH
          Darling, we're not getting in that, are
          we?

                    BEN
          Uh-huh!

Ruth not used to this type of treatment, gives Ben
her pie-eyed look.

EXT. BLUE PICKUP TRUCK - DAY

The truck travels along a long stretch of desert
road. In the foreground we see cactus, lava rocks,
and brush.

Nothing but lava fields can be seen for over five
miles in any direction. On the driver's side, in
the distance, the landscape changes from black and
tan to the brilliant blue Pacific water.

EXT. TWO LANE ROAD - DAY

The sky starts to cloud up, threatening to rain.
The desert scenery has changed to plushness; trees
and lush bushes line the road. More cars travel in
both directions.

We see cowboys on horses.

                    RUTH
          Oh, look, cowboys!

                    BEN
          Paniolo.

SCREENPLAY

                         RUTH
          What?

                         BEN
          Paniolo, Hawaiian cowboy. Dis de
          Parker Ranch.

EXT. WAIMEA TOWN - DAY

A light rain starts to fall as the blue truck
drives past a rustic sign reading WAIMEA. A small
strip mall has a large modern supermarket next to
the Bank of Hawaii. The heavy traffic moves at five
miles an hour.

                         RUTH
          This traffic is like the States.

                         BEN
          Dis is Hawaii. We ARE a State.

                         RUTH
          Darling, the traffic shouldn't be like
          this in paradise.

EXT. LONG STRETCH OF ROAD THROUGH RAIN FOREST - DAY

The rain continues as the blue truck goes down a
long stretch of road lined with large trees and
lush vegetation.

                         BEN
          We almost der, fifteen minute.

EXT. TWO LANE ROAD - DAY

The shower stops as the blue truck slows down,
turning right onto a minor unimproved road.

INT. BLUE PICKUP TRUCK - DAY

Ruth bounces all over the cab. To stabilize
herself, she grabs the strap hanging from the
ceiling. It comes off in her hand. She looks at
it.

Her left-hand holds down the pet carrier. Mrs.
Wiggins MEOWS her protests.

The truck slows down. A car comes towards them, and
Ben, with both hands on the steering wheel, raises
his left hand and waves at the oncoming vehicle.

The other driver does the same.

The truck continues its journey up the austere
road.

                         RUTH
          I'm not feeling good.

                        -89-

Ben looks at her.

> RUTH (CONT'D)
> I can't take it anymore. All this
> bouncing around is making me unwell.

EXT. PAVED ROAD - DAY

> RUTH
> Darling, stop the truck now! I'm going
> to be sick!

The truck turns into a ginger and tree-lined
driveway and stops.

Ruth opens the door and sticks her head out, ready
to throw up. She regains her composure.

Ruth glances down at the end of the driveway and
sees a beautiful blue-and-white trimmed, three-car
garage. Behind it, a sizeable modern blue-and-white
trimmed house.

> RUTH (CONT'D)
> That's a beautiful house! Do you know
> who lives there?

> BEN
> Uh-huh.

> RUTH
> Do you think they would let me stay
> there until I feel better?

> BEN
> Uh-huh.

Ben starts the truck. Ruth closes the door.

> RUTH
> Good.

Ben pulls up to the garage.

> RUTH (CONT'D)
> Well, who lives there?

> BEN
> You do.

The truck moves to the garage and stops.

EXT. RUTH'S GARAGE - DAY

Ben gets out, retrieves the luggage, and ambles
towards the house.

Ruth gets out and reaches for the carrying case.
She looks inside it.

-90-

                    RUTH
                 (to the cat)
          Darling, we live here; isn't this
          wondrous?

She turns the case, letting Mrs. Wiggins take in
the terrain.

As Ruth starts to follow Ben. One of her high heels
gets caught, and she loses her balance causing the
cat carrier to swing violently. The cat lets out a
long, sorrowful MEOW.

EXT. RUTH'S HOUSE - DAY - CONTINUOUS

Ruth, carrying Mrs. Wiggins, follows Ben as they
move around the corner toward the front door.

Ruth sees the vast macadamia nut orchard. Various
citrus trees with large fruit form the boundary
between the front yard and the orchard.

She sees chickens pecking at the ground. The wild
turkey and néné (Hawaiian geese) hear Ruth and
scurry from the yard to the orchard.

An expansive lanai wraps the exterior of the blue
house with white trim. It's all floor-to-ceiling
windows.

Without using a key, Ben opens the front door.

Ruth follows Ben in.

INT. RUTH'S HOUSE - DAY

Ruth moves to the living room floor-to-ceiling
window and looks down the hill, through the trees,
is the ocean. She smiles.

Ben ambles up behind her, carrying her luggage.

                    BEN
          Nice view.

Ruth nods.

                    RUTH
          Darling, this is truly paradise.

Ben starts towards Ruth's bedroom.

                    BEN
          I put your stuff in da master suite.
          If you need me, I live in the other end
          of the house.

Ruth puts the pet carrier down and opens the door.
Mrs. Wiggins runs out, heading down the hall. She
hears Ben and runs towards Ruth and back into the
carrier.

Ben comes back into the living room.

Ruth starts for the front door.

>   BEN (CONT'D)
>   You need Cutters.

Ruth ignores Ben, continuing towards the door.

EXT. RUTH'S HOUSE - DAY

Ruth goes outside, taking in the view of the orchard and the fauna. Orange, lime, and lemon trees abound. A fence of ginger, bird of paradise, and anthurium plants separate the orchard and the house. She takes a deep breath and smiles.

Through the window, we see Ben watching Ruth. He disappears.

Ruth starts slapping her arms and legs. She runs inside.

INT. RUTH'S KITCHEN - DAY

The enormous kitchen, with large floor-to-ceiling windows stretching from one end to the other, has all the modern appliances one could ever want. A flower arrangement with bird of paradise, anthuriums, and ginger sits on the granite-topped island.

Ben holds out a can of Cutters bug spray.

Ruth approaches Ben.

>   RUTH
>   Darling, you didn't tell me about the
>   mosquitoes.

>   BEN
>   It rain a lot here. Da haole use
>   Cutters.

Ben sees Ruth cocking her head and mouthing the word "haole."

>   BEN (CONT'D)
>   Haole, it mean white people or tourist.

INT. RUTH'S BEDROOM - NIGHT

Light from solid full moon streams through the big window, illuminating the large room.

Ruth is asleep in bed, wearing a silk night mask. Mrs. Wiggins curled up next to her, snoring.

Outside, we hear GRUNTING and SCRATCHING sounds.

Ruth wakes up, removes the night mask, sitting upright in the bed. She listens. The sounds persist.

She grabs Mrs. Wiggins and holds the cat close to her.

                    RUTH
          It's going to be alright.

Ruth, stroking Mrs. Wiggins, glances at the clock. It's 4:31.

                                        DISSOLVE TO:

INT. RUTH'S BEDROOM - NIGHT

The clock reads 5:18.

Ruth seated upright, holds a purring Mrs. Wiggins.

The sounds of frogs CROAKING and an occasional bird CHIRPING.

Ruth places the cat on the covers next to her. She puts the silk night mask back on and lies down.

                                        DISSOLVE TO:

INT. RUTH'S BEDROOM - DAWN

The clock reads 6:25.

A rooster CROWING breaks the quietness.

The sound startles Ruth. Removing her mask, she gathers her bearings.

The rooster continues CROWING.

Ruth takes the pillows and covers her head.

INT. RUTH'S KITCHEN - DAY

Ruth, seated at the kitchen table, sips a cup of coffee. She reads a throw-away magazine called "The Big Island."

INSERT: AN ARTICLE TITLED "WAIPIO VALLEY" with photographs of the black sand beach, palm trees, cliffs, and waterfall.

Ben enters and pours himself a cup of coffee.

Ruth puts the magazine down.

                    BEN
          How did you sleep?

                    RUTH
     Sleep? Darling, most of the night, I
     heard you grunting. You need to keep it
     down when I'm here.

                    BEN
     Grunt? I no grunt.

                    RUTH
     Then what was that sound if it wasn't
     you?

                    BEN
     It da pig! Wild boar. Dey come for the
     mango and mac nut. Not every night,
     some night, when dey get hungry.

Ruth glances at the magazine.

                    RUTH
     Darling, I want to go shopping and see
     the island.

                    BEN
     I drive you.

                    RUTH
     I want to do it myself. Darling, I want
     a car.

                    BEN
     You take truck.

                    RUTH
     I do not drive trucks. I can barely
     drive cars.

                    BEN
     You need four-wheel drive to get
     around. Truck mo betta.

                    RUTH
     Darling, I said, I don't drive trucks.
     You have to find me a car.

INT. RUTH'S LIVING ROOM - DAY

Ruth waters plants with a Tiffany glass container.

AUNTIE (60's), a robust, jubilant, and over-
gesticulating Hawaiian-Asian woman who speaks in
singsong Hawaiian pidgin except where noted, bursts
into the house without knocking. She sees Ruth.

Ruth, startled by Auntie, drops the glass
container, which shatters.

                    AUNTIE
     Oh! You clumsy lady. Where Ben? He
     kokua you, klinim mess, den he kam my
     place. Da keiki's need him. Where he?

                         RUTH
          Darling, who are you?

                         AUNTIE
          Me, Auntie.

                         RUTH
          Who ... what gives you the right to
          burst into my house without knocking?

                         AUNTIE
          Ben wok fo me.

                         RUTH
          Darling, he works for ME!

                         AUNTIE
          Oh, dat oh-kay.
               (beat)
          You tell him, come plenny wikiwiki.

Ben enters the living room.

                         AUNTIE (CONT'D)
          Oh, der you are! Da keiki's need you.

Auntie turns to leave, pointing to the broken
pitcher.

                         AUNTIE (CONT'D)
               (to Ben)
          You klinim here first. Den kam
          wikiwiki.

Auntie leaves.

                         RUTH
          Darling, what was that all about?

                         BEN
          What?

                         RUTH
          That lady, what is with her?

                         BEN
          Dat Auntie. I work for her, too.

                         RUTH
          I don't like the way she just burst
          into my house. I want to be left alone.

                         BEN
          I talk to her.

EXT. AUNTIE'S GREENHOUSE - DAY

Ben meanders up, opening the end door of a large,
opaque plastic Quonset hut greenhouse.

INT. AUNTIE'S GREENHOUSE - DAY

An elaborate watering system hangs from the canopy.
Marijuana plants abound.

Auntie trimming a mature plant. Ben enters.

> BEN
> A-lo-ha.

> AUNTIE
> A-lo-ha, she plenny tight.

Ben takes a pair of trimming shears and starts
trimming.

> BEN
> Oh, she oh-kay. She no like Luka, she
> like Ruth.

> AUNTIE
> Luka, Hawaiian name. Ruth haole name.
> She plenny haole. Ruth, mo betta.

EXT. RUTH'S LANAI - DAY

The sky is dark and ominous, with low, wafting
clouds brushing the tops of the evergreen trees.

Ruth, wearing a sundress and house slippers, sits
on an Adirondack chair with a laptop on her lap,
typing. Next to her a can of Cutters.

EXT. RUTH'S YARD - DAY - CONTINUOUS

Mrs. Wiggins lies on the grass in front of Ruth.

The thick squall looking like a wall of water
rushes through the yard toward the house.

With full force, the squall hits the house.

A soaked Mrs. Wiggins looks up at Ruth, letting out
a long sorrowful MEOW.

Ruth jumps up, having difficulty maintaining her
balance as she heads to save Mrs. Wiggins from the
downpour.

Ruth reaches down for the cat and loses her
balance. As she falls, she grabs the soaked cat.

Ruth lands on her rear end and starts to slide down
the hill, along with all the water and mud from the
squall. She cannot stop nor do anything but ride
with the torrent of water and soil.

Ruth continues sliding towards a thicket of bushes,
holding Mrs. Wiggins in the air.

EXT. AYALA HOUSE - DAY

As Ruth plows through the thicket of bushes, her
dress moves up to her thighs. About to hit the
house, she braces her legs for impact, holding the
cat close to her.

THUD! Ruth hits the house.

The deluge continues as Ruth's Hawaiian-Filipino
neighbors, NALANI (mid 30's) and MEKA (mid 30's),
run to the uphill side of their house to find Ruth
and the cat.

                    NALANI
          Rain stop soon.

Ruth brushes her soaked hair from her eyes.

                    RUTH
          Eh, wha? Ohhh!

Mrs. Wiggins' yellow eyes pierce through her mud-
soaked body.

                    MEKA
          Give Nalani cat.

As Ruth holds Mrs. Wiggins up, the heavy rain
washes the mud from her body.

Nalani takes Mrs. Wiggins.

Meka reaches down and helps Ruth up. Ruth grabs her
back.

                    NALANI
          You wait on lanai for rain to stop.
          Then you go.

As they move to the lanai, Nalani hands Mrs.
Wiggins back to Ruth.

EXT. AYALA LANAI - DAY

Nalani escorts them to four rickety chairs
surrounding a table.

                    NALANI
          Sit.

Ruth sits.

                    MEKA
          I'm Meka.

Meka points to Nalani.

                    MEKA (CONT'D)
          Dis Nalani, da misses.

SCREENPLAY

                    RUTH
          Darlings, it is nice to meet you. I'm
          Ruth Newcomb. I live next door, up the
          hill. Does it always rain like this?

                    MEKA
          Sometimes.

Nalani notices Ruth's slippers.

                    NALANI
          No WON-DA you fall. House slippahs no
          good in Hawaii; too slippery. You need
          zori.

Ruth cocks her head as if she doesn't understand
Nalani.

                    RUTH
          Zori?

                    NALANI
          Haole call em Flip-flops.

INT. RUTH'S KITCHEN - DAY

Ruth, wearing a dress, and Ben have their morning
coffee.

                    RUTH
          Darling, have you found a car?

                    BEN
          Yes.

                    RUTH
          Where is it?

                    BEN
          It not ready.

                    RUTH
          Why not?

                    BEN
          No windows.

                    RUTH
          Darling, what good is a car without
          windows?

                    BEN
          Dat is all I could find. You take
          truck?

                    RUTH
          Ben, I don't want to use your truck. I
          want to own my own car. Where do we go
          to get a car?
               (BEAT)
          One with windows?

SCREENPLAY

                        BEN
          Hilo, it closer than Kona.

                        RUTH
          Fine, we go to Hilo and buy a car.

                        BEN
          Auntie need me.

                        RUTH
          She can wait. I need a car now!

EXT. HILO SUV DEALERSHIP - DAY

Ruth and Ben, with a SALESMAN, stand in front of an
SUV.

                        SALESMAN
          Dis SUV will get you from Hilo to Kona
          on Saddle Road like you are riding in
          first class. No bouncing, smooth ride.
          It's great when you get caught in a
          downpour. You can go anywhere on the
          island.

                        RUTH
          Darling, what about Waipio Valley?

The salesman nods.

                        SALESMAN
          Dis da best four-wheel drive SUV. You
          won't slide off the road like other
          SUVs and trucks do when you go to
          Waipio.

                        RUTH
          Okay, I'll buy it on one condition.

                        SALESMAN
          What?

                        RUTH
          You show me how to operate it.

                        SALESMAN
          It's easy. But first, you must always
          take off your high heels when you
          engage da four-wheel drive. Safety
          first.

                                        DISSOLVE TO:

INT. SUV AT HILO DEALERSHIP - DAY

Ruth in the driver's seat, the salesman in the
passenger's seat. Ruth reaches for the gearshift
and starts to shift. The sound of GRINDING GEARS as
the SUV lurches forward and comes to an abrupt
stop.

SCREENPLAY

EXT. SUV AT HILO DEALERSHIP - DAY

The salesman indicates something to Ruth. Again, the sound of GRINDING GEARS.

Ben, standing nearby, watches the entire episode and starts to laugh.

                              DISSOLVE TO:

EXT. SUV AT HILO DEALERSHIP - DUSK

CLOSE ON BEN.

His eyes closed, slowly open as the SOUND OF A SUV uninhibitedly changes gears.

INT. SUV AT HILO DEALERSHIP - DUSK

The exhausted salesman sighs as Ruth drives the SUV forward.

EXT. SUV AT HILO SUBARU DEALERSHIP - DUSK

CLOSE ON BEN.

Ben smiles, stands, and starts to clap.

EXT. RUTH'S LANAI - DAY

Ruth sits in a chair, typing away at her laptop; Mrs. Wiggins is curled up on the chair next to her.

A dish filled with dry cat food is at the bottom of the stairs.

                    RUTH (V.O.)
          If you ever saw The Trouble with Angels
          with Haley Mills and June Harding, that
          would typify my schooling at St.
          Francis Academy. I was more the Haley
          character, whereas Sarah Martin was
          June's. As in the movie, we had fun
          devising schemes to be defiant. Even
          today, I don't like rulers; they remind
          me of the nuns using the back of our
          hands for target practice.

Ruth hears PECKING near the steps. She notices two wild turkeys eating cat food.

Nearby a couple of chickens and néné head for the food.

Ruth lunges forward towards the birds, waving her arms.

                    RUTH
          Shoo, shoo!

The birds scurry away from the cat food, running down the stairs through the orchard.

Mrs. Wiggins looks up at the commotion and stares.

EXT. HONOKAA - DAY

Ruth's SUV drives through the relatively small town. The wooden buildings, with paint peeling, have seen better days.

The post office is the only modern structure.

EXT. HONOKAA POST OFFICE - DAY

Ruth, wearing a designer dress and shoes, collects her mail from her outdoor post office box.

DANNY MAKUA, the local television station manager and producer wearing Aloha wear, collects mail from a mailbox. He sees Ruth and smiles.

Ruth notices, but does not acknowledge Danny.

EXT. MR. WOO'S MARKET - DAY

Ruth struts up to the weathered wooden building.

INT. MR. WOO'S MARKET - DAY

The store has a variety of items, primarily single-use or sample-size items.

Ruth goes through the aisles, searching for something. She spots a small jar of peanut butter. She picks it up, studies it, frowns, and shakes her head.

Ruth notices the not-quite-perfect farm fresh produce and carrots.

Ruth goes to the sole cash register near the front door, behind which stands THE GROCER (70's), a jubilant Asian, wearing a white apron.

> RUTH
> Darling, do you have a big jar of peanut butter?

> THE GROCER
> Have only small. Big ones at da supermarket in Waimea.

EXT. WAIMEA SUPERMARKET - DAY

Ruth's SUV pulls into the supermarket. She gets out, smiling and nodding.

INT. WAIMEA SUPERMARKET - DAY

The supermarket has large, wide, well-stocked aisles.

Ruth finds the peanut butter aisle.

MRS. STRONG (mid 60's) high school counselor and mainland transplant, wearing a muumuu, searching for peanut butter.

Ruth sees the sole large jar of peanut butter on the shelf. She reaches for it.

Mrs. Strong also reaches for the jar.

Ruth hostilely grabs the jar, holding it close to her chest.

                    MRS. STRONG
          I was reaching for that jar.

                    RUTH
          Darling, it's MY peanut butter. Mrs.
          Strong observes the overdressed Ruth.

                    MRS. STRONG
          Your first time on the island, isn't
          it?

                    RUTH
          Darling, I live here.

Mrs. Strong reaches for a smaller jar of peanut butter.

                    MRS. STRONG
          A long time ago, I was like you.

                    RUTH
          Darling, I AM the only one like me.

Mrs. Strong shakes her head and extends her hand to Ruth.

                    MRS. STRONG
          I'm Charlene Strong, Honokaa's high
          school counselor.

Ruth refuses to shake hands.

                    MRS. STRONG (CONT'D)
          When I first arrived from the mainland,
          I used to be uptight like you. We are
          now on the Big Island, not the
          mainland. Life is different here. In
          time, you, too, will change, become
          more relaxed, and enjoy our Big Island
          ways.

Ruth turns and leaves.

SCREENPLAY

                              MRS. STRONG (CONT'D)
                    Have a great day, A-lo-ha!

                                              DISSOLVE TO:

EXT. RUTH'S HOUSE - DAY

WILLIAM AYALA (18), a portly, happy-go-lucky,
heart-of-gold, son of Nalani and Meka, carries a
Hawaiian floral arrangement in a glass vase and
opens the unlocked front door.

INT. RUTH'S LIVING ROOM - DAY

William places the arrangement on the living room
coffee table. He looks around the room and examines
Ruth's changes to Martin's former home.

Noticing new photos in the bookcase, he examines
the photographs of Ruth with the Clintons and
Donald Trump, Jackie Onassis, Princess Diana and
Prince Charles in the bookcase. He spotted the Emmy
prominently placed in the center of the bookcase,
picking it up and almost dropping it because it was
heavy. He examined the gold statuette and the
plaque that read "OUTSTANDING INFORMATIONAL SERIES
- 2001, RUTH NEWCOMB - HOST, FROM THE BIG APPLE",
and returns it to its resting place, turning his
attention to the collection of hardback books,
which include The Adventures of Tom Sawyer, The
Adventures of Huckleberry Finn, Catcher in the Rye,
Uncle Tom's Cabin amongst Dante, Dickens, and other
classics.

He picks up the flower arrangement and heads for
the kitchen.

INT. RUTH'S KITCHEN - DAY

William enters, placing the flower arrangement in
the center of the granite island.

He returns to the living room.

INT. RUTH'S LIVING ROOM - DAY

Ruth enters, carrying a paper grocery bag.

Ruth spots William entering from the kitchen. She
screams, dropping the bag.

                         RUTH
                    What are you doing here?

                         WILLIAM
                       (innocently)
                    Noth-thing.

                         RUTH
                    You are stealing something, aren't you?

                              -103-

SCREENPLAY

William shakes his head no.

Ben comes running in the front door and notices William.

> BEN
> William, what are you doing here?

> WILLIAM
> Noth-thing.

> BEN
> You go home.

William starts to leave.

> RUTH
> No, I want to know what he is doing here.

> WILLIAM
> I do noth-thing.

> RUTH
> You're here. That's enough.

> WILLIAM
> I do noth-thing, I just leaving.

> BEN
> William, you go.

William heads for the door.

> RUTH
> Darling, where I come from, people don't wander into other peoples' homes. It's a violation.

As William reaches the door, Auntie comes bursting in.

> AUNTIE
> (to Ben and William)
> You come, wikiwiki! Da keiki's no wait!

> WILLIAM
> I go.

William leaves.

Auntie observes the bag on the floor.

> AUNTIE
> (to Ruth)
> You fo'ever drop dings.

Ruth gives Auntie a look of disdain.

>   AUNTIE (CONT'D)
>   I no like yu stink-eye. I go.

Auntie leaves.

>   RUTH
>   Talk about violations. People enjoy
>   popping in around here, don't they?

>   BEN
>   Hu-huh.

>   RUTH
>   Darling, what are those keiki things
>   that lady is always talking about? Why
>   are they so important?

>   BEN
>   Keiki, it Hawaiian for little ones or
>   children. If everything oh-kay, I go
>   Auntie's.

INT. RUTH'S KITCHEN - DAY

Ruth goes over to the rotary wall phone, picks it
up, and pauses momentarily. She hangs up. Opening a
cabinet door, she pulls a worn AT&T telephone book
and places it on the island.

She notices the flower arrangement.

Ruth studies the cover of an AT&T. She shakes her
head, opens the book, locates a number, and dials.

>   RUTH
>   Police?

INT. RUTH'S LIVING ROOM - LATER

Ruth reads Dante's <u>Purgatory</u>.

The front door bursts open as OFFICER #1 and
OFFICER #2 enter.

Ruth startled.

>   RUTH
>   What the heck! Doesn't anyone knock
>   around here?

>   OFFICER #1
>   You want to report a break-in?

>   RUTH
>   Darling, why else would I have called
>   you?

>   OFFICER #2
>   What was broken?

SCREENPLAY

                    RUTH
          I even know who he is and where he
          lives. He's the neighbor boy next door.

The officers glance at each other, smile, and nod.

                    OFFICER #1
          Oh, William ... William Ayala, he's
          harmless. He won't cause you no harm.
          He's a curious kid.

                    RUTH
          I don't like that he was in MY house.
          In New York, this isn't done.

                    OFFICER #1
          Dis is Hawaii, not New York.

                    OFFICER #2
          Did you lock da door before you left?

                    RUTH
          Yes, but Ben, my caretaker, also lives
          here.

                    OFFICER #2
          So he didn't lock da door?

                    RUTH
          I don't know.

                    OFFICER #2
          No harm done. Nothing taken. Is der
          anything else you need?

                    RUTH
          Darling, I want something done.

                    OFFICER #2
          There isn't anything for us to do if
          nothing was taken.

Ruth shook her head.

                    OFFICER #2 (CONT'D)
          We're here. We check on Auntie.

EXT. RUTH'S LANAI - DAY

Ruth, on the lanai, reads <u>The New Yorker</u> magazine.

Ben comes down the hill from Auntie's.

                    RUTH
          Ben, come here, please.

Ben ambles over to Ruth and sits on the other
Adirondack chair.

                              RUTH (CONT'D)
               Darling, I don't want to be disturbed.
               I want to be left alone.

                              BEN
               You want me to leave?

Ben starts to rise.

                              RUTH
               No, Ben, sit.

Ben sits back down.

                              RUTH (CONT'D)
               What I don't like is everyone keeps
               bursting into my house, not knocking
               from Auntie, to the police, to William.

Ruth lays down the magazine, open to an elaborate
security system advertisement, showing it to Ben.

                              RUTH (CONT'D)
               So, I want you to install a security
               system like this one.

                              BEN
               Door has lock.

                              RUTH
               No, Ben, I want a security system.

                              BEN
               Dis not New York, dis Hawaii. No-one
               has security system.

                              RUTH
               Darling, I don't care if we are in
               Timbuktu. When can you install it?

                              BEN
                  (scratches his head)
               I don't know where to get security
               system.

Ruth points to the phone number on the
advertisement.

                              RUTH
               Here's the number. I want it done. Do
               you understand?

INT. RUTH'S KITCHEN - DAY

Ruth, in a sundress, and Ben, in an Aloha shirt and
jeans, finish their morning coffee.

Ruth glances at the flower arrangement.

                    RUTH
        Darling, I forgot to thank you for the
        lovely flowers.

                    BEN
        Flowers? I thought you put them there.

                    RUTH
        I wonder how they got here.

Ruth and Ben look at each other.

                    BEN
        William!

Ruth looks at the flowers and smiles.

                    BEN (CONT'D)
                (Nodding)
        Dat what he do here!

                    RUTH
        Darling, why didn't he tell us?

                    BEN
        You scare him.

                    RUTH
        He scared me! That was very kind of
        him.

Ruth turns her attention to the throw-away magazine
with Waipio Valley on the cover.

                    RUTH (CONT'D)
        Darling, is Waipio Valley as beautiful
        as these photographs?

                    BEN
        Uh-huh.

                    RUTH
        How long does it take to get there?

                    BEN
        Too dangerous to drive. You hike.

                    RUTH
        Hike from where?

                    BEN
        You park at top, hike down to beach. Da
        hike takes half an hour to get down and
        over an hour to go up.

                    RUTH
        I have an SUV. I can drive.

                    BEN
        Some people don't make it.

                    -108-

> RUTH
> The salesman told me I could do it.

> BEN
> Oh-kay, use only first gear and drive
> very slowly. Going down is hard; going
> up easy. You need carrots with stalk
> attached.

Ruth gives Ben a curious look.

> RUTH
> Carrots?

Ben gets up.

> BEN
> You need carrots when you get to
> bottom. I go to Auntie's.

Ben puts his cup into the dishwasher and leaves.

EXT. RUTH'S HOUSE - DAY

Ruth, dressed in a designer outfit and high heel
shoes, double-checks the front door, ensuring it is
locked. She smiles.

EXT. MR. WOO'S MARKET - DAY

Ruth exits Mr. Woo's holding a bunch of carrots by
the stalk.

EXT. WAIPIO VALLEY ROAD - DAY

The sun was shining brightly. The parking lot is
filled with cars. The road ahead of the SUV has
barriers on both sides, narrowing down from a two-
lane well-paved road to a one-lane paved road. A
large sign on one side of the road states, STOP,
RESTRICTED ROAD, ONLY 4-WHEEL DRIVE VEHICLES
PERMITTED, ONE LANE ROAD, DOWNHILL TRAFFIC MUST
YIELD TO UPHILL TRAFFIC. On the other side was
another sign, WARNING, PROCEED AT YOUR OWN RISK,
STEEP GRADE, ENGAGE ALL WHEELS, ENGAGE FIRST GEAR,
FALLING ROCK.

INT. SUV - DAY

Ruth studies the signs, reaches down, takes off her
high heel shoes, looks at the gears, and shifts the
SUV into first gear.

EXT. WAIPIO VALLEY ONE LANE ROAD - DAY

Ruth drives slowly down the steep, bumpy paved one-
lane road.

Tourists hike single file down the road.

EXT. BOTTOM OF WAIPIO VALLEY - DAY

Ruth navigates over the dirt road with numerous potholes filled with water and mud.

INT. SUV - DAY

Ruth concentrates on the road. To her right, the hull of a rusted car comes into view, cut in half by a tree.

EXT. WAIPIO VALLEY ROAD - DAY

Ruth stops the SUV, staring at the car.

She gazes into the trees to see a rusted carcass of a pickup truck perched in the tree.

Continuing to inspect the area, Ruth sees another truck, a car, and another and another. The trees are littered with rusted cars and trucks. It's a forest of rusted cars!

EXT. WAIPIO BEACH - DAY

The SUV follows the sandy path leading through the palm trees.

Wild horses meander over to Ruth.

Ruth gets out, grabs the carrots, and closes the door.

She takes a carrot holding it by the stalk and sticks out her hand. A horse comes over and takes the carrot from her. Jubilant, she smiles to the point of almost laughing.

Ruth takes another carrot, holding it by the stalk again, and another horse takes it from her. The five horses pin her against the SUV, WHINNYING and nuzzling Ruth as she continues feeding them carrots.

Ruth, now out of carrots, holds both hands up showing the horses she doesn't have anymore.

> RUTH
> All gone.

As the horses leave, four more horses approach her. Ruth gets pinned between the horses and the SUV. Again, she holds her hands up.

> RUTH (CONT'D)
> My little darlings, I have no more. All gone.

The horse's WHINNY, meandering away.

Ruth starts to walk down to the beach. The moment she steps off of the grassy area, her shoes sank deeply into the sand. She was trapped, unable to move. It takes some effort to slide out of the heels and go barefoot. She carries her shoes as she strolls down to the sand beach.

She reaches the beach, goes to the water, and turns around, taking in the beauty of the virtually deserted palm-lined beach.

To her left, she sees a waterfall originating at the top of the cliff, cascading into the Pacific.

Ruth takes a deep breath, sighs, and smiles.

EXT. WAIPIO VALLEY ONE LANE ROAD - DAY

Ruth, in the idling SUV, at the bottom of the steep road.

INT. SUV - DAY

Ruth looks at the shift and starts to put it into first gear. We hear the GRINDING of the gears.

Ruth, looking at the shift, the SUV lurches forward.

THUD. The SUV struck something. Ruth stops the SUV and looks up.

EXT. WAIPIO VALLEY ONE LANE ROAD - DAY

She doesn't recognize William, who is sprawled on the SUV hood.

Ruth gets out, going over to the man.

                    RUTH
          Darling, are you okay? I'm so sorry.

William looks up at Ruth.

Ruth recognizes William.

                    WILLIAM
          I am oh-kay, Mrs. Newcomb.

                    RUTH
          Darling, I didn't see you there. I'm so
          sorry. You aren't going to sue me, are
          you?

                    WILLIAM
          Huh?

                    RUTH
          Are you going to sue me?

-111-

                    WILLIAM
          Why would I sue you?

                    RUTH
          I'm from New York, and everybody sues.

                    WILLIAM
          I won't sue you. Can you give me a lift
          to da top?

                    RUTH
          Yes...

Ruth starts to get into the driver's seat.

                    RUTH (CONT'D)
          Darling, are you SURE you're not hurt?

                    WILLIAM
          I am alright.

William gets into the passenger side.

INT. SUV - DAY

Ruth slowly drives the SUV up the road. Ruth and
William bounce all over the place.

Ruth concentrates on the road.

William stares out the window.

EXT. WAIPIO VALLEY ONE LANE ROAD - DAY

The SUV slowly makes drives up the road.

EXT. PAVED TWO-LANE ROAD - DAY

The SUV drives through a cane field, passing an
occasional wooden house.

INT. SUV - DAY

Ruth and William do not talk.

William stares out the open window as they approach
Honokaa.

                    RUTH
          Darling, about yesterday. Thank you for
          the flowers.

                    WILLIAM
          You're welcome.

                    RUTH
          You know you shouldn't go uninvited
          into other people's homes, right?

                    WILLIAM
          Uh-huh.

                    RUTH
          Darling, it's not right, intruding like
          that.

As they approach Honokaa High School, William
slinks down in the seat. He's almost on the floor.

                    WILLIAM
          I'm sorry, Mrs. Newcomb.

EXT. HONOKAA HIGH SCHOOL - DAY

A green and white sign announces the school.

Mrs. Strong, the school counselor, and the peanut
butter lady stands at the curb, arms folded,
looking down the street as the SUV approaches.

INT. SUV - DAY

Ruth looks down at William

                    RUTH
          There's no need for you to be down
          there.

The SUV passes the school.

William moves back up into the seat.

Ruth realizes William doesn't want to be seen by
Mrs. Strong.

                    RUTH (CONT'D)
          Darling, are you supposed to be in
          school?

                    WILLIAM
          Uh-huh.

                    RUTH
          Then why aren't you in class?

                    WILLIAM
          I don't like English. I go to beach
          instead.

                    RUTH
          Darling, you need English. School is
          important.

                    WILLIAM
          Dat what Mrs. Strong, my counselor,
          says.

EXT. ROAD - DAY

The SUV makes a U-turn, heading back towards the
school.

SCREENPLAY

                    WILLIAM
          What are you doing?

                    RUTH
          Darling, I am taking you to school.

EXT. HONOKAA HIGH SCHOOL - DAY

The SUV pulls up, stopping in front of Mrs. Strong.

William gets out, head down, as he approaches Mrs.
Strong.

                    WILLIAM
          Hello, Mrs. Strong.

Ruth listens to the conversation through the open
window.

                    MRS. STRONG
          William, you're early today. How was
          the beach?

William looks at Ruth, then Mrs. Strong.

                    WILLIAM
          It oh-kay.

Mrs. Strong leans down, recognizing Ruth from the
market.

                    MRS. STRONG
          William, you get to Dr. Tilton's class.
          He's expecting you.

Mrs. Strong leaned down, looking into the passenger
window.

                    MRS. STRONG (CONT'D)
          It's you.

Ruth recognizes Mrs. Strong.

                    MRS. STRONG (CONT'D)
          Thank you for bringing William. At
          least he'll be able to catch part of
          his English class. I forgot to tell
          you the other day at the market. This
          may be The Big Island. However, we are
          a tight little island where everyone
          knows everyone else and what goes on.
          Thank you for bringing him to school;
          you performed an excellent service.

EXT. RUTH'S LANAI - DAY

A heavy fog engulfs the area as Ruth types on her
laptop. Hearing a noise and looked up to see what
it is. She sees a figure heading for her. She
starts to pick up the laptop to go inside when she

SCREENPLAY

recognizes it is William and puts the laptop back down.

>   WILLIAM
>   Aaa-looo-haaa, Mrs. Newcomb. What you
>   doing?

>   RUTH
>   I am writing my memoirs.

>   WILLIAM
>   Why?

>   RUTH
>   Darling, I had a wonderful life; people
>   will love reading it. How did it go in
>   school today?

>   WILLIAM
>   Oh-kay.
>   (beat)
>   I got to help Auntie with her keiki's.
>   Aaa-loooo-haa!

EXT. RUTH'S ORCHARD - DAY

Ruth forges through the macadamia orchard. Her slippers sink into the thick grass.

Nuts cover the ground beneath the trees.

Ruth frowns, shakes her head, and turns and starts towards the house.

EXT. RUTH'S HOUSE - DAY

Ben leaves the house and starts up the hill towards Auntie's. Ruth sees Ben.

>   RUTH
>   Ben...

Ben does not hear Ruth.

>   RUTH (CONT'D)
>   (Louder)
>   Ben...

Ben turns.

>   RUTH (CONT'D)
>   Ben, I need to talk to you.

Ben starts moving towards Ruth.

>   RUTH (CONT'D)
>   Darling, how is it going with the
>   security system?

>   BEN
>   Ah, I still look for system.

SCREENPLAY

                    RUTH
          It shouldn't take this long to locate a
          system.

                    BEN
          Dis Hawaii, take long time to get
          stuff.

                    RUTH
          You've been spending too much time with
          Auntie.

Ben stares at the ground.

                    BEN
          No, I haven't.

                    RUTH
          Look at this place.

Ruth makes a sweeping motion with her hand.

                    RUTH (CONT'D)
          The grass needs mowing.

Ben glances at the grass.

                    BEN
          Uh-huh.

                    RUTH
          Look at all the nuts under the trees.
          They need to be collected and sold.

                    BEN
          Uh-huh.

                    RUTH
          For years, the Martins raved about how
          good of a caretaker you are. Darling, I
          just haven't seen it, Ben.

                    BEN
          I sorry, da keiki's need attention. Dey
          no wait.

                    RUTH
          Darling, I know children, I mean the
          keiki's, need attention, and so do my
          macadamia nut trees and the lawn.
          Please take care of it this week.

                    BEN
          Oh-kay...

Auntie comes down the hill towards Ruth and Ben.

SCREENPLAY

                    AUNTIE
              (To Ben)
          Oh, der you are!
              (To Ruth)
          How you?

                    RUTH
          I'm fine. I need Ben to spend more time
          with me.

                    AUNTIE
          No, he need to spend time wit me and da
          keiki's. Dey important right now.

                    RUTH
          Darling, my lawn and macadamia nuts are
          important too.

                    AUNTIE
          Da mac nut wait. Keiki's no wait. Ben
          you come.

Ben starts up the hill.

                    RUTH
          This week, Ben.

                    BEN
              (Over his shoulder)
          Uh-huh.

INT. SUV - DAY

Ruth, in her designer dress and high heels, drives
down the two-lane road toward town. She sees
William hitchhiking.

Ruth pulls the SUV over, picking up William.

                    WILLIAM
          Aaa-looo-haaa, Mrs. Newcomb.

                    RUTH
          Get in.

EXT. TWO LANE ROAD - DAY

William gets into the SUV. The SUV pulls away.

INT. SUV - DAY

                    RUTH
          Going to school?

                    WILLIAM
          No, Waipio.

                    RUTH
          Why don't you want to go to school?

                    WILLIAM
          Dr. Tilton makes us read aloud. It
          embarrasses me.

                    RUTH
          There is nothing to be embarrassed
          about. Public speaking is easy.

                    WILLIAM
          Dr. Tilton is not human! People say he
          is da ghost of an old kahuna.

                    RUTH
          Darling, Dr. Tilton can't be all that
          bad.

                    WILLIAM
          He is. He makes us read da big words.

The SUV approaches the school.

                    RUTH
          When I lived in New York, I volunteered
          to help people learn to read. I can do
          the same for you, darling.

William smiles.

                    RUTH (CONT'D)
          Please go to Dr. Tilton's class. Try
          your best.

William frowns.

                    RUTH (CONT'D)
          Then after school, please come to my
          place, and we will work on your
          reading.

William smiles.

                    WILLIAM
               (enthusiastically)
          Sometimes, Auntie helps me too.

Ruth stops the SUV at the school entrance.

EXT. HONOKAA HIGH SCHOOL - DAY

William gets out and goes up the front walkway
toward school. He glances over his shoulder.

Ruth watches.

William continues meandering up the stairs and
opens the front door. He glances over his shoulder
again.

Ruth watches.

SCREENPLAY

William enters. The door closes. Through the front door window, William looks out.

Ruth watches.

The door opens, and Mrs. Strong steps out, mouths thank you, and waves at Ruth.

EXT. RUTH'S LANAI - DAY

Ruth types away on the laptop. On the table next to her lies a Time Magazine with Ruth's face on the cover, with the headline in red lettering, FROM THE BIG APPLE NO MORE, A TRADITION ENDS.

William meanders through the orchard and approaches Ruth.

                    WILLIAM
          Aaa-looo-haaa, Mrs. Newcomb.

                    RUTH
          Hello, William.

William sees Ruth's photograph on the cover of Time Magazine.

                    WILLIAM
          That's you, isn't it?

                    RUTH
          Yes, darling.

                    WILLIAM
          Why is your picture on da magazine?

Ruth picks up the magazine.

                    RUTH
          Darling, the headline says it all.

                    WILLIAM
          I don't understand.

                    RUTH
          It's simple.

Ruth opens the magazine to the page where the article on her starts and hands the magazine to William.

William takes the magazine and studies it. He glances at Ruth.

                    RUTH (CONT'D)
          Why don't you read the article aloud to
          me? Sit down, and I'll help you with
          the words you don't understand.

William sits down.

                    WILLIAM
          Ruth Newcomb, former host of the syn-d--

                    RUTH
          --Syndicated.

                    WILLIAM
          --syn-di-cated television show "<u>From
          the Big Apple</u>" was born in East
          Hampton, New York. The so--

                    RUTH
          Socialite.

Ruth and William don't notice the wild turkey,
chickens, and néné eating Mrs. Wiggins' food.

                    WILLIAM
          The so-cial-ite attended St. Francis
          Academy for girls and graduated mag-na
          co-me la-

                    RUTH
          That's magna cum laude, it means...

The SOUND OF THE BIRDS PECKING draws Ruth's
attention. She gets up and chases them away.

                    RUTH (CONT'D)
          Shoo, shoo!

William starts laughing.

                    RUTH (CONT'D)
          Darling, what's so funny? Every day
          they come, every day the same thing.

                    WILLIAM
          Why don't you give them food too?

                    RUTH
          That's Mrs. Wiggins' food. I don't want
          to feed the entire island!

                    WILLIAM
          They eat bugs. They good for you.

                    RUTH
          I'm not going to feed them, and that's
          final!

EXT. HONOKAA POST OFFICE - DAY

Ruth, wearing heels, collects her mail from her
post office box.

Danny, the local television producer, collects his
mail.

SCREENPLAY

DANNY
Excuse me...

Ruth looks at Danny.

DANNY (CONT'D)
You're Ruth Newcomb, aren't you?

RUTH
Yes, Darling, who else would I be?

DANNY
Aaa-loooo-haa! I'm Danny Makua,
station manager at KBI, Big Island TV,
channel 32.

RUTH
Nice to meet you.

DANNY
I'm sure you have made quite a few
adjustments to life here on da Big
Island.

RUTH
Darling, more than you would ever want
to know.

DANNY
Da first few months are hard, but
you'll adjust.

Ruth closes her box.

DANNY (CONT'D)
Would you be interested in doing a
broadcast or two?

RUTH
Darling, I am not interested in
television, radio, or anything. I want
to be left alone.

Danny reaches into his pocket, pulls out a business
card, and hands it to Ruth.

DANNY
Here, take my card. If you change your
mind, call me.

Ruth sticks the card in with her mail and leaves.

EXT. RUTH'S GARDEN AREA AND LANAI - DAY

Ruth, wearing slacks for the first time and a large
hat covering her face from the sun, kneels in the
garden, clipping flowers and placing them in a
Tiffany ceramic basin.

The lanai is behind her.

William sits in an Adirondack chair, reading an article from <u>The New Yorker</u>. He places the magazine on the table.

> WILLIAM
> I finished, Mrs. Newcomb.

Ruth puts down the clipping shears. She gets up and sits in the Adirondack chair next to William.

A new paperback edition of <u>The Adventures of Huckleberry Finn</u> rests on the table.

> RUTH
> Excellent, William.

William smiles.

> RUTH (CONT'D)
> You have made a significant improvement in your reading.

> WILLIAM
> It's coming a lot easier, thanks to you and Auntie.

Ruth reaches for the paperback.

> RUTH
> I think reading is an adventure and it's about time you start reading a novel. We'll start with an easy and fun one, <u>The Adventures of Huckleberry Finn</u>.

Ruth hands William the paperback.

William studies the cover. He flips through the book.

> WILLIAM
> What type of name is Huckleberry? Is he related to Huckleberry Hound, that cartoon dog?

> RUTH
> No, but that's not important. What is important is that you enjoy Huck's adventures.

> WILLIAM
> Huck?

> RUTH
> Darling, that's short for Huckleberry. You will get into the story and won't be able to put the book down.

> WILLIAM
> Ma-ha-lo, Mrs. Newcomb.

William opens the book, flips to chapter one, and starts to read.

                    WILLIAM (CONT'D)
          It says he was in another book called
          <u>The Adventures of Tom Sawyer</u>.
          Shouldn't I read that book first?

                    RUTH
          Darling, I think this book is better.

                    WILLIAM
          Oh-kay, but he sure writes funny.

                    RUTH
          That's known as colloquial writing.
          Colloquial is like Auntie, when she
          speaks, that is known as Hawaiian
          Pidgin. In the case of the book, that
          is how Huck speaks. It will take you no
          time to pick it up. Continue reading,
          William.

William starts reading. His lips move with each word as though he were reading aloud.

Ruth watches William.

INT. RUTH'S LIVING ROOM - NIGHT

Ruth watches television. Mrs. Wiggins curled up on her lap. Ben enters through the front door.

                    BEN
          Good evening, Mrs. Newcomb.

                    RUTH
          Good evening.
              (beat)
          Darling, have you found a security
          system yet?

                    BEN
          No.

                    RUTH
          I want you to check on it in the
          morning, okay?

                    BEN
          Oh-kay.

Ben continues to his room.

INT. RUTH'S BEDROOM - NIGHT

Ruth sleeps wearing her silk night mask.

GRUNTING and SCRATCHING sounds awaken Ruth. She removes her silk night mask and sits on the edge of the bed.

SCREENPLAY

Mrs. Wiggins waddles into the bedroom, meowing.

Ruth reaches into the nightstand and takes out a flashlight. She turns it on.

EXT. RUTH'S ORCHARD - NIGHT - CONTINUOUS

Ruth, using the flashlight to guide her, heads towards the grunting and scratching sounds. She wears slippers.

Ruth turns the flashlight on the giant, hundred-and-fifty-pound pig, GRUNTING, scratching the ground near the base of a macadamia tree. The pig slams against the tree with all its weight, and nuts fall. More grunting as the pig eats the nuts.

The pig looks at Ruth, grunts, and waddles away into the darkness.

EXT. RUTH'S ORCHARD - DAY - CONTINUOUS

Ruth wonders the orchard, disgusted with the ankle-high grass and macadamia nuts all over the ground.

                    RUTH
          (yelling)
     Ben!
          (beat)
     Ben!

Ruth starts marching, passing the house, heads up to Auntie's.

                    RUTH (CONT'D)
     Ben!

EXT. AUNTIE'S GREENHOUSE - DAY

Ruth passes through the trees and shrubs separating her property from Auntie's. She spots the greenhouse and heads for it.

                    RUTH
     Ben!
          (beat)
     Ben!

Ruth finds the door to the greenhouse and enters.

INT. AUNTIE'S GREENHOUSE - DAY

Ben and Auntie pick marijuana buds from the mature plants. They stare at Ruth.

                    AUNTIE
     You, kokua?

                    RUTH
     No, I came for Ben.

-124-

SCREENPLAY

Ruth takes a moment to study the greenhouse. She does a slow burn. Her jaw drops as she realizes what she is looking at.

> RUTH (CONT'D)
> That's marijuana!

> AUNTIE
> Haole call it marijuana. We call it pakalolo. You kokua?

> RUTH
> (to Ben)
> What you are doing is wrong. Ben, I want you down at my place now!

> BEN
> Oh-kay...

Ruth turns to leave.

> AUNTIE
> (to Ben)
> No! You stay. Keiki's need kokua now.

Ruth turns towards Auntie.

> RUTH
> No! Darling, Ben will come with me to my place. He gets paid to take care of my place.

> AUNTIE
> I pay Ben, too. Da pakalolo help people and make more money den mac nuts, Kona coffee, an orchids.

> RUTH
> What you all are doing is wrong; growing marijuana is illegal.

> AUNTIE
> Dis is medicinal marijuana.

> RUTH
> I don't care.
> (to Ben)
> Ben, come!

Ben shakes his head.

> RUTH (CONT'D)
> Ben, you have been hired to take care of my place. You haven't mowed the lawn in over a month. The nuts need attention and the security system...
> (beat)
> Well, what about the security system?

SCREENPLAY

                    BEN
          I work it.

                    RUTH
          Enough of this, Ben. I have had all I
          can take of you and your lack of work.
          If you like it so much here, Ben, get
          your stuff out of my place and move up
          here with Auntie.

                    AUNTIE
          He no live wit me.

                    RUTH
          I want Ben out of my place tomorrow.
          You understand?

EXT. RUTH'S LANAI - DAY

Ruth types on the laptop. Mrs. Wiggins curled up in
her chair.

William comes meanders up, carrying The Adventures
of Huckleberry Finn. He smiles.

                    WILLIAM
          Aaa-looo-haaa, Mrs. Newcomb... Am I
          disturbing you?

                    RUTH
          No, Darling. Have a seat.

William sits in his usual spot.

                    WILLIAM
          You were right, Mrs. Newcomb. I
          couldn't put Huck Finn down. It is a
          great book! I could identify with Huck
          'cause we have a lot in common. I like
          how he uses pigs' blood to fake his
          death.

                    RUTH
          It was good, wasn't it?

                    WILLIAM
          Yes, Mrs. Newcomb. Ma-ha-lo!

William hands the book to Ruth, who places it on
the table next to Catcher in the Rye.

                    RUTH
          You know, William, Catcher in the Rye
          is a great book. You'll like it too.

She picks Catcher in the Rye, handing it to
William.

                    WILLIAM
          Ma-ha-lo!

                    -126-

                         RUTH
          Darling, I need help around the house,
          mowing the lawn, collecting the nuts,
          and doing odd jobs. Do you know of
          anyone?

                         WILLIAM
          Ben, he's da bomb. There is no one
          better than Ben.

                         RUTH
          So you don't know of anyone?

William shakes his head.

                         RUTH (CONT'D)
          Darling, would you help me?

                         WILLIAM
          I'm not Ben. I do not have the tools or
          experience like him. I need to help
          Auntie.

                         RUTH
          Why are you helping her with THAT
          stuff? You shouldn't engage in such
          activities.

                         WILLIAM
          That stuff? Such activities?

                         RUTH
          You know what I mean, William.

                         WILLIAM
          No, I don't, Mrs. Newcomb.

                         RUTH
          Darling, what you are doing is wrong.

                         WILLIAM
          There's nothing wrong with helping
          Auntie.

                         RUTH
          William, I agree with you to a point.
          However, helping someone tend to
          marijuana is not.

                         WILLIAM
          It ohana, da Hawaiian way.

                         RUTH
          If you go up there and help her, I
          don't want you around here anymore.

William gets up.

                         WILLIAM
          What-ever...

SCREENPLAY

William leaves, holding <u>Catcher in the Rye</u>.

INT. RUTH'S BEDROOM - NIGHT

Ruth sleeps, wearing her silk night mask. The sounds of Mrs. Wiggins in a CAT FIGHT mixed with GRUNTING SOUNDS awaken Ruth. She removes the night mask and gets out of bed.

> RUTH
> Mrs. Wiggins!

EXT. RUTH'S ORCHARD - NIGHT CONTINUOUS

The sounds of a horrific fight continue, the GROWLING and HISSING from the cat and those of a pig GRUNTING.

Ruth, with a flashlight in hand, runs frantically into the orchard toward the sounds of Mrs. Wiggins HISSING and the pig GRUNTING.

Ruth reached the scene, shining her flashlight on the pig, watching it meander away, leaving Mrs. Wiggins sprawled on the grass.

> RUTH
> Oh, no! Mrs. Wiggins!

EXT. RUTH'S GARDEN AREA - DAY

Ruth, with a shovel in hand, dug a hole in the soft, red volcanic pumice soil. Next to the hole, Mrs. Wiggins, wrapped in Ruth's New York RED WOOLEN SCARF, looks like a mummy.

Ruth places Mrs. Wiggins in the hole, filling the cavity with soil and finishing by placing a handmade wooden cross at one end of the grave. Ruth stands, leaning on the shovel.

CLOSE ON RUTH

Ruth shakes her head and starts to cry.

PULL BACK TO REVEAL

The orchard, the house, and the vastness of the island as clouds obscure the island.

> FADE TO WHITE:

EXT. RUTH'S LANAI - DAY

Ruth sits with the laptop open. She stares pensively at the screen, not typing. She shakes her head and closes the laptop.

Ruth gets up and strolls down the lanai steps.

SCREENPLAY

EXT. RUTH'S GARDEN AREA - DAY

Ruth meanders to Mrs. Wiggins' grave site. She
stands there observing the cross.

Auntie quietly moves up to Ruth, placing her hands
before her, and bows her head.

Ruth doesn't notice Auntie standing next to her.

                    AUNTIE
               (in perfect English)
          It's tough when you lose loved ones,
          isn't it?

Startled, Ruth turns and looks at Auntie.

                    AUNTIE (CONT'D)
          It will take time, and you will get
          over it. You need a hug...

Auntie opens her arms to Ruth.

                    AUNTIE (CONT'D)
          Come to Auntie.

Reluctant Ruth approaches Auntie.

                    AUNTIE (CONT'D)
          It's okay. I am here for you.

Ruth starts to raise her hands to hug Auntie and
pauses.

                    AUNTIE (CONT'D)
          It would help if you had someone right
          now.
               (beat)
          Auntie is here.

Ruth can't resist. The two of them hug.

Ruth starts crying.

                    AUNTIE (CONT'D)
          There, there...

Auntie starts patting Ruth as if she were consoling
a young, scared child.

                    AUNTIE (CONT'D)
          Everything is going to be alright.

                    RUTH
               (Sobbing)
          Mrs. Wiggins was the last thing I had.
          I wanted to have solitude but not be
          alone like this.

Ruth and Auntie break their embrace.

                    AUNTIE
          Sometimes, what we want is not what we
          truly need. Often, what we are looking
          for is right before us, and we don't
          see it. We look elsewhere because we
          believe it is there and not where it
          truly is. You came from the fast-paced,
          wikiwiki world of the Big Apple to the
          more relaxed laid back life of the Big
          Island. The two cannot coexist. You are
          here now, but for how long?

Ruth shrugs her shoulders.

                    RUTH
          I sold everything and am here for good.

                    AUNTIE
          You're a multi-millionaire. You can
          move back to the Big Apple any time you
          want.

                    RUTH
          There's nothing left for me there
          anymore.

                    AUNTIE
          Then you must adjust to the Big Island
          life. Here, we help each other. We are
          all one big family; it's the Hawaiian
          way. The Hawaiians call it ohana. Ohana
          is the Hawaiian word for family. It
          doesn't only mean our blood family, but
          also our extended family, who are there
          for us in the here and now. William is
          not my son, but I treat him like he is.
          That's ohana. Hawaii was built on
          ohana; it is the magic of the Hawaiian
          people.

                    RUTH
          I think I understand. My needs and
          wants are out of whack; they are not
          set for the Hawaiian way. They are
          currently set for the Big Apple.
          That's in the past. I need to move on.
          As Mrs. Strong said when she arrived
          from the mainland, she used to be
          uptight, and that life is different
          here, and she changed; she said, in
          time, I too would change and become
          more relaxed and enjoy da Big Island
          ways.

Auntie glances towards her house and back at Ruth.

                    AUNTIE
          Would you like to have a punch?

                    RUTH
          I'd love to.

                         -130-

SCREENPLAY

Ruth and Auntie stroll towards Auntie's house.

>   RUTH (CONT'D)
>   You are speaking perfect English now.
>   So why do you speak pidgin?

>   AUNTIE
>   It's expected. I have my Ph.D. in
>   horticulture from Purdue, and if I were
>   to speak proper English, things would
>   be completely different. Besides, I
>   enjoy speaking pidgin. Very few people
>   know I have my doctorate. I keep that
>   and speak perfect English to a select
>   group who have at least a master's
>   degree, like the Baccio's, Charlene
>   Strong, and Dr. Tilton; other than
>   them, people think I'm that sweet crazy
>   Auntie born and raised on Oahu. In due
>   time, you'll be speaking pidgin too.

EXT. LAVA FIELDS - DAY

Ruth's SUV drives towards Kona through the lava
fields.

EXT. KONA MACY'S - DAY

Ruth, wearing a designer dress and high heel
designer shoes, and Auntie, in her muumuu, enter
Macy's.

>   AUNTIE
>   (In perfect English)
>   We need to change your mainland attire
>   to that of a kama'aina.

>   RUTH
>   A what?

>   AUNTIE
>   Kama'aina is the Hawaiian for a child
>   of the land or better known as a local
>   person. Haole used to mean white
>   person, but now, to be politically
>   correct, it means foreigner. This is
>   all part of what I have been talking
>   about, changing your mindset to be a
>   part of da Big Island. We have a
>   secret.

Ruth leans into Auntie.

>   AUNTIE (CONT'D)
>   As I told you earlier, you know
>   something few other people do.

>   RUTH
>   Darling, what could I possibly know
>   that no one else knows?

                    AUNTIE
          My education and use of pidgin! It's
          between us girls. From now on, I will
          only speak pidgin. And it would help if
          you cut that darling stuff. Using
          darling may work in the Big Apple, but
          not here on da Big Island. We do things
          differently here.

Auntie leans into Ruth.

                    AUNTIE (CONT'D)
               (In pidgin)
          You understand, sista?

Ruth laughs as they enter Macy's.

                                        DISSOLVE TO:

EXT. KONA MACY'S - DAY

Ruth exits Macy's wearing a muumuu and zoris for
the first time. Ruth and Auntie carry bags.

EXT. LOWE'S - DAY

Ruth and Auntie stroll into Lowe's.

INT. LOWE'S GARDEN DEPARTMENT - DAY

Ruth takes in the assortment of smaller potted
flowers. She places a few in her cart.

Auntie's cart has four bags of potting soil and two
bags of fertilizer.

                    AUNTIE
               (Patting the fertilizer)
          Dis kokua, da keiki's.

                    RUTH
          I don't understand why you are growing
          that stuff.

Auntie leans close to Ruth.

                    AUNTIE
               (Whispering in perfect
               English)
          It's one way I can afford to live here.

                    RUTH
          So you see nothing wrong with what you
          are doing?

                    AUNTIE
          There is nothing wrong with it. It's
          not like I'm trafficking or selling to
          kids.

                         -132-

SCREENPLAY

                    RUTH
          So that makes it okay?

Auntie nods.

                    AUNTIE
          Yes, I'm registered with the feds on an
          experimental horticultural program
          researching growing medicinal marijuana
          which we hope sometime in the future
          will help many suffering people. Did
          you know cannabis cures specific types
          of cancer? The Chinese have been using
          it for thousands of years. Cannabis is
          in its infancy. With more research, it
          will be the wonder drug.

                    RUTH
          So, why does Ben spend so much time
          with you?

                    AUNTIE
          He usually doesn't, it's harvest time,
          and I can use all the help I can get.
          You're welcome to help any time.

Auntie moves back from Ruth.

                    AUNTIE (CONT'D)
               (In pidgin)
          It da Hawaiian way!

Ruth spots the chicken feed and grabs a large bag,
placing it in the cart.

INT. RUTH'S KITCHEN - DAY

Ruth, wearing a Hawaiian Missionary dress and
zoris, takes Mrs. Wiggins' bowl and fills it with
chicken feed. She goes to the lanai.

EXT. RUTH'S LANAI - DAY

Ruth moves down the lanai steps, placing the cat
dish at the base.

EXT. RUTH'S GARDEN AREA - DAY

Ruth plants the flowers she bought around Mrs.
Wiggins' grave. As she does, she hears a noise
coming from the lanai steps. She observes chickens,
wild turkeys, and néné fighting for the chicken
feed. She smiles.

                                        DISSOLVE TO:

EXT. RUTH'S ORCHARD - DAY

Ruth, wearing zoris, jeans, and a T-shirt, attempts
to navigate a large lawn tractor.

On the way to the orchard, she tries to learn how
to cut the grass before getting to the orchard and
engages the mower.

At first, she wasn't doing a good job. She could
not drive straight nor control the mower. The
chickens, wild turkey, and néné scurry out of the
way only to follow the tractor pecking the ground.
She heads directly for a large macadamia tree but
turns; branches brush her face as she misses the
tree.

EXT. RUTH'S ORCHARD - DUSK

Ruth rides the lawn tractor, smiling. She navigates
expertly through the orchard before finishing.

EXT. RUTH'S LANAI - DAY

Ruth, wearing a missionary dress for the first
time, types on the laptop.

William comes up to Ruth.

                    WILLIAM
          Mrs. Newcomb, here's <u>Catcher in the
          Rye</u>.

William hands Ruth <u>Catcher in the Rye</u>. He turns to
leave. Ruth places the book on the table.

                    RUTH
          William, please come back.

William turns back towards Ruth.

                    RUTH (CONT'D)
          William, I want to apologize for my
          rudeness the other day. It was wrong of
          me.

                    WILLIAM
          Dat oh-kay, Mrs. Newcomb. Ben's
          brother, Michael, lives in New York. He
          says New Yorkers can be very rude.

                    RUTH
          We New Yorkers are not rude, William,
          but sometimes the customs and the way
          of life of other cultures, even our own
          here in the United States, are
          misunderstood and taken as being rude
          or unacceptable.

                    WILLIAM
          I think I understand. Do you have
          another fun book?

Ruth thinks for a moment. She snaps her fingers.

                    RUTH
          I have it! Come with me.

INT. RUTH'S LIVING ROOM - DAY

Ruth scans the bookshelf, book after book until she
reaches the thickest book on the shelf James
Michener's <u>Hawaii</u>.

                    RUTH
          Ah, here it is.

Ruth hands the book to William.

William studies the thick book, and his eyes go
wide.

                    WILLIAM
          It's soooo thick.

                    RUTH
          William, it's a good read. You will
          enjoy it.

                    WILLIAM
          Thank you, Mrs. Newcomb. I am sure I
          will like it as I did the other books.

William starts to leave.

                    WILLIAM (CONT'D)
          Auntie's keiki's need me.

                    RUTH
          Mind if I tag along?

William shakes his head.

Ruth closes the laptop and places it on the table
beside the chair. She gets up and follows William.

EXT. RUTH'S ORCHARD - DAY - CONTINUOUS

Ruth and William stroll through the orchard heading
for Auntie's.

                    WILLIAM
          I thought you didn't like what we are
          doing, and now you want to help?

                    RUTH
          William, let's say I need to adjust
          from my New York ways and customs to
          those here on the Big Island.

                    WILLIAM
          That brings up a question. Is New York
          as wicked and phony as Holden Caulfield
          says it is?

SCREENPLAY

> RUTH
> From Holden's perspective, it is. From mine, New York isn't really that way.

> WILLIAM
> I didn't think so, because you aren't like the characters in the book.

> RUTH
> I don't know if I should take that as a compliment or not.

> WILLIAM
> Oh, a compliment, Mrs. Newcomb. I couldn't put da book down. Reading is fun, just like you, Auntie, Mrs. Strong, and Dr. Tilton told me. I discovered so much about New York.

> RUTH
> Just think about it, William. You were able to accomplish it without leaving the island. And now you will discover Hawaii. It's a fictional account of Hawaii, and it is reasonably accurate about what happened and how the islands became the way they are.

INT. AUNTIE'S GREENHOUSE - DAY

William enters, followed by Ruth.

Ben and Auntie harvest buds.

Ben looks up as if caught in the middle of doing something wrong.

> RUTH
> Ben, I want to apologize about DA other day.

This is Ruth's first use of the word DA for THE. Ben and Auntie react by smiling.

> RUTH (CONT'D)
> You can come back.

> BEN
> Mahalo, I thought you didn't like what we are doing here.

> RUTH
> I've thought helping each other is da Hawaiian way, isn't it?

> BEN
> Huh-huh...

SCREENPLAY

                    RUTH
          I'm here to help.
              (BEAT)
          Ah, I mean, I am here to kokua.

                    AUNTIE
          You go, sista!

Auntie notices William carrying <u>Hawaii</u>.

                    AUNTIE (CONT'D)
              (to William)
          Dat good book. It Hawaii to da max.

                    WILLIAM
          It is a BIG book.

William holds the book as if he were weighing it.

                    WILLIAM (CONT'D)
          It heavy.

                    AUNTIE
          You read. You like. Yes?

William nods.

                    WILLIAM
          Mrs. Newcomb said I would like it, too.

Ruth notices Auntie and Ben with shears and
buckets.

                    RUTH
          Where do I get a bucket?

                    BEN
              (whispering to Auntie)
          She never done dis before.

                    RUTH
          What can be so hard about trimming?

                    BEN
          There's a special way I'll show you.

                    AUNTIE
          No, she learn from da masta. I show
          her! Come.

Ruth moves towards Auntie.

                    AUNTIE (CONT'D)
          Here scissor.

Auntie hands the scissors to Ruth.

William places <u>Hawaii</u> on the counter, picks up a
small bucket and shears, and starts harvesting
buds.

Auntie shows Ruth how to harvest the buds and places them in the bucket.

> AUNTIE (CONT'D)
> See, it not hard. You try.

Ruth follows the same procedure shown to her by Auntie, placing the buds in the bucket.

> AUNTIE (CONT'D)
> You do plenny good. You get bucket.

Ruth goes over and picks up shears and a small bucket and starts harvesting buds, smiling.

All watch Ruth.

INT. RUTH'S LANAI - DAY

Ruth types on the laptop.

Ben meanders up the steps carrying a large open UPS cardboard box. He has his tool belt on.

Ruth stops typing and turns her attention to Ben.

> BEN
> What do you want done first?

> RUTH
> What are you talking about, Ben?

> BEN
> You asked for a security system. I got da system. It's here in da box. Do you want da front door or your bedroom done first?

> RUTH
> Ben, I no longer need a security system.

> BEN
> Since you got here, you wanted a security system; now you don't?

> RUTH
> DIS is Hawaii. You said Hawaii is laid-back. No one has an alarm system. We don't need it. Please give it to me. I'll return it.

INT. RUTH'S BEDROOM - NIGHT

Sounds of the INSECTS CHIRPING and FROGS CROAKING are abruptly broken by a pig's nearby GRUNTING and POPPING sounds. Ruth reaches into her nightstand, grabs the flashlight, and leaves the room.

SCREENPLAY

EXT. RUTH'S GARDEN AREA - NIGHT

The sounds come from Mrs. Wiggins' gravesite and a
nearby mango tree. Ruth points the flashlight
towards the gravesite and saw the flowers were
gone, apparently eaten by the pig.
Hearing a LOUD THUD followed by a GRUNT, she points
the flashlight towards the mango tree, illuminating
the pig ramming the trunk with its body as a ripe
mango fell to the ground. The light attracts the
attention of the pig, who looks at her as it eats
the mango and trots away into the darkness.

INT. AUNTIE'S LANAI - DAY

Ruth and Auntie are having coffee.

                    AUNTIE
               (in perfect English)
          The pigs are a major issue on the
          island and need to be kept in check.
          It's tough to do where we live because
          our properties are near a state park
          where the pigs are protected. I believe
          the pigs figured out that they are safe
          and cavort there.

          Usually, fences do a great job of
          keeping the pigs out. I've been
          thinking that we have Ben put up fences
          around our properties once harvesting
          is over. My concern is they may get to
          the pakalolo. Can you imagine what
          would happen with a pig high on
          marijuana?

Ruth and Auntie laugh.

                    RUTH
          What do we do to keep them out?

                    AUNTIE
          Keeping the fences in check is our
          first line of defense. Right now, we
          have to have Ben trap and dispatch
          them.

                    RUTH
          Dispatch them?

                    AUNTIE
          Kill them, donating their carcasses to
          needy families, a local luau, or
          someone who would love fresh pork. For
          the other undesirables, such as
          mongoose, Ben dispatches them to what
          we locals call another zip code,
          meaning a field a few miles from here
          so they don't return. Having Ben around
          is such a help for us women.
                    (MORE)

                    AUNTIE (CONT'D)
Paul once shot a 200-pound pig. A few
days later, the Martins had Ben prep
and cook da pig in their Imu, the
sizeable earthen barbecue pit near your
shed, and had a luau for their friends
and ohana before they returned to New
York.

                    RUTH
I remember them telling us about that
adventure. They said the pig was tender
and succulent.

                    AUNTIE
The rifle should still be somewhere in
your house.

                    RUTH
It's in my closet. Are you suggesting I
shoot the pig?

                    AUNTIE
Oh, not at all. There may be a night
when you must protect yourself from da
pigs. They sometimes get aggressive and
may charge you. When they charge you,
you have two choices: climb a tree or
shoot. When I hear them at night, I
always take my rifle. Luckily the
flashlight usually scares them, and
they trot away like what happened to
you last night.

                    RUTH
I have at least two mongoose running
around my place. I thought they would
be like the squirrels in Central Park
looking for a handout. They run away
from me when I approach them. They
don't seem to be an issue. So why
would Ben dispatch them?

                    AUNTIE
Mongoose aren't really an issue. They
love to consume eggs. With all the
chickens around, we have a plethora of
fresh eggs. Wait here!

Auntie leaves Ruth on the lanai, returning moments
later carrying a bowl with two eggs, one slightly
smaller. Auntie takes both eggs from the bowl and
places them beside the coffee mugs. She points to
the smaller egg.

                    AUNTIE (CONT'D)
This egg is from one of the feral
chickens. See how it's slightly smaller
than the store-bought egg.

SCREENPLAY

Auntie took the larger egg into her hand, cracked it open into the bowl, followed doing the same thing with the smaller egg, and handed it to Ruth to inspect.

> AUNTIE (CONT'D)
> Notice the difference in the yokes?

> RUTH
> The yoke from the smaller egg is much larger than the store-bought egg. Why is it?

> AUNTIE
> It means the egg is feral; on the mainland, they use phrases like organic or free-range eggs. You probably haven't seen any eggs because your mongoose are eating them before you know they are there. We'll have Ben dispatch the mongoose to another zip code. Most of all, the feral eggs are free and much tastier than the store-bought ones. Would you like scrambled eggs for breakfast?

EXT. KBI-TV - DAY

A rusted tan metal Quonset hut with a big faded sign above the door announces KBI-TV, Big Island TV, Channel 32.

Ruth, wearing a missionary dress, marches up, opening the wooden door.

INT. KBI-TV - DAY

A large thumping window air conditioner rattles and vibrates in the austere reception area. At the desk the KBI RECEPTIONIST plays solitaire.

Ruth enters and goes to the KBI Receptionist.

> KBI RECEPTIONIST
> May I help you?

> RUTH
> Yes, I'm here to see Danny.

> KBI RECEPTIONIST
> He's back there.

The KBI Receptionist points.

> KBI RECEPTIONIST (CONT'D)
> Second door to da right.

> RUTH
> Thank you.

Ruth goes down the hall.

SCREENPLAY

INT. DANNY MAKUA'S OFFICE - DAY

Looks like a 1940s-style military office. A
television monitor plays a re-run of <u>Gilligan's
Island</u>. Danny sits at his desk typing on a
computer.

A KNOCK at the door.

                    DANNY
          Come in.

Ruth enters.

                    DANNY (CONT'D)
          Aloha!

Danny gets up.

                    DANNY (CONT'D)
          Have a seat.

Ruth and Danny sit.

                    DANNY (CONT'D)
          Well, Ruth, may I call you Ruth?

                    RUTH
          Yes, of course, darling, ah, Danny.

                    DANNY
          I was hoping you would call. I like
          your thoughts about doing a monthly
          show about da Big Island.

Ruth smiles.

                    DANNY (CONT'D)
          If it's anything like <u>From the Big
          Apple</u>, both locals and tourists will
          like it. What do you think about
          calling da show <u>From the Big Island</u>?

                    RUTH
          Love it!
             (beat)
          <u>From THE Big Island </u>doesn't sound quite
          right.

                    DANNY
          I think it's perfect.

                    RUTH
          I do too. We need to make a minor
          change; change the THE to DA.

Danny raises his eyebrows, smiles and nods.

                    RUTH (CONT'D)
          It's da Hawaiian way.

SCREENPLAY

                    DANNY
          I like it!

                    RUTH
          It will make all da difference. We'll
          call it <u>From da Big Island</u>. However,
          we need something else.

                    DANNY
          Like what?

                    RUTH
          A logo or something, what about
                    (thinking)
          A palm tree?

                    DANNY
          Overdone.

                    RUTH
          Hibiscus flower?

                    DANNY
          Overdone.

Danny stares into space for a moment, and snaps his
fingers.

                    DANNY (CONT'D)
          I got it!

                    RUTH
          What?

                    DANNY
          FBI!

                    RUTH
          FBI?

                    DANNY
          Yes, FBI: From da Big Island.
                    (beat)
          Get it?

Ruth nods.

                    DANNY (CONT'D)
          We have FBI in large yellow letters
          with <u>From da Big Island </u>in a smaller
          font.

                    RUTH
          Won't people get confused with THE FBI?

                    DANNY
          I don't think so, this is Hawaii, not
          da mainland. We'll even put the da in
          small letters between the F and B.
                    (MORE)

                    DANNY (CONT'D)
          How could anyone misinterpret that logo
          between us and the Federal Bureau of
          Investigation?

Ruth cracked a smile.

                    RUTH
          We still may have legal issues. And
          there are other big islands around the
          world. We must better identify our Big
                    (MORE)
                    RUTH (CONT'D)
          Island of Hawaii from other big
          islands.

          When we came up with da logo for <u>From
          the Big Apple</u>, we put the name of da
          show inside a line drawing of an apple.
          What if we did something similar, such
          as encapsulating da letters FBI inside
          an outline of the island? That way, we
          have something unique, thereby reducing
          any confusion.

                    DANNY
          What a fantastic idea, Ruth. Have you
          thought about what you would like to do
          for your first installment?

                    RUTH
          I was thinking of doing something in
          Waipio Valley.

                    DANNY
          I don't think that would be a good
          idea. It's been overdone and on da
          tourist channel.

                    RUTH
          Yes, but not my angle.

EXT. WAIPIO VALLEY ONE LANE ROAD - DAY

RUTH, AS SEEN THROUGH THE CAMERA

Ruth wears a hibiscus above her ear. This is the
first time we have seen her with a hibiscus.

                    RUTH
          Many tourists and locals attempt to
          make the arduous journey down to Waipio
          Valley, and some don't.
                    (BEAT)
          Okay, let's get shots of da cars.

BACK TO THE SCENE.

We see Danny, MICKEY (30's), the cameraman holding
a video camera, and the SUV parked off the
roadside.

SCREENPLAY

                    DANNY
          Mickey, get plenty of cut-a-ways.

Mickey takes the camera into the brush to get
angles of the rusted cars in the trees.

                    DANNY (CONT'D)
          This is an excellent idea of yours,
          Ruth. It's unique.

                    RUTH
          Everyone knows about da cars, but no
          one talks about them.

                    DANNY
          I remember a year ago when a couple of
          drunk tourist kids thought they would
          take their rental car down here to
          party on da beach. They almost made it.
          Da only thing that saved them from all
          being killed was da tree.

                    RUTH
          Do you know where their car is?

Danny studies the trees, searching for the car.

                    DANNY
          It's somewhere here. I really can't
          remember exactly where it is. You can
          tell which one it is because it isn't
          as rusted as da others.

INT. RUTH'S LIVING ROOM - NIGHT

CLOSE ON TELEVISION

                    RUTH
          That's it from the Waipio Valley
          graveyard of cars in the trees. Until
          next time, this is Ruth Newcomb, From
          da Big Island. Aaa-looo-haaa!

BACK TO THE SCENE AS CREDITS ROLL BY

Ruth, Ben, and Auntie drink red punch and eat
brownies watching the credits roll by.

                    AUNTIE
          Dat gut! You do gooood job!

                    BEN
          It funny, too.

Ruth is beaming.

                    RUTH
          Ma-ha-lo!

SCREENPLAY

                    AUNTIE
          Der you go. You become mo Hawaiian.

Ruth takes a bite from a brownie.

                    RUTH
          Auntie, these brownies are fabulous!
          Whatever do you put in them?

Auntie and Ben smile.

                    AUNTIE
          Coconut water make da punch.

                    BEN
          Da brownies are from an old Hawaiian
          family recipe.

EXT. BIG ISLAND GRILL - DAY

The Big Island Grill in Kona looks like a converted
fast-food restaurant.

Ruth and Madam Gloria La Fong, wearing Aloha wear,
enter the restaurant.

INT. BIG ISLAND GRILL - DAY

On a wall inside by the door is a POSTER displaying
many fish with their Hawaiian and mainland names.
Next to it, a CHALKBOARD is handwritten with FRESH
FISH TODAY - OPAH AND HAPU'UPU'U.

Ruth and Gloria study the chart finding that
Hapu'upu'u was grouper and Opah was moonfish.

They are seated and review the menu.

INT. BIG ISLAND GRILL - DAY (LATER)

Ruth and Gloria are seated eating seafood.

                    RUTH
          Gloria, what do you think about the
          fish?

                    GLORIA
          When you told me this is the best place
          on the island for seafood, and the only
          downside was it doesn't have a
          waterfront view, I thought you were
          joking. Have you been to a hukilau yet?

                    RUTH
          Not yet. I think it's a wonderful idea
          to shoot a real hukilau from throwing
          out the hukilau nets to the beach
          festival and dance that follows.

GLORIA
I'm sure you could integrate the
hukilau song in the segment.

RUTH
You are filled with ideas.

GLORIA
Ruth, you've been avoiding telling me
how you are adjusting. How are you
really doing?

RUTH
Gloria, remember how a wreck I was
after Zach's death? I thought his death
was brutal, but worse was how I lost
Mrs. Wiggins to that damned pig. What a
way for her to go.
     (she shakes her head)
It still makes me mad when I think
about it. The pigs are becoming a
significant issue here on the island.
We did a segment on <u>From da Big Island</u>
about the pig issue. It was well
received, but we can do nothing to
reduce the population explosion. Ben
has been making extra money dispatching
pigs.

GLORIA
Dispatching? I don't understand

RUTH
Killing and selling them for luau's or
donating them to needy families.

GLORIA
What a great thing for him to do: care
for those in need. Do the pigs taste
any different than what we get in the
States?

RUTH
Gloria, Hawaii IS a state. It's best to
say mainland. However, to answer your
question, I haven't had any yet. I
understand nothing is better than a pig
cooked the Hawaiian way in an Imu, a
Hawaiian underground oven, for the
entire day. I have one by the shed and
hope to use it.

GLORIA
You still are avoiding answering my
question about how you are doing.

RUTH
Gloria, I prefer to spend our time
together not as your patient, but as a
friend. In that respect, things are
          (MORE)

-147-

                    RUTH (CONT'D)
          going great, and I am keeping busy with
          <u>From da Big Island</u>, writing my memoirs,
          and helping a local high school senior
          with his reading.

INT. DANNY MAKUA'S OFFICE - DAY

Ruth wearing a Missionary dress, sits at Danny's
desk, behind which Danny shuffles legal papers.

                    DANNY
          Ruth, I think I have everything in
          order. Da two of us are da executive
          producers. Partial funding comes from
          da visitors bureau and our head offices
          in New York.

                    RUTH
          Danny, did they put it in writing?

                    DANNY
          Ruth, it's right here.

Danny hands the contract to Ruth with his finger
resting on the middle of the page.

                    DANNY (CONT'D)
          See?

Ruth studies the contract.

                    DANNY (CONT'D)
          From da Big Island.

                    RUTH
          I was afraid that with the show going
          into syndication, they would want to
          change da name to <u>From THE Big Island</u>.

Ruth scans the contract.

                    DANNY
          They loved it and agreed to partner
          with da visitors bureau to develop an
          advertising campaign. Da logo will go
          on T-shirts, coffee mugs, and the like.
          They're going all out.

Ruth smiles.

                    DANNY (CONT'D)
          Since you did a great job conveying so
          much information about da Big Island in
          so little time, everyone agreed to keep
          to the original short format. Da
          visitors bureau can utilize our
          segments as public service
          announcements worldwide.

Ruth hands the contract to Danny.

SCREENPLAY

                    RUTH
          That is terrific news, Danny. We've
          come a long way in a short time. Our
          segments have been viral, from our
          first one with cars in da trees segment
          to da one we did on da sports fishers
          throwing chum into the water, drawing
          da sharks that were attacking da
          swimmers.

          And we cannot forget da pigs! The way
          you set everyone up with da pig issue.
          Dat scene where da pigs were eating da
          ears of corn, then cutting to da pig at
          da luau with da ears of corn
          strategically placed around da pig, was
          precious.

They both laugh.

                    RUTH
          Danny, I was so busy filming that pig
          segment I didn't have a chance to enjoy
          the event or the food. One of these
          days, I will.

EXT. MAUNA KEA HOTEL CLAM BAKE - DUSK

An elaborate beachside buffet feast of fresh island
lobster, fish, sushi, sashimi, prime rib, and other
excellent food adorn tables, servers assisting
guests all wearing Aloha wear.

At one table are Ruth and Auntie with Joe and
Eileen Baccio, all in Aloha wear.

                    AUNTIE
              (in perfect English)
          What we need to see happen, Joe are
          changes in the law to make medicinal
          marijuana available nationwide. It's a
          shame to exclude something that can
          cure ailments like certain cancers and
          allow AIDS and HIV patients to eat
          where they couldn't before. I think
          we're heading in the right direction.

                    JOE
          I couldn't agree with you more.
          Hopefully, the government will approve
          medicinal use one day, and people won't
          have to go underground to get their
          medications. Thank you for what you are
          doing, and keep up the good work.

SCREENPLAY

                    EILEEN
To change the subject, Ruth, I've
noticed this is the first time we've
been out, and we haven't been
interrupted by your fans. I thought the
show was very popular here.

                    RUTH
Eileen, the show is very popular. We're
on the islands, and people are
different here. They respect my
privacy. Occasionally, some fans from
the mainland will recognize and
approach me for an autograph. What's
nice is it doesn't happen all that
frequently.

                    EILEEN
We were watching TV last night and saw
your segment on Queen Lili someone.

                    RUTH
You're talking about Queen
Liliuokalani, the last Hawaiian monarch
overthrown by the narrow-minded
missionaries.

                    EILEEN
It was a tremendously informative
segment.

                    JOE
Eileen and I liked that she wanted to
tax prostitution, the lottery, and
opium because people would do it
anyway, and it was a revenue stream. I
hope our government will also change
its mind and tax medicinal marijuana as
it did with the lottery. Only time will
tell.

INT. AUNTIE'S GREENHOUSE - DAY

Ruth, Auntie, Ben, and William harvest the keiki's.
Their buckets filled with buds.

                    AUNTIE
            (to Ruth)
You do plenny good, Luka.

                    RUTH
Luka, what's that?

                    WILLIAM
Dat Hawaiian for Ruth.

The door to the greenhouse opens, Officer #1 and
Officer #2 nonchalantly enter.

Ruth's eyes widen. She glances at Auntie.

>   OFFICER #1
>   Aaa-loooo-haa!

>   AUNTIE, BEN, AND WILLIAM
>   Aaa-looo-haaa!

Relieved, Ruth smiles.

>   RUTH
>   Aaa-loooo-haa!

Auntie goes over to the table, picks up a brown
paper bag, and hands it to Officer #1.

>   OFFICER #1
>   Ma-ha-lo!
>   (looking at Ruth)
>   Oh, Mrs. Newcomb, we congratulate you
>   on your Emmy nomination.

>   RUTH
>   (inquisitively)
>   What are you talking about?

>   OFFICER #2
>   It came over the radio that From da Big
>   Island was nominated for an Emmy.

Everyone turns their attention to Ruth and clap.

>   RUTH
>   I was nominated for an Emmy!

>   AUNTIE
>   You go New York?

William looks at Ruth.

>   WILLIAM
>   New York! Can I go with you?

>   RUTH
>   With me, where?

>   WILLIAM
>   To New York!

>   AUNTIE
>   Dat's were da Emmy's are, aren't they?

>   RUTH
>   (nodding)
>   Yes, they are in New York City. I
>   really don't want to return to New
>   York.

>   BEN
>   It's important, isn't it?

Ruth nods.

SCREENPLAY

                    AUNTIE
          Oh, Luka, you must go. Dis is important
          to you, to us, and most of all da
          island.

EXT. 747 FLYING OVER NEW YORK CITY - DUSK

Air to air shot.

EXT. MARRIOTT MARQUIS HOTEL MAIN ENTRANCE - NIGHT

The glimmering lights of Broadway spill into the
covered hotel entrance as a black limo pulls up.

A DOORMAN opens the limo door. A PORTER starts
taking the baggage out of the trunk.

Ruth, dressed in a muumuu, steps out. She was
followed by Danny, who turns around and reaches
into the limo, helping Auntie out, all wearing
Aloha wear.

Ruth, Auntie, and Danny gaze into the limo.

                    RUTH
          It's oh-kay. Come.

William sticks his head out the limo door, studying
the doorman while noticing the people hurrying by.

                    WILLIAM
          Ben say he doesn't like all the people
          in New York. Dat's why he didn't come.

                    RUTH
          Remember Holden Caulfield in <u>Catcher in
          the Rye</u>. It's okay!

William slowly steps out, wearing an Aloha wear.

The passersby stare at the foursome.

                    RUTH (CONT'D)
          We've had a very long flight. Let's
          check in and get some rest.

                    WILLIAM
          Can we see Times Square? Can we? Can we
          now, Mrs. Newcomb?

                    RUTH
          We'll explore it tomorrow.

                    WILLIAM
          Please?

                    AUNTIE
            (to Ruth)
          Da boy need to see Times Square at
          night. It unforgettable.

SCREENPLAY

                    RUTH
          Auntie's right. We'll go now.
               (to the porter)
          Take these upstairs. We'll be up in a
          bit.

The porter nods.

                    RUTH (CONT'D)
               (To the group)
          Let's go.

Ruth leads William, Auntie, and Danny out of the
Marquis entrance.

EXT. TIMES SQUARE AT 46TH STREET - NIGHT

Ruth, William, Auntie, and Danny enter Times
Square. The lights illuminate their awed faces as
cars and people rush about.

                    RUTH
          Here it is. This is Times Square.

William studies the square, turning his gaze
upward.

                    WILLIAM
          Da buildings are so tall! Higher than
          the waterfall at Waipio.

                    RUTH
          Have you seen the New Year's ball
          dropping?

William nods.

                    RUTH (CONT'D)
          It happens over there.

Ruth points to the One Times Square building.

People breeze by the foursome as they look towards
the building.

                    DANNY
          Too many people.

                    AUNTIE
          Dey to busy to enjoy life.
               (shaking her head)
          Too, wikiwiki!

                    WILLIAM
          I don't think I like it here.

SCREENPLAY

                    RUTH
     William, you just arrived. We are in
     the busiest area of New York. Central
     Park is not far from here and isn't
     anything like this.

                    WILLIAM
     I'm tired. Can we go to our room?

INT. MARRIOTT MARQUIS PRESIDENTIAL SUITE - NIGHT

The bellhop holds the door open Ruth, Auntie,
William, and Danny enter the enormous suite.

                    DANNY
     I've never seen a hotel suite this big
     before.

                    WILLIAM
     Dis is bigger than my house.

Auntie spots the grand piano.

                    AUNTIE
     Oh, a piano!

                    WILLIAM
     Where do I sleep? Da sofa?

Ruth opens a door.

                    RUTH
     William, this is your room.

                    WILLIAM
     I get my own room?

                    RUTH
     It's the presidential suite. We each
     have our own room.

EXT. TAVERN ON THE GREEN PATIO - DAY

Ruth, wearing a muumuu, and JIM, Ruth's former
television station owner, eat lunch.

                    JIM
     Ruth, the Emmys are this evening. No
     matter the outcome, I would like to
     offer you a contract.

                    RUTH
     Jim, I don't want to accept your
     contract. Danny and I have a perfect
     one with Al.

                    JIM
     The one I am offering you is better.

                    RUTH
          Jim, how do you know what I have with
          Al?

                    JIM
          It's better. Trust me. The contract is
          for a show much more incredible than
          From the Big Apple or From da Big
          Island could be.

Jim takes a sip from his Manhattan.

                    JIM (CONT'D)
          It's an international travelogue-type
          show.

                    RUTH
          What do you mean?

                    JIM
          I think you'll like the idea. You go to
          different places throughout the country
          and the world, showing us the out-of-
          the-way places to see. It's never been
          done before.

                    RUTH
          It's an exciting idea, and I like my
          semiretired life in Hawaii.

                    JIM
          You like New York, too, don't you?

Ruth nods.

                    JIM (CONT'D)
          And you like Hawaii, don't you?

Ruth nods.

                    JIM (CONT'D)
          It's the best of both worlds, Ruth.
          You can still live in Hawaii, come here
          and do the show.

                    RUTH
          The eleven-hour flights are too much
          for me, Jim.

                    JIM
          Eleven hours isn't that bad when you're
          traveling first class.

                    RUTH
          I lose a day each way! Perhaps most of
          all, all those new post-9/11
          restrictions are taking the fun out of
          air travel; like air travel was ever
          fun.

They both laugh.

SCREENPLAY

                    JIM
          It's an opportunity for you to reinvent
          yourself and make more money. Think
          about it, Ruth.

EXT. CENTRAL PARK - DAY

Auntie and William wearing Aloha wear and zories,
stroll through the park walking by a pond loaded
with DUCKS.

                    AUNTIE
          William, you remember da duck pond in
          <u>Catcher in the Rye</u>? Dis is da duck
          pond.

                    WILLIAM
          Der plenty of duck here.

William notices squirrels chasing each other around
the base of a tree, and one scurries up a tree.

                    WILLIAM (CONT'D)
          What dat? It look like mongoose, but
          they climb trees!

William points to the squirrels.

                    AUNTIE
          Dey squirrel, dey all over da mainland.

EXT. CENTRAL PARK - DAY (LATER)

Auntie and William are near the <u>Alice in Wonderland</u>
statue.

SOUNDS OF A UKULELE are heard. Michael is singing a
Hawaiian song.

Auntie and William reach the crowd around Michael.

Michael spots Auntie and William and stops
strumming and singing.

The crowd stares at Auntie and William.

                    MICHAEL
          Auntie! William!
               (beat)
          Aaa-loooo-haa!

                    AUNTIE AND WILLIAM
          Aaa-loooo-haa!

                    MICHAEL
          What you do here?

                    AUNTIE
          We here to see you, Michael.

                    MICHAEL
          You come all the way from da Big Island
          to see me?

                    AUNTIE
          Yups. We miss you. Ben and I need your
          kokua, Michael. It time you return to
          da island.

                    MICHAEL
          I do okay here. I make plenny money.

                    AUNTIE
          You make plenny money wid me on da
          island. You be mo happy.

                    WILLIAM
          Ben misses you, and we need you in
          Hawaii.

                    AUNTIE
          Come back wid us.

                    WILLIAM
          Please.

INT. MARRIOTT MARQUIS PRESIDENTIAL SUITE - NIGHT

The door to the Presidential Suite swung open by
Danny holding an Emmy in one hand, the door in the
other. Ruth entered carrying an Emmy. She was
followed by Linda and Pauline, her sister and
niece. Behind them followed Auntie and William, all
wearing formalwear. Danny closes the door behind
him. The group moved into the suite sitting on the
sofa and in the chairs surrounding the coffee
table.

                    PAULINE
          We knew you two would win.

                    WILLIAM
          Yeah, <u>From da Big Island</u> is da bomb.

Ruth and Danny place their Emmys on the coffee
table.

The group moves into the suite, sitting on the sofa
and in the surrounding chairs.

                    DANNY
          Don't they look great together? I never
          knew they were as heavy as they are.

                    RUTH
          That reminds me of the first time I won
          one. I almost dropped it on the stage.

SCREENPLAY

PAULINE
Aunt Ruth, Mother, and I remember our
going to Sardi's after the ceremony.
Are we going this evening?

LINDA
(to Ruth)
Darling, Sardi's is a great place to
celebrate.

RUTH
Linda, it never entered my mind to
celebrate at Sardi's.

Linda and Pauline make pouting faces.

LINDA
Sis, you've been away way so long.
Don't you miss it here?

RUTH
Rarely.

LINDA
Darling, you've been away too long. We
always celebrated at Sardi's. Don't you
miss it here, Darling?

RUTH
I used to, but not anymore.

LINDA
Darling, Pauline said Jim was going to
make you an offer. Did he?

RUTH
Yes, Linda, he did.

LINDA
Why don't you take it and move back
here? You can stay with us until you
find a place.

Pauline perks up.

PAULINE
Oh, Aunt Ruth, that would simply be
fabulous. Did Jim tell you I'd be the
producer of your show?

RUTH
We discussed it.

WILLIAM
Are you thinking of leaving us?

AUNTIE
Oh, Luka, you can't do it. Think about
us. Da island.

                    DANNY
          What would dat do to <u>From da Big
          Island</u>?

                    RUTH
          I never said I accepted Jim's offer.
          Jim made an offer. I turned it down.

                    LINDA
          Ruth, I've told you many times Hawaii
          is no better than a third-world
          country.

                    AUNTIE
          It not bad!

                    LINDA
          Darling, the people are ill-educated.

                    WILLIAM
          I'm almost educated. I graduate next
          month.

                    LINDA
          All night, all I've been hearing is
          fragmented talk.

Linda glances at Auntie, Danny, and William.

                    LINDA (CONT'D)
          It's hard to understand you.

                    AUNTIE
          It come wit time.

                    LINDA
               (to Ruth)
          Darling, you see what I mean? And you
          are willing to put up with it?

Ruth nods.

                    LINDA (CONT'D)
          Come back to civilized New York.

                    WILLIAM
          I'm civilized.

                    AUNTIE
          Hawaii civilized.

                    LINDA
          Darling, you call THAT language
          civilized?

                    AUNTIE
          What you say, sista?

SCREENPLAY

                    LINDA
          Darling, that's my point exactly. Come
          back here. Listen to that deplorable
          language.

                    AUNTIE
          What wrong wit pidgin?

                    LINDA
               (addressing Auntie)
          Darling, listen how you speak. No one
          with a real education speaks like that.

                    AUNTIE
          Wat you mean, sista?

                    LINDA
          Darling, you need to come to the United
          States and get a real education.

Ruth was becoming agitated with Linda.

                    RUTH
          Linda, Hawaii is a state! How do you
          know where Auntie was educated?"

                    AUNTIE
          You go, sista!

Linda was looking a little confused.

                    LINDA
          Darling, what's going on?

                    RUTH
               (emphasizing darling)
          I'll tell you what's going on, DARLING.
          Auntie speaks pidgin because she wants
          to speak that way, DARLING. She enjoys
          it, DARLING, and most of all, it is
          expected DARLING. You can stop using
          that damn DARLING stuff because you
          cannot remember people's names.
               (points to each person as
               she says their names)
          This is Auntie, this is William, and he
          is Danny.

Auntie, William, and Danny give Linda a howdy wave.

                    LINDA
          Ruth, darling, you surround yourself
          with people like them. What kind of
          life is that?

                    RUTH
          It's the kind of life I need and want.
          I enjoy my life on da Big Island. I
          chose to live there, not because I have
                    (MORE)

                    -160-

                         RUTH (CONT'D)
          to because I like it there. I
          didn'tknow how much I liked it until
          this trip. New York no longer does it
          for me, all the rushing around and
          superficial people.
               (motions towards Auntie,
               William, and Danny)
          These people are my new family; the
          Hawaiians call it ohana. To put it
          succinctly, I have more friends on da
          Big Island than I ever had here in the
          Big Apple!

Ruth looks at Auntie, William, and Danny, then
Linda and Pauline.

                         RUTH (CONT'D)
          We have a long flight tomorrow. It's
          late, and we need to rest before our
          long flight.

Ruth stands.
                         RUTH (CONT'D)
          Now, Linda and Pauline, let's call it
          an evening.

Linda and Pauline get up.

                         PAULINE
          Aunt Ruth, what about the show?

                         RUTH
          I am not going to do the show. Jim will
          find someone else. Pauline, you will
          still be the producer.

Pauline hugs Ruth.

                         PAULINE
          Love you, Aunt Ruth.

INT. RUTH'S BEDROOM - NIGHT

Ruth sleeps, but she doesn't have the silk night
mask.

GRUNTING AND SCRATCHING sounds awaken Ruth.

Ruth sits on the edge of the bed. Slips on her
zoris and reaches into the nightstand, taking out a
flashlight. She goes to the closet and takes out
the rifle.

EXT. RUTH'S ORCHARD - NIGHT - CONTINUOUS

Ruth, using her flashlight to guide her, makes
heads towards the GRUNTING and SCRATCHING sounds.

The flashlight illuminates a giant pig scratching
the ground near the base of a macadamia tree.

SCREENPLAY

Ruth, with the flashlight in one hand and the rifle in the other, raises the rifle feebly aiming and fires. The recoil of the rifle causes Ruth to drop the flashlight. The flashlight illuminates the pig, who looks at her, grunts then eats more fallen nuts.

In the distance from Auntie's house, we see a flashlight approaching Ruth through the orchard.

It is Auntie also carrying a flashlight and rifle.

> AUNTIE
> Luka, what da heck are you doing?

> RUTH
> (defiantly)
> I'm going to get that pig!

Auntie sees Ruth's flashlight illuminating the pig and directs her flashlight on the pig.

> AUNTIE
> Thank God! I thought it was da local boys trying to steal my keiki's.

Ruth and Auntie laugh as the pig started to trot towards Auntie's.

> AUNTIE (CONT'D)
> Oh, no! I don't want him to get into da keiki's; he'll go lolo.

Using the light from Auntie's flashlight, Ruth takes aim at the pig and carefully pulls the trigger.

EXT. AUNTIE'S LANAI - DAY

In lounge chairs, Ruth, Auntie, and Ben, each sip red punch while eating brownies.

> AUNTIE
> We tell no one that Luka kill pig.

> BEN
> (Looking at Ruth)
> Luka, you in plenny trouble.

> RUTH
> Trouble?

> BEN
> We next to state park. You can only kill pig with bow and arrow. We need to get rid of da evidence.

> RUTH
> Evidence?

                          BEN
          Da pig!

                          AUNTIE
          We have luau!

INT. HONOKAA GYMNASIUM - DAY

Graduation day. The bleachers are filled with
families, most wearing green and white Aloha shirts
and muumuus, the school's colors. Ruth, Ben,
Auntie, Danny, Nalani, and Meka are in the stands.

A green and white CONGRATULATIONS GRADUATES sign
hangs from the rafters.

Mickey and another CAMERAMAN, wearing <u>From da Big
Island</u> T- shirts, set up and shoot the graduation
from different angles.

On the court facing the bleachers are forty empty
seats and a podium.

Off to one side, Michael sits with his ukulele and
a microphone in front of him, glances behind the
bleachers, nods, starts strumming the ukulele, and
sings to Queen Liliuokalani's <u>Aloha Oe</u>.

Students, including William, dressed in green caps
and green and white muumuus or green and white
aloha shirts, march from behind the stands to the
seating area and wave to their families.

The families in the stands clap.

INT. HONOKAA GYMNASIUM - LATER

Mrs. Strong wearing a green and white muumuu,
stands at the podium.

A STUDENT returns to her seat.

                          MRS. STRONG
          And now for the most improved graduate,
          William Ayala. Please approach the
          podium.

The audience claps.

William gets up and goes to the podium.

                          MRS. STRONG (CONT'D)
          Not only is he the most improved
          student, and also the first member of
          his family to ever graduate from high
          school.

William approaches the podium. Mrs. Strong extends
her hand. William shakes it. In the other hand, she
has a plaque.

                    MRS. STRONG (CONT'D)
          William, stand here for the
          photographer.

A high school-aged PHOTOGRAPHER snaps Mrs. Strong
handing the award to William. The From da Big
Island crew video continues to film the ceremony.

Mrs. Strong moves back to the podium.

                    MRS. STRONG (CONT'D)
          William, would you like to say a few
          words?

                    WILLIAM
          Yes, Mrs. Strong.

William faces the crowd.

                    WILLIAM (CONT'D)
          I want to thank my mother and father.
          They had to put up with a lot from me.

LAUGHTER from the crowd.

                    WILLIAM (CONT'D)
          But most of all, I want to thank Mrs.
          Strong, Dr. Tilton, Auntie, and Mrs.
          Newcomb for helping me get here.
          Ma-ha-lo.

William starts to leave but turns around and
returns to the podium.

                    WILLIAM (CONT'D)
          Oh, I almost forgot. Da pig for
          tonight's luau come from Mrs. Newcomb.
          Ma-ha-lo.

Everyone claps.

EXT. HONOKAA PARK - NIGHT - CONTINUOUS

Picnic tables abound with students and family. The
only light comes from the tiki torches lining the
luau, illuminating the CONGRATULATIONS GRADUATES
sign.

Two folding tables are filled with all the
trimmings of a luau; one has chicken, the partially
eaten pig, hamburger buns, and an assortment of
utensils to cut and pull the meat off the pig. The
other has poi, brownies, plates, glasses, and a
giant Thermos jug filled with red punch.

Mickey and the other video cameraman set up a shot
at the picnic table with the pig.

At one picnic table, William, Nalani, Meka, and
Danny. The other side has Ruth, Auntie, Ben, and
Michael eating.

                    MEKA
          Ben, I still don't understand where da
          pig come from.

                    BEN
          Meka, I told you da pig kill Luka's
          cat. I use crossbow and kill da pig.

                    MEKA
          You never use crossbow for pig before.

                    RUTH
          There is always a first time for
          anything, isn't there?

Ruth using her spoon, takes a scoop of poi. She
tastes it and grimaces.

                    RUTH (CONT'D)
          This pudding is funny tasting. What is
          this purple stuff?

                    NALANI
          It poi. No use spoooon! Use finger like
          this.

Nalani brings her fore and middle fingers together,
showing Ruth how to scoop up and eat the poi.

                    WILLIAM
          It called two-finger poi!

Mickey arrives at the table, giving Danny the
thumbs up.

                    DANNY
          Luka, they are ready for you to shoot
          da closing.

Ruth looks at Mickey.

                    RUTH
          Bring the camera over here. I want to
          shoot my poi lesson before we do da
          closing.

                    MICKEY
          Luka, I'm already set up for da
          closing. Can we shoot that first, then
          shoot the poi sequence?

                    RUTH
          That will work for me.

Ruth and Danny get up from the table and approach
the pig. Mickey hands Ruth a wireless lavaliere
unit, which she puts on her muumuu.

SCREENPLAY

> RUTH (CONT'D)
> I don't want to do a run-through. Let's
> shoot it.

Mickey has the camera pointed on Ruth, who looks
into the camera.

RUTH, AS SEEN THROUGH THE CAMERA

> RUTH (CONT'D)
> We learned a lot in this episode,
> including how to eat poi. I want to
> dedicate this episode to William Ayala.
> I know he has a great future ahead of
> him. Until next time, this is Luka
> Newcomb, <u>From da Big Island</u>. Aaa-looo-
> haaa!

                                        FADE OUT.

NOTES

SCREENPLAY

NOTES

THE NOVEL

From da Big Island

New York defined her – Hawaii changed her

by

BILL HUTCHINSON

Published by Bill Hutchinson
Web Site: FromDaBigIsland.com

Paperback ISBN-13: 978-0-9996268-0-1
Hardback ISBN-13: 978-0-9996268-1-8
eBook ISBN-13: 978-0-9996268-2-5
Large print ISBN-13: 978-0-9996268-3-2
Screenplay and Novel ISBN-13: 978-0-9996268-7-0

10 9 8 7 6 5 4

NOVEL

Dedication

This book is dedicated to my beloved husband, Allyn, for all his help, inspiration, and creativity over the years.

NOVEL

NOVEL

Characters

Auntie: Ruth's uphill neighbor and horticulturist.

Ben Kokua: Ruth's live-in handyman and gardener.

Danny Mauka: Hawaii television producer and station manager.

Eileen Baccio: Wife of Joe Baccio.

George Epstein: Zach Newcomb's law partner.

Gloria La Fong: Ruth's therapist.

Jim: Network CEO.

Joe Baccio: Head of a New York crime syndicate and client of Newcomb and Epstein Law Offices.

Linda: Ruth's sister and mother of Pauline.

Meka Ayala: Ruth's downhill neighbor, husband of Nalai, and William's father.

Michael Kokua: Ben's musician brother.

Mrs. Charlene Strong: Honokaa High School counselor.

Mrs. Wiggins: Ruth's cat.

Nalani Ayala: Ruth's downhill neighbor, wife of Meka, and William's mother.

Paul Martin: Sarah's husband and owner of a house in Hawaii.

Pauline: Ruth's niece and a television production assistant.

Ruth Newcomb: The protagonist, Zack's wife, and star of the syndicated television show *From the Big Apple*.

Sarah Martin: Ruth's childhood friend, Paul's wife, *From the Big Apple* television show producer, and owner of a house in Hawaii.

William Ayala: Son of Meka and Nalani, Ruth's downhill neighbors and an at-risk high school student who would rather surf than be in class.

Zach Newcomb: Ruth's husband and George Epstein's law partner.

NOVEL

Table of Contents

NOVEL

NOVEL

PROLOGUE

Ruth Newcomb and I go back many years, more than either would like to admit. She is very staid in her ways, sticking more to the familiar than the unfamiliar. Even though she had been on the Big Island of Hawaii for what would seem decades, it had only been a little more than one.

Ruth is part of my ohana. Ohana is Hawaiian for what most would call extended family. Every time I return to the Big Island, we get together, sitting for hours on her lanai (Hawaiian for veranda or porch), talking about life and old stories from before we met, bringing each other up to date with our lives, and other things friends enjoy discussing.

On one particular trip, we were seated on Ruth's lanai talking, just as we have always done. What made this time different, more than any other was Ruth's recollection of when we first met and the events surrounding her arrival on the Big Island. Not that I was contesting it, nor anything like that; she wanted to validate her memory. Period!

Ruth told me to remain seated, got up, and went to her small living room library to get a journal, one of the many volumes she had written since reading *The Diary of Anne*

Frank. Little did Ruth realize then that her first diary would become numerous volumes, filling the lower shelves of her library. Seeing her return with one of the journals in hand, that's when it struck me; I'm a journalist, why not write a book about Ruth's transition from the Big Apple to the Big Island of Hawaii, using her journals as a basis for turning them into this book you are now reading.

William Ayala
Huntington Beach, CA
September 11, 2017

RUTH

"Ruth, Ruth Newcomb, is that you?" an elderly woman yelled, running after Ruth, a red-haired lady, who continued her brisk walk down New York's post 9/11 Fifth Avenue, oblivious of the Christmas shoppers and the woman calling her name. It wasn't hard to miss Ruth, as not many people have copper-hair to begin with, and most of the other women wore scarves or hats to protect their heads from the wind. However, to Ruth, it is her red hair and staunch demeanor that anyone who sees her will instantly recognize her as television personality Ruth Newcomb. If that were not enough, Ruth was always impeccably dressed and wore the latest designer fashion. Her clothes were always skintight to show off her slender, well-proportioned body, fitting her like a glove, not bad for a lady in her sixties. So it was no surprise that the older woman had instantly recognized Ruth Newcomb.

The elderly woman finally reached Ruth and tapped her shoulder, "Aren't you Ruth Newcomb, *From the Big Apple?*"

Ruth stopped and turned, "Of course, Darling! Who else could I be?"

NOVEL

The elderly woman dug through her purse, "I'm such a big fan of your show." a stall technique Ruth had heard many times before as fans searched for a pad and pen. Finding both, the woman held them before Ruth and asked, "May I have your autograph?"

Happy to oblige a fan, Ruth took the pen and pad, scribbled something, signed it, and handed them back to the older woman who studied it. The autograph was not the normal one would expect from famous people. The signature was unique and instantly recognizable to her vast television audience. She would sign her name Ruth Newcomb surrounding her signature with the sizeable stylized apple associated with her show, *From the Big Apple*. The woman looked back at Ruth, smiling, "Oh, thank you. Thank you. It's such a wonderful and unusual autograph that I will cherish for years to come."

"Thank you, Darling," Ruth responded. She always used darling when responding to people as it was a general response people expected and liked, and perhaps most of all, she adored using darling because it was easier than remembering the person's name. Ruth turned to continue her walk through the Fifth Avenue Christmas crowd as a light evening snow began to fall. As Ruth reached 52nd Street, the light crossing hand popped up. She stopped with the hordes of people. The aroma of cooking steaks caused Ruth to look to her right, where she spotted the steel jockeys lining the front of The 21 Club.

A man accidentally bumped into Ruth and, in a thick Italian accent, said, "Excusa me." For some reason, perhaps the combination of seeing The 21 Club and the Italian accent caused Ruth to flashback to that unusual evening many years ago when Mario Manzoni, the head of one of New York's key crime families, was assassinated in front of the restaurant.

It was the evening of June 17th, 1965. A warm, pleasant breeze blew down 52nd Street past The 21 Club. A large crowd of spectators surrounded the red carpet and the chrome stanchions holding the rope leading from the entrance to the street to the two awaiting stretch limousines. A television news crew set up near the entrance of the club. Bob, the cameraman, had his camera on Pat, the local New York television commentator, standing next to one of the limousines. Looking at the camera, speaking into his microphone, Pat announced, "This is Pat Patterson at The 21 Club, where in a few moments mob boss Mario Manzoni, his lieutenant Joe Baccio, attorney Zach Newcomb, and their wives will be exiting. It is rumored they have been discussing a resolution to the turf wars between the Manzoni and the Sarducci crime families."

In the nighttime crowd next to Pat stood a tall, black-haired man who wore an unbuttoned long black raincoat, which would be more suited for winter than a warm June evening. No one seemed to notice the man was concealing a gun under his raincoat.

"Manzoni," continued Pat, "prefers the use of the legal system to resolve a conflict over the use of force as some of the other crime families do."

The doorman opened the door for two bodyguards in their early 20s dressed in black with slicked-back black hair. Pat noticed the two bodyguards leaving and changed his commentary, "it looks like they are exiting the 21 Club."

The bodyguards made their way to the limousines, scanning the crowd, not noticing the man in the long heavy raincoat. The doorman opened the door, this time for gray-haired Mario Manzoni, who wore a white tuxedo. His blond bombshell of a wife, some twenty years younger, wore a white sequenced Dior evening dress, followed by Joe Baccio, dressed in a white tuxedo, and Eileen, his wife, dressed in a vivid blue evening gown.

"Here comes Mario Manzoni, Joe Baccio, and their wives."

They were followed by Ruth, dressed in a brilliant shimmering green evening dress, and Zach, her husband, in a white tuxedo.

"Here's Zach Newcomb and his wife, Ruth Newcomb, our very own junior reporter."

As Ruth left the club, she saw Pat and mouthed, "I love you, darling." and threw him a kiss.

Mario, not one to miss an opportunity for publicity, waved and approached Pat.

"Mario, do you have anything you are willing to tell us?" Pat asked. The assassin in the raincoat stealthy pulled out the gun and shot Mario at point-blank range.

Mario fell to the ground. His wife screamed and grabbed him as blood gushed out, covering his white tuxedo and splattering his wife and Pat with blood. The assassin turned, bumping Pat. At the same instant, one of the bodyguards fired his gun, hitting Pat, who collapsed next to Mario and his wife.

Meanwhile, the surrounding crowd dropped to the ground. The bodyguards started to chase the running assassin. More gunshots rang out. This time, the assassin fell dead on the sidewalk.

Ruth and Zach, being in the middle of the assassination, surveyed the carnage.

"I think we're safe now that the assassin is dead," Zach assured Ruth. "I'm glad you're alright. I love you. We need to wait for the police."

"Pat's dead!" Ruth exclaimed, shaking her head in disbelief. "I need to get this news story to the newsroom now!"

NOVEL

She noticed Bob had captured the entire bloodbath and was filming the blood-covered body of Mario being held by his wife, much like the Pieta, with Pat lying to the side in a pool of blood.

"Bob, darling, when you have an opportunity, don't forget to get a wide shot for the closing showing restaurant with the jockeys," Ruth commanded. She looked at Pat and spotted the blood-covered microphone. Trembling, she bent down, using her thumb and forefinger, picked the microphone up by the wire mesh, which didn't have blood, and wiped Pat's blood off on his blue news jacket. As Ruth regained her composure, she pointed the microphone down and, in a firm whisper, said, "Bob! Bob, darling! Turn the camera on me. I'll finish the piece. Then get the footage back to the studio. We need to make the eleven o'clock news!"

Bob turned the camera around towards Ruth and gave her the queue. Taking a deep breath, Ruth brought the microphone up, looking into the camera, "This is Ruth Newcomb, coming to you from The 21 Club, where a few moments ago, we witnessed the brutal murder of Mario Manzoni, the reputed mob boss, and television commentator, Pat Patterson, by a lone assassin ..."

"Andiamo, we go, light change!" Ruth was knocked back into the present day as the light at 52nd Street changed, and the man with the Italian accent pushed his way past her. Ruth continued her short walk down Fifth Avenue, finally reaching Rockefeller Center. When she entered the plaza, she was greeted by the illuminated Rockefeller Center Christmas tree, the piped-in Christmas music playing, skaters enjoying the rink, and the smell of chestnuts roasting wafting from a nearby vending cart. Ruth smiled, nodded her head in approval, and thought it was Christmastime in New York City.

* * *

Inside the Rockefeller Center television studio, cables, flats, propping, cameras, and personnel watched the broadcast unfold. Ruth was seated at the desk on the From the Big Apple set in a glimmering silken red dress. Behind her was a large red stylized apple, just like the one she used in her autograph, with red lettering announcing the show, *From the Big Apple*. Next to the camera was a monitor pointed towards Ruth playing the prerecorded segment of the Rockettes Christmas Spectacular. A floor manager stood next to the camera, holding one hand up, flashing five seconds to go. The countdown continued as he yelled, "4, 3, 2." On his signal, Ruth looked at the camera and read from the Teleprompter, "So don't miss the Rockettes Christmas Spectacular at Radio City Music Hall through January second.

"Darlings, I adore the New York Public Library Reading is Fundamental program. I love it so much that I will read Charles Dickens, *A Christmas Carol*, at the New York Public Library mid-town branch this Saturday at two PM.

"So don't forget to be there because reading is fun-da-mental.

"This wraps up another edition of *From the Big Apple*. Tomorrow we will have..." pausing, she tilted her head and looked curiously at the Teleprompter, which read, "TOMORROW WE WILL HAVE ???? UNTIL NEXT TIME..."

Realizing that the question marks were for her to fill in, Ruth quickly recouped, "... a wonderful show for you.

"Until next time, this is Ruth Newcomb, *From the Big Apple*." Ruth looked directly at the camera, smiling. The tally light went out.

"We're clear," yelled the floor manager.

NOVEL

Ruth's smile faded as she looked into the camera, "What the heck was that?"

"What was what?" The floor manager responded.

"Darling," addressing the floor manager, "you and Sarah know what I mean."

The floor manager shrugged and gave Ruth a curious look as she continued, "I mean the question marks!"

Sarah Martin, the show's producer, and Ruth's childhood friend, ran up.

"I thought we had the next show planned," Ruth asked Sarah.

"We don't!" Ruth's niece Pauline, a twenty-something production assistant who wants to be a producer, was carrying a clipboard, following Sarah like a puppy, and was the first to speak.

"Pauline, darling, would you be a doll and get Auntie some water?"

As Pauline left, Ruth looked at the television monitor next to the camera, showing a commercial with palm trees, sandy beaches, Diamond Head, and Waikiki Beach.

"In any event," Sarah continued, "George called during the segment and canceled."

"So what if he canceled, Sarah. You could have had Teleprompter Bob put something on the Teleprompter other than those damn question marks in the Teleprompter. Darling, you know how I hate that."

"You did a good job faking it."

Ruth returned her gaze to the monitor when the commercial ended with *Come to Hawaii.*

"Sarah, I could have said, 'Tomorrow we will be coming to you from Hawaii!'"

"Coming from Hawaii?"

Ruth raised her voice, "Yes, Hawaii! Ever since Thanksgiving, that *Come to Hawaii* ad has aired. We might as well do the show from Hawaii. What's going on here?"

Sarah tried not to be defensive, "It's cold; people want to escape to a warm climate like Hawaii. You know, warm, friendly, happy people, tropical drinks, ukuleles, luaus, hukilaus, and Hula dancing."

"Not everyone has a little grass shack like you and Paul do in Hawaii. Some people like to ski, go to a cozy mountain cabin, and enjoy the snow."

"And then there are those like you who never leave New York."

Pauline returned with Ruth's water. "Thank you, Darling."

Sarah looked at Ruth, "we need to think of something for the next show."

"Maybe we could do *The Nutcracker*."

Both Sarah and Pauline grimaced and, in unison, declared, "Not again!"

Pauline continued, "We've never done an inside tour of Tiffany's. We can tie into the re-release of *Breakfast at Tiffany's*. Or maybe we can cover the medicinal marijuana trial Uncle Zach is working on. Sparks are flying, and I'm sure we can do an interview with Uncle Zach about why the Baccio trail is so important."

Across the room, a production assistant yelled, "Pauline, telephone." Pauline turned and walked quickly to the phone.

Sarah agreeing with Pauline's line of thinking, responded, "We did *The Nutcracker* last year. Think of something. We'll talk about it first thing tomorrow, before the production meeting."

"Darling, I was thinking of an easy way out."

NOVEL

"I'm with you." Sarah put her hand on Ruth's shoulder, "We're still on for Charlie Chan tonight, aren't we?"

"Starts at seven," Ruth responded. Sarah removed her arm and turned to leave. Ruth continued, "I have the chopsticks, so don't forget the sushi."

"Big Apple or Mr. Okomoto's Sushi?"

NUMBER 3 BEEKMAN PLACE

Ruth's movie room resembled a 1930's style theater with red curtains flanking a large projection screen. Zach, Ruth's husband, and Paul, Sarah's husband, were seated together in an overstuffed leather loveseat, eating popcorn. Next to them on another loveseat were Ruth and Sarah. Mrs. Wiggins, Ruth's portly elderly black cat given to her years ago and named by Carol Burnett, was curled up on Ruth's lap. In front of them are empty Mr. Okomoto Sushi containers and freshly prepared Manhattans.

"Manhattan's, sushi, popcorn, and Charlie Chan... cheers!" Zach said as they all toasted. He reached for the remote and pressed the button. On the screen, *Charlie Chan and the Black Camel* started, and the credits rolled by, followed by a scene of surfers surfing in the foreground and Diamond Head in the background. A few moments later was a shot of 1930's Waikiki Beach from the surfer's point of view with the only two multistory hotels; the Royal Hawaiian and the Halekulani.

Paul whispered to Zach, "That reminds me..."

"Shhh..." Sarah said quietly.

NOVEL

Paul ignored Sarah and continued in a lower voice, "That reminds me, Charlie liked to have his Manhattan's at the Halekulani House Without a Key Bar under the kiawe tree."

"Hal-le-ku-lani? kiawe tree?" Zach responded.

Ruth and Sarah gave the guys disapproving looks. Ruth, unable to concentrate on the movie, asked, "Can't you guys let us enjoy the movie?"

Zach grabbed the remote, pausing the movie.

"What are you doing?" Ruth protested.

"Paul was saying something about Charlie and the Hall-le-ku-lani House Without a Key Bar ..."

"Oh, that!" Sarah retorts. "It's nothing. The real Charlie Chan hung out at the Halekulani Hotel and its House Without a Key Bar. It is as simple as that."

"Honey, I thought you liked your tropical drinks and listening to the live Hawaiian music under the kiawe tree at sunset," Paul exclaimed.

"I do, darling, it's a fantastic hotel, but we're here to watch a movie, not talk about Hawaii," Sarah responded.

Zach pressed the button on the remote, and the movie continued. The girls were content and smiled.

"Thanks!" The girls respond in unison.

Neither Zach nor Paul are interested in the movie. Their eyes wander around the room. Zach starts whispering to Paul again, "I thought you liked the remoteness of your vacation home on the Big Island."

"We do, eccentric neighbors and all; it's like something straight out of a Ma and Pa Kettle movie or *The Beverly Hillbillies*."

Ruth glared at the two of them, grabbed the remote, pressed the pause button, and asked, "So you want to watch Ma and Pa Kettle?"

"No, we're talking about our house on the Big Island of Hawaii," Paul responded.

"Darling," Sarah addressing Paul, "they already told us they don't want to go to Hawaii. Why push it?" Sarah then looked at Zach, "Zach always has an excuse of being tied up on this or that trial. And..." Sarah looked at Ruth, "Ruth doesn't want to leave the comfort of the Big Apple." Sarah looked at the screen. "Now that everything is cleared up let's watch the movie." Ruth pressed the play button, and everyone turned their attention toward the screen and resumed watching Charlie Chan.

* * *

Auntie Mame was always Ruth's favorite novel, so much so that she vowed that when she grew up, she would live in the place Auntie Mame lived, Number 3 Beekman Place. It took years for Ruth and Zach to obtain the apartment with the terrace overlooking the East River on the secluded two-block-long residential street just north of the United Nations building.

The Christmas decorations filled the penthouse sunroom as the light from the rising sun over the East River cast a golden glow across the room. Mrs. Wiggins was playing with one of the Christmas ornament balls hanging nearby.

Dressed in woolen robes, Ruth and Zach were seated at the table, drinking coffee and having breakfast. Ruth took a sip from her Tiffany coffee cup and glanced at Zach finishing his half-eaten bagel and reading the *New York Times*. Ruth noticed the headline *Defense Atty Newcomb Drops Bombshell at Baccio Trial*. "What's this about a bombshell?"

"A bombshell?" Zach exclaimed. "It's only the beginning! The medicinal marijuana issue came to a head yesterday."

"Darling, you know marijuana is bad. I don't understand why you are for it."

"I'm not. Joe thinks since states have started to allow medicinal marijuana, it's another way to make money."

"Darling, I don't understand it at all. People are using the medicinal excuse to get high."

"We have documentation that it does help some people."

Ruth, having finished her breakfast, got up. "Got to run." She kissed Zach, who smiled as she left the terrace.

THE NUTCRACKER

The studio office corridor was filled with business people dressed in holiday colors scurrying about. Pauline stood by the elevator, repeatedly looked at her watch, and took an occasional sip from her coconut water while she waited for Ruth. Ding, the elevator door opened, and people exited; while others entered, the door closed. Another look at the watch followed by a sip. Ding, the elevator door opened, people left, door closed. Ding, the third elevator door opened. This time, Ruth, dressed in her woolen coat and scarf, stepped out of the elevator.

"Aunt Ruth, great show yesterday. Nothing like the Rockettes!"

Ruth nodded, "You said it, Pauline."

Ruth strode towards her office. Pauline ran to keep up.

"So we're doing another segment on *The Nutcracker*?"

"Haven't decided yet."

"When are you and Uncle Zach seeing it?"

"Tomorrow."

Sarah caught up with Ruth and Pauline. "I was able to get Alec Baldwin for today's show."

NOVEL

"Great!" Ruth and Pauline respond in unison.

Ruth noticed Pauline taking a sip from her coconut water. "Pauline, why are you drinking that stuff?"

"Coconut water is an excellent alternative to other drinks as it is all-natural, healthy, and potassium-rich. Some call it 'Mother Nature's sports drink.'"

"Sounds like you're an advertisement," Ruth responded as they entered her office. Ruth hung her coat and scarf on the coat stand. The office was clean, with a unique feminine air about it. There are flowers on the desk, a plant in the corner, a goldfish bowl on the credenza next to an Emmy, and a needlepoint "I Love New York" pillow on the plush leather sofa. On the wall was a framed "Reading Is Fun" poster from the New York Metropolitan Library with Ruth holding *The Adventures of Huckleberry Finn* in the center. Pictures of Ruth with the Clintons, Donald Trump, Jackie Onassis, Princess Dianna and Prince Charles adorn the walls, diplomas from New York and Columbia Universities, and a plaque for the Nobel Prize in Journalism. Behind her desk was a spectacular view of the New York skyline. Ruth sat at the desk and placed her purse in the top right drawer. Sarah and Pauline took seats across from Ruth's desk.

"We need to work on the show," Sarah stated. "We cannot do another year of *The Nutcracker*."

"Darling," Ruth responded, "I was trying to make things easy, and we're seeing it tomorrow night."

"We will need a different angle than what we've done. Any suggestions?"

"I see, making me do all the work! Hmm…"

"We might as well run last year's show."

Ruth laughed. "You're so funny, Sarah. How about the fight scene between the soldiers and the mice or the costumes and make-up?"

Sarah started taking notes. "That's a thought."

"Sure, the conflict, the intrigue, the combat. Finally, the soldiers are all dead ..." Ruth said jokingly, "Not unlike living in New York." They all laughed.

"It is Christmas!" Sarah exclaimed, "and fights don't mix. The Sugar Plum Fairy and the Nutcracker dance sequence is more Christmassy."

"Do we always have to sugarcoat it?" Ruth asked.

They all laughed again.

"You know what I'm talking about. You're the one who mentioned *The Nutcracker.*"

"I was trying to keep things simple," Ruth admitted.

Pauline glanced at the framed New York Metropolitan Library *Reading is Fun* poster. "Aunt Ruth, you did a great job reading *A Christmas Carol* last night. Maybe we could do a segment on that instead of *The Nutcracker.*"

"That's an idea," Sarah exclaimed. "Let's keep our options open. Best of all, we are going to see *The Nutcracker* tomorrow."

* * *

The following evening, Ruth and Zach were in their master bathroom vanity area, getting dressed in formal attire. Zach was unsuccessfully attempting to put on his black onyx cuff links. Ruth noticed he was having difficulty and helped Zach put them on. She reached into her jewelry case and took out her triple-strand pearl necklace. Zach lovingly took the necklace from her without saying a word and put it on Ruth's neck. As he does so, she turns her back to him to make it easier for Zach to attach the necklace. After fastening the clasp, he stood back, giving Ruth an affectionate whack on her derrière. "You're so beautiful! And these pearls make you look fantastic!" Ruth smiled as Zach turned her around for a long hug and affectionate kiss.

* * *

At Lincoln Center, a light snow was falling, adding to the magic of the evening performance of *The Nutcracker*. Limousines pulled up alongside taxis and cars. Ruth, Zach, Sarah, and Paul were exiting a limousine, all dressed formally. The foursome walked with the other theatergoers as the falling snow glistened, reflecting the lights illuminating the fountain. Large posters announce *The Nutcracker* as they approach the golden-lit Lincoln Center entrance.

Ruth and Sarah looked at each other during the performance, smiling as the Nutcracker and the mice began to battle. Sarah noticed Ruth had reached into her purse, pulled out a notepad, and whispered, "Enjoy it! Don't take notes."

"Darling, you know me. I need to."

Sarah placed her hand on the notepad and shook her head. Ruth started to pay attention to the ballet.

* * *

The mezzanine was filled with people dressed in black ties and Christmas-colored evening gowns, sipping Champagne or wine. Ruth, Zach, Sarah, and Paul were sequestered in a corner sipping Champagne. Ruth enthusiastically exclaimed, "The fight sequence was better than in past years. However, I don't think we have enough to do an entire eight-minute segment on this version being different."

Paul smiled, retorting, "Wait until the third act."

"During the Sugar Plum Fairy and the Nutcracker dance," Zach added.

Paul leaned into the girls, "We heard a rumor that they are seeing each other."

"Who's seeing whom?" Sarah inquired.

"The Sugar Plum Fairy and the Nutcracker, who else?" Zach answered.

"Oh, stop it, you two," Ruth exclaimed.

"We're not kidding. In real life, Rudolph and Natasha are seeing each other. I heard that scene makes the show." Paul responded.

Zach noticed Joe and Eileen Baccio, now in their sixties, walking up to the foursome. "Joe, I didn't know you were going to be here tonight," Zach said, extending his hand to Joe. "Are you enjoying the show?"

"Fantastic!" Joe responded. "The tension between the Sugar Plum Fairy and the Nutcracker is unbelievable! I don't recall that from prior performances."

"Zach put you up to this, didn't he, Joe?" Sarah asked.

"Up to what?"

"Oh, never mind." Sarah shook her head and continued. "How's the trial going?"

Millie, a rather tall woman carrying a *Playbill* program and pen, makes her way to the group with Billy, her meek short, balding husband in tow and interrupts the conversation. "You're Ruth Newcomb of *From the Big Apple*, aren't you?"

"Darling, who else could I be?"

"I *adore* your show. May I have your autograph?" Millie pushed the *Playbill* program and the pen toward Ruth.

"Darling, what's your name?"

"Millie ... Millie Greenwald."

Ruth looked at Millie's husband, who looked down, avoiding eye contact with Ruth and the others in her party.

"Do you want me to add your husband's name, too?"

Millie smiled, clasped her hands together, and looked up at Ruth. "Oh, could you? Please! His name is Billy." The husband smiled.

"Ah, Millie and Billy, what a pair!" Ruth laughed, followed by everyone else, as she signed the front of the *Playbill* program. "To Millie and Billy, My favorite fans, Ruth Newcomb." She drew her stylized *From the Big Apple* logo around her signature. Ruth handed the program back to Millie. Millie and Billy looked at the signature on the *Playbill* program smiling as they received the best Christmas gift ever.

"Oh, thank you so much, Mrs. Newcomb. Thank you, and Merry Christmas."

Millie and Billy both bowed as if they were in the presence of royalty. Turning, they left the group.

"Ruth, every time we get together, your fans interrupt. Don't you ever get tired of it?" Eileen asked.

"Not in the least, Eileen." Ruth answered, "It's expected. Now, where were we?"

"Sarah asked me how things were going with the trial," Joe responded. "I think it's going better than expected. We're dealing with medicinal marijuana; it is enough to cause significant issues."

The first chime rang. The audience started to head into the theater. A few looked at Ruth and smiled, giving her a nod as they passed the group. Ruth nodded back.

"I believe the medicinal marijuana is the way to go," Joe continued. "Legalize it, not only here, but nationwide, and tax it. The government and I make money, and everyone will be happy." The second chime. "We better get back to our seats. I hope you all have a wonderful evening. See you later. Merry Christmas!" Joe and Eileen turn and join the theater-going crowd as they return to their seats.

* * *

As the audience exits Lincoln Center, they are greeted by heavy snow that already blanketed the plaza. Ruth, Zach, Sarah, and Paul made their way through one of the shoveled paths to the awaiting limousines at street level. After a few moments, their limousine pulled up. Inside, they brushed the snow from their jackets as the limousine headed down Broadway toward Columbus Circle. Ruth starts the conversation, "Let's focus on the Rudolf and Natasha romance."

"We can't," Sarah responded.

"Why not, Darling? I think that's what made the show so good."

"We need to verify if it is true."

"Pshaw!" Ruth responded as the limousine entered Columbus Circle with the other cars, trucks, taxis, and limousines whizzing unencumbered through the snow, ice, and slush. Over Sarah's shoulder, through the limousine window, Ruth watched in horror as a large truck skidding sideways was headed directly towards the side of the limousine where Sarah was seated. Ruth stiffened and yelled, "Brace yourselves!"

POST MORTEM

Ruth was in a hospital bed, eyes closed. Bottles filled with Ringer's and other solutions hung from hooks attached to a bar attached to the bed. All the tubes connected to her arm. Ruth opened her eyes, blinking, and scanned the room. The counter is filled with flowers and cards; larger flower arrangements have condolence ribbons. On the floor next to the counter was a large *From the Big Apple* logo flower arrangement with black and white carnations on its stand with a ribbon stating, "Our thoughts are with you."

Pauline and Linda, Pauline's mother and Ruth's look-alike albeit blonde sister, entered the room carrying a large bouquet of flowers.

"Everyone sends their condolences. I never knew black flowers were so hard to come by." Pauline declared as she moved one of the flower arrangements on the counter to make room for her display.

"Darling, you look much better than we expected, considering what you've been through," Linda remarked. "We are all surprised that anyone survived that nasty crash."

"It's been on every news channel," Pauline added.

"What are you talking about?" inquired Ruth.

"The accident," Sarah added, "you were the sole survivor. The impact of the truck was so hard it trapped everyone inside. The fire department got you out before the limo exploded in flames killing everyone else. You're so lucky!"

* * *

A persistent rain fell at the Brooklyn cemetery filled with cars, limousines, news trucks, and extensive canopies protecting the mourners surrounding the Newcomb headstone. Ruth was prominently seated front row center, flanked by Linda and Pauline, consoling her. Next to Pauline sat Madam Gloria La Fong, Ruth's born-again hippy therapist, who wore a black Indian tunic. Next to Linda were Joe and Eileen Baccio, along with George Epstein, Zach's law partner and executor of the estate.

The funeral was hard on Ruth. During the ceremony, she was in a daze, which was quite understandable considering what she had gone through and losing those dearest to her. She knew the clock could not be turned back and nothing would be the same as it once was, knowing the deaths would cause a significant void in her life, generating unwanted and unneeded changes. Ruth disdained change and wished things would be like before the accident.

* * *

Back at Number 3 Beekman Place, in the walk-in closet, Ruth stood in her designer woolen bathrobe, holding Zach's bathrobe, bringing it up to her, taking a long smell, remembering intimate moments with Zach. She shook her head, sighed, and pensively replaced his robe on its hook.

Ruth meandered into the living room and looked around. A comforting fire in the fireplace added to the melancholy warmth of the room. On the mantel, pictures of Ruth holding an Emmy with Zach and the Martins at her side, along with photographs of Ruth and Zach having dinner with Jackie Onassis and John F. Kennedy, Jr. at Tavern on the Green, and Ruth and Zach with Donald Trump and Bill and Hillary Clinton all in golf attire. Ruth walked to the Emmy photograph and picked it up. She took it with her to a plush chair next to the fireplace. Studying the photograph for a moment, she gently stoked it and smiled. A purring Mrs. Wiggins nudged her leg, letting out a short meow. Ruth put the photograph on the side table, reached down, and stroked the black cat, who took the stroking as an invite and leaped up on Ruth's lap, nudging her little black head against Ruth's arm and purring. "You're the only one I have left. What are we going to do?"

* * *

A cold wind blew down Fifth Avenue as the post-holiday crowd hurried about. Ruth was bundled up in her designer long black woolen coat and red woolen scarf that obscured most of her face. However, she stood out not only wearing her designer outfit but due to her walking significantly slower than others, moving at a snail's pace. A few people recognized Ruth, smiling and nodding to her. Wanting to avoid the attention, Ruth decided she could walk through Central Park to visit one of her favorite spots, the Alice in Wonderland statue she had not seen in years. She was right; the paths were less crowded except for an occasional squirrel. As she meandered closer to the statue, Ruth heard the sounds of a ukulele and a man singing *My Little Grass Shack*. Curious, Ruth followed the music to the statue, where she saw Michael, a Hawaiian Man who wore Ray Bans and an Aloha shirt over his parka. She stopped and listened to the music.

As the song ended, Ruth reached into her purse, took out a twenty-dollar bill, and gently placed it into the open ukulele case with a few dollar bills and coins.

"Ma-ha-lo!" Michael responded, delighted to see the twenty dollars. "Dat mean thank you in Hawaiian."

Ruth started to walk away.

"Aaa-loooo-haa!" Michael said. She paused and looked over her shoulder at him. "Dat mean hello and farewell. Da boss goin do plenny good stuff fo you."

Michael smiled and winked, continuing, "Change, she come soon." before playing the ukulele again.

"I'm just a little Hawaiian,

A homesick island boy,

I want to go back to my fish and poi,

I want to go back to my little grass shack."

* * *

Ruth is sitting alone at a cleared table in the 21 Club, stirring her coffee. A solitary candle illuminated her melancholy face.

The maître de escorted a middle-aged couple to their table. As they passed Ruth's table, the woman recognized Ruth and nudged her husband, who also recognized Ruth. They stopped at her table. The maître de continued walking, unaware that the couple had stopped following him. Ruth was engrossed in her melancholy and continued to stir her coffee, oblivious to anything and everyone around her.

"It must be a terrible loss," the woman interrupted.

Ruth stopped stirring but did not look up. "Terrible," the woman's husband added, shaking his head, "we miss your show."

Ruth looked up, forcing a slight but noticeable smile. The maître de returned to retrieve the couple. "Please follow me."

Ruth took a sip from her coffee. The couple followed the maître de.

Later, the maître de returned to her table. "I'm sorry, Mrs. Newcomb. I should have kept them on a tighter leash."

"Darling, sometimes it cannot be avoided. You did your best under the circumstances."

MORE TIME, PLEASE

The winter was relentless, cold, and wetter than previous ones. A cold spring wind blew through the overcast city. Ruth wore her long woolen coat and scarf, standing in front of the modern Upper East Side marble façade of Zach's office building and gazed pensively at the lavishly embossed *Law Offices of Newcomb and Epstein* shiny brass sign. Reaching up with her forefinger, Ruth solemnly traced the outline of her last name. Although the tracing of the word Newcomb took less than a minute, to Ruth, it seemed like an eternity. Sighing, she left the sign for the entrance.

"Good morning, Mrs. Newcomb," the legal assistant said. "Is there anything I get you before you see George?"

"No, darling, I'm fine. Is George ready?"

"Yes, go right in."

A stack of legal papers almost obstructs Ruth's view of George seated behind the desk. The short, stocky well-dressed, balding man had on his reading glasses. As Ruth entered, George stood up and motioned to her to sit opposite him. Smiling, he asked, "Do you like Hawaii?"

"George, you know I've never been."

"Now's your chance."

"Darling, what do you mean?"

"You now own the Martin's house in Honokaa on the Big Island of Hawaii."

Ruth's was flabbergasted.

George continued, "What's also great is the Martins had entered into a ten-year contract with the caretaker, Ben Kokua, who lives on the property. He takes care of the six acres, including the macadamia nut orchard."

Ruth shook her head in disbelief.

"It's the perfect vacation home; you don't have to worry about anything."

"If everything has been taken care of, why didn't they will it to ... what's his name?"

"Ben," George paused briefly, "Ben has a heart of gold, is a great caretaker, and is, how should I put it, a little inept."

"Darling, what would I do with a place in Hawaii?"

"At the funeral, you told me you wanted to get away from it all, right?"

Ruth nodded.

"What better place than Hawaii?"

"It's so far away."

"You're right; that's what makes it perfect for a vacation home."

"I don't want it."

"It's prime real estate, in a rain forest, with a great view."

"Then make arrangements to sell it."

* * *

Ruth and Jim, the network CEO, entered her office as she went to her desk. "Darling, I need more time," as she sat.

Jim stood before the desk, "Ruth, I understand you need more time."

"Jim, darling, I can't continue with the show."

"You've been through a lot, Ruth, and you need to move on. We can't continue the re-runs."

"The show can go on an extended hiatus."

"You realize you are putting many people out of work."

"Stop it, Jim. You're the owner of this network. You will find something to fill the gap until I am ready, and you need to fill Sarah's producer position. So let's stop playing games. I'm not into it right now."

"You know me all too well. For you, Ruth, I will reluctantly agree to put the show on hiatus, keeping a small contingent of staff to research show ideas for when you return, and we will keep this office for you to use. Let me know when you're ready to restart From the Big Apple, and I'll get the ball rolling."

MADAM LA FONG

Madam Gloria La Fong, Ruth's Earth Mother therapist, wore a long tie-died dress with a Native American Indian turquoise and silver squash blossom necklace, looking much like a born-again hippy, was seated in an overstuffed multi colored bean bag chair with notepad and pen at the ready. The gentle sound of water rippling from a relaxation fountain and the pleasant, tranquil aroma from aromatherapy candles were barely noticeable. The walls were adorned with vintage 1960's Joplin, Elvis, Woodstock, and other posters and memorabilia. Ruth was comfortably seated on one of the numerous bright-colored bean bag chairs encircling Madam La Fong.

"I hate it here. I hate my job. I hate that people stare at me. Everywhere I look, I remember things Zach and I did. I can't get him out of my mind."

"You two were together for going on forty years." Madam La Fong put down her notepad, thinking for a moment. "Ruth, what happened to you is monumental. There's been a significant change in your life; your world has been turned upside down. You not only lost Zach, but you also lost Sarah, your childhood friend as well."

NOVEL

"Gloria, that's why I'm here. I'm looking to you for guidance."

"It takes people years to get over similar circumstances. Your entire life is changing; you are at the crossroads of life with many paths to take. Over the years, you've been given crumbs to help you find your way through changes such as this, and when you reach the crossroads, you can make a more informed decision."

"Oh, stop it, Gloria. Everything and everyone I love is gone."

"Are they?"

"Yes!"

"What would make you happy?"

"I don't know."

"You do!"

Ruth became more uncomfortable, adjusting her body in the bean bag. She didn't want to hear what Madam La Fong was telling her.

"You must discover what you want for yourself." Madam La Fong continued, "No one can make your choices. You have more money than you know what to do with. Think of people who would give anything to be in your situation, given the opportunity to change their life and direction. You have to let loose, let go of the old, and think of something you've always wanted to do and never had time to do it. Open up, Ruth; you can do it! What is it that you want or need?"

"I spent my entire life here in New York or the Hamptons. I'm a New Yorker. And now, I hate it!"

Madam La Fong observed Ruth showing more frustration with the status quo. "Now, we're getting somewhere! What is it that will make you happy?"

"I want to be alone!" Ruth paused a few moments, "and write my memoirs."

"Well, you are not going to be alone here in New York. You said so yourself; you're too well known; everywhere you go, people know you. Privacy and solitude cannot be found here. It would help if you had a place somewhere you can go. Do you?"

Ruth shook her head no.

Madam La Fong continued, "Think of those breadcrumbs that have been laid before you. The answer is right before you, and you choose not to see it. Think. Think about a place where you will have peace and solitude."

Ruth absorbed what she heard, became less agitated, looked up in deep thought, and then looked around the room at the posters before focusing on the 1966 Elvis Presley *Blue Hawaii* poster with his hands stretched with Diamond Head in the background, the palm trees, the beach, Hula girls, the outrigger canoe, and other elements of that vintage poster seemed to beckon her. Madam La Fong watched as Ruth experienced her aha moment.

Ruth grinned, looking almost giddy, nodding and exclaiming, "The breadcrumbs have been there all along, haven't they? The allure of Hawaii beckons me. The change will be wonderful, won't it?"

* * *

Ruth closed the door to Madam La Fong's and took out her cell phone to call George when it started to ring.

"Hello?" Ruth answered.

"It's George. Good news!"

"Darling, me, too. I'm moving to Hawaii!"

"What? Joe Baccio just made an offer for the property in Hawaii."

"Darling, tell him no, and I'll explain it later."

"Ruth, you've never been there, not even on a vacation. How do you know you will like it?"

"Sometimes, one must move out of their comfort zone and do something they have never done before; have the courage to take that chance and not be afraid of the unknown."

"But, Ruth!"

"Darling," Ruth continued, "a new door has opened for me, and I refuse to let it close. This is an opportunity of a lifetime that will provide me many new challenges and adventures."

"Ruth, this is a decision you cannot make lightly." George retorted. "Remember how many years it took you to obtain Beekman Place?"

"Darling, I do remember." Reminiscing for a moment, "There is nothing here for me anymore. I want to be alone and want a place to go where no one knows me. Hawaii is the place. Sell Beekman place."

HONOLULU

"We're starting our final approach to Honolulu International Airport. Out the right side of the aircraft are Diamond Head and Waikiki Beach. Please place your seatbacks in an upright position."

Ruth was seated at a first-class window seat, looking out the window at Diamond Head and Waikiki Beach below.

The plane was still taxiing when a flight attendant announced, "We ask that you remain seated until the captain turns off the seat belt sign. Mahalo."

Another flight attendant approached Ruth.

"Mrs. Newcomb, can you gather your belongings? Please."

Ruth nodded, smiled, and asked, "The captain hasn't turned off the seat belt sign."

"It's okay. You need to deplane first."

Ruth beamed; she was dressed more for attending the opera than for the comfort of flying, and glad she was well dressed. She leaned forward and reached under the seat in front of her, pulling out her purse and a nylon pet carrier. Inside, Mrs. Wiggins yellow eyes peer out, surveying the passengers.

Another flight attendant opened the front cabin door. Ruth got up and followed the flight attendant. The other passengers observed the "special treatment" that Ruth was receiving. A few passengers start to stand up. Another announcement, "Please remain seated until the captain has turned off the seat belt sign. Mahalo."

At the door, a man in a Hawaii Department of Agriculture uniform was waiting for Ruth. "Mrs. Newcomb, can you come with me, please?"

He turned and exited the aircraft, followed by Ruth. On the jetway, the officer stopped and turned to address her. "Can I have your pet carrier, please?"

Ruth reluctantly handed over the pet carrier. The officer took the carrier and opened the exit door to the exterior stairs.

"Please be careful; the sun is quite bright." The officer said as he held the door open for Ruth.

"Where are we going?"

"Down to the van."

"Darling, I ordered a limo, not a van."

"Follow me."

"Darling, why aren't we going down the jetway to the terminal?"

"We have business to take care of. Please follow me."

Ruth held her purse up to shield her eyes from the bright sun and followed the officer down the stairs.

"What is going on?" Ruth inquired.

"We're going to the Airport Animal Quarantine holding facility."

"What?"

"I'm here to quarantine your cat. There is a quarantine law to protect our residents and pets from rabies. Hawaii is rabies-free."

NOVEL

"Darling, I assure you Mrs. Wiggins doesn't have rabies!"

"I'm sure she doesn't."

"You can't quarantine her; she's all I've got!"

"Rules are rules, even in Hawaii."

The airport animal quarantine holding facility looked like any other kennel. Ruth was at the counter, with the officer on the other side with Mrs. Wiggins cat carrier.

"You realize your cat is a little old to be going through something like this."

"Darling, I know, and she is all I have."

"The quarantine law states that your cat must stay in quarantine for 120 days."

"Darling, 120 days?"

"However," the officer responded as he started to smile. "If you have the proper paperwork, you qualify for our five-day quarantine."

* * *

In the baggage claim area, a few passengers were still milling about claiming their bags; most were gone. A door opened next to where the bags come out as Ruth exited carrying only her purse. She looked around and noticed her Louis Vuitton bags were on the baggage carousel. She then spotted a lone limo driver holding a cardboard sign with Mrs. Newcomb professionally printed. Ruth went over to him. "Darling, I'm Mrs. Newcomb. My bags are over there."

As the limo made its way through downtown Honolulu, Ruth was transfixed as she observed century-old buildings next to modern-day ones and how they blended so well. When they reached Waikiki Beach, most buildings were modern multistory, not unlike New York City, but on a much smaller scale, with palm trees.

The limo pulled up to the modern Halekulani Hotel. A porter, wearing a blue and white hibiscus Aloha shirt and black slacks, opened the limo door for Ruth. On stepping out, she saw the Halekulani hibiscus logo and noticed the fresh smell of the air, the aroma of the ocean, and the sweet smell of the tropical flora. Another porter took her luggage from the limo, placing them on a waiting cart. She observed people wearing muumuus and Aloha shirts and not walking briskly but enjoying the sights. Some gave her a nod of recognition as she entered the hotel lobby.

* * *

Ruth opened the door to her lanai. The curtains billowed as she went to the handrail to view Diamond Head in the distance, Waikiki Beach, and the hotel pool some ten stories below her corner room. She smiled and nodded approvingly; the hotel was no different from any metropolitan city.

She turned her attention to the ocean. In the distance, she saw catamarans and surfers catching waves. She smiled and sighed deeply, relieved that she had decided to give up her life in Manhattan for Hawaii.

* * *

The sun was ready to bid another fond Aloha to Waikiki and the guests at Halekulani's House Without a Key bar; painting the sky a golden hue with orange clouds on the horizon only added to the beauty of the approaching sunset. Ruth, dressed in a designer evening dress, was seated at a table under palm trees swaying with the trade winds, sipping a Manhattan while other guests enjoyed exotic cocktails with

NOVEL

orchids, pineapple, and tiny umbrellas in them. Everyone enjoyed listening to a trio playing and singing *My Little Grass Shack*. At the same time, a woman dressed in an eloquent muumuu performed the Hula to the song. The colors continued to shift as the sunset on the horizon. Ruth remembered her conversations with the Martin's about the beauty of the sunset and how Charlie Chan would frequent the bar she was enjoying.

* * *

Back in Ruth's hotel suite, a slight breeze blew the white lace balcony curtains, revealing a full moon rising behind Diamond Head and the tropical flowers strategically placed throughout. A basket of fresh Hawaiian fruits adorned the coffee table. On one wall was a fully stocked bar with assorted glasses. Ruth searched her purse, pulled a piece of paper, and headed for the phone. She dialed the number and waited; there was no answer, and she hung up.

* * *

Kalakaua Boulevard, Waikiki's main oceanfront street, was crowded with locals and tourists alike, men in shorts and Aloha or T-shirts, while women wore muumuus or missionary dresses. All are wearing zoris (Hawaiian for flip-flops) or sandals. However, if one individual stood out from the sea of other people, it was Ruth. Ruth walked confidently, wearing a designer dress and high heel shoes. Formal or designer dresses and high heels were rarely worn in the tropics; it wasn't done except for a special occasion like a formal event. Even when attending church, missionary dresses or muumuus are called for, not formal dresses; formal dresses were not the Hawaiian way. Most women don't like getting their heels caught in uneven surfaces or sinking down to their heels in the sand.

Ruth had no real destination in mind, as she wanted to see what Hawaii and Waikiki were all about. She was happy people did not stop and ask her for her autograph. They looked but did not disturb her; Ruth was quite pleased with the freedom Hawaii brought her.

* * *

It was the evening before she could pick up Mrs. Wiggins and fly to the Big Island. She had been unsuccessful in reaching Ben to inform him of her arrival. She tried again, waiting for Ben to pick up the phone impatiently waiting. Finally, the phone was picked up.

"Thank God. It's about time." She thought.

"Hello, are you Ben?" Ruth asked, continuing, "Darling, I'm Ruth Newcomb, the new owner.

"Yes, that's right, I'm in Waikiki. I'll be arriving tomorrow on the noon flight.

"Yes, it *arrives* in Kona at noon. You'll be there, right?

"Good! I want a limo with a full bar and sushi.

"Darling, do what you can do.

"I'm looking forward to meeting you. You'll have a sign so I know who you are, won't you?

"Good! See you then. Goodbye."

Ruth hung up. Hearing the Hawaiian music filtering up from The House Without a Key bar, she walked to the lanai. When she reached the railing, Ruth smiled at the scene around her; the shimmering lights emanated from the city, the full moon, and its light shimmering on the ocean surface below. Ruth nodded, proclaiming, "No wonder they call this paradise."

THE BIG ISLAND

Ruth wore a fashionable designer dress and high heel designer shoes, carrying her purse and the pet carrier with Mrs. Wiggins' yellow eyes peering out, and she passed security to the Kona Airport baggage claim area. Lei greeters met many people, and a plethora of limo drivers held up signs. Ruth examined each one and failed to see her name. She continued to look for Ben and did not see anyone holding a sign resembling anything close to her name. Ruth watched her Louis Vuitton bags pass as passengers or limo drivers picked up their bags. Being the lone passenger in the baggage claim area, she took each one of her bags to a bench near the exit. Ruth sat looking at her gold Rolex, which read half past noon. Nearby, a tourist magazine rack caught her attention. She got up and chose *101 Things to Do on the Big Island* and *The Big Island*. She returned to the bench and started to read *The Big Island*. A little later, she examined her watch, which read one o'clock. Looking around, she spotted a pay phone. She left her luggage and headed for the pay phone, reaching into her purse and pulling out a paper and a quarter, putting it into the pay phone, and dialing the number. After numerous rings, she shook her head and hung up, returning to the bench.

A middle-aged Hawaiian man, wearing Ray Ban sunglasses, an Aloha shirt, and blue jeans, looking oddly like the Central Park ukulele man, walked in from the street holding a sheet of lined notebook paper with Luka Newcomb crudely written with a marker.

Ruth could not help but notice her last name and went to the man who was the first to speak. "Aaa-loooo-haa! I am Ben Kokua. Are you Mrs. Newcomb?"

"Darling, it's about time! I've been waiting for over an hour. I did say noon, didn't I?" Ruth asked, then pointed to the sign Ben was holding. "Darling, I'm Ruth Newcomb, not Luka Newcomb."

"Dat okay. You go shi-shi, we have long drive."

"Shi-shi, what's shi-shi?"

"You go baf-room. I wait, watch bags. You go! Baf-room over der."

Ruth left her luggage and cat carrier with Ben and took her purse.

Later, in the Kona Airport parking lot, Ruth followed Ben to the passenger side of a stretch limo as Ben heaved her bags into the back of a rusty mud-encrusted blue pickup truck. Ruth looked at the truck dumbfounded. "Darling, we're *not* getting in *that*, are we?"

* * *

The truck, with both windows rolled down, made its way along a long stretch of road high up on the cloudless mountainside, the savannah scattered with parched dried trees in desperate need of water, along with cactus, dried tan grass, lava rocks, and flows could be seen for miles in any direction.

Every now and then, a goat or two grazed along the roadside. In the distance below, the landscape changed from the black of the lava flows and the tan of the parched grass to lush green vegetation nestled along the brilliant deep blue waters of the Pacific.

"Darling, where are the beaches?"

"Da beaches are way down there," Ben replied, pointing down the hill towards the ocean.

Later, the savannah gave way to plushness; trees and bushes sporadically lined the road. The clear blue sky had given way to menacing rain clouds as more cars traveled in both directions. On the right side of the truck were cowboys riding horses.

"Darling, look, cowboys!" Ruth exclaimed.

"Paniolo."

"What?"

"Paniolo, dat Hawaiian for cowboy. Dis da Parker Ranch; the largest ranch in the United States."

A light rain started to fall as the truck entered a more populated area of one-story houses and tropical vegetation. They drove past a rustic wooden sign that announced Waimea, a small town nestled on a plush plateau between two volcanos. They reached a traffic light. While waiting for the light to change, Ruth noticed a strip mall with a large modern supermarket. The light changed, but Ben could only go a few miles an hour due to traffic.

"This traffic is like the states." Ruth declared.

"Dis is Hawaii. We *are* a state."

"Darling, the traffic shouldn't be like this in paradise. What is going on?"

"Rush hour."

"You have rush hour here, in Hawaii?"

"Uh, hu! Every day."

"Darling, why, where is everyone going?"

"Shift change."

"Shift change, darling?"

"Dey go to and from da resorts on the sunny side of da island."

The gentle rain gave way to a heavy downpour. Fearing getting wet, Ruth rolled up her window while Ben left his down. The truck made its way down a long stretch of road, both sides lined with large trees and lush vegetation. Ben noticed Ruth repeatedly looking out the window, visibly bored, looking at her watch, at him, and the cat carrier. Ben attempted to comfort Ruth, "We almost der ... fifteen minute."

The truck slowed down, making an abrupt right onto a smaller one-lane road that had seen better days as it headed up Mauna Kea through sugar cane fields, fertile vegetation, and trees lining the side of the road. The rain had all but abated, giving way to the fog that engulfed the freshly rinsed truck. Ruth rolled her window down and was greeted with a sweet, sugary aroma.

"Darling, what is that smell? It is so sweet, smelling almost like sugar or candy."

"It cane. Dat where sugar, molasses, and rum come from."

"You mean that funny stuff that looks like bamboo?" Ruth pointed towards a rogue clump of sugar cane off to the side of the road.

"Uh-huh."

Ruth studied the sugar cane taking in deep sniffs, and smiled at the entire scene. The old road by this time had become extremely bumpy, knocking Ruth and Mrs. Wiggins about. To stabilize herself, she grabbed the strap hanging from the roof of the cab above her door; it came off in her hand. She looked at it, then at Ben. She held down the pet carrier with her left hand as Mrs. Wiggins loudly protested.

The truck slowed down as a car approached them. Ben pulled the truck off to the right to allow the car to pass. As it did so, Ben raised his left hand and waved at the oncoming car, and the driver waved back.

Every few hundred yards of the bumpy tree-lined road were well-paved driveways leading to houses hidden behind the lush tropical rainforest vegetation. Ben made abrupt jerks of the truck to avoid hitting fallen branches, turkeys, or chickens. This combined with the bumpiness, made for an extremely uncomfortable ride for Ruth and Mrs. Wiggins.

"Darling, I'm not feeling well." Ben looked at Ruth, whose skin color was slowly turning gray. "I can't take it anymore. All this bouncing around is making me unwell." The truck continued to bounce.

"Darling, stop the truck now! I'm going to be sick!"

The truck turned into a ginger, tree-lined, impeccably maintained driveway and stopped. Ruth opened the door and stuck her head out, about ready to throw up, but quickly regained her composure. She looked down the driveway where she saw an inviting beautiful blue and white trimmed three-car garage. Behind it was a larger modern blue and white trimmed house with a matching blue metal roof.

"What a beautiful house!" Ruth exclaimed.

"In Hawaii, we say hale for house."

"I must start to learn new Hawaiian words. Darling, do you know who lives there?"

"Uh-huh. You do."

HALE NEWCOMB

Ben pulled the truck closer to the garage and parked. He retrieved the luggage and walked towards the house. Ruth reached for the carrying case and looked inside to find a shivering and cowering Mrs. Wiggins in the back, tail twitching.

"It's okay, Mrs. Wiggins." Upon hearing Ruth's calming voice, Mrs. Wiggins moved forward. Ruth turned the carrier away from her, sharing the surrounding terrain with Mrs. Wiggins.

"Darling, we live here; isn't this wondrous?"

Ruth followed Ben down the concrete and grass pathway from the garage to the house. She was more enthralled with the beauty of the scenery around her than walking when she accidentally stepped into the grassy section, which caused her heel to sink slightly into the grass. She momentarily lost her balance, causing the cat carrier to swing violently. Mrs. Wiggins let out a short sorrowful meow. Ruth quickly regained her balance, paying more attention to where she was walking as she followed Ben toward the main house.

Beyond the house, a vast macadamia nut orchard came into view. Various citrus trees with large fruit line the boundary between the front yard and the orchard. Chickens, wild turkey, and néné (Hawaiian geese) pecked the ground. The birds scurried for protection in the orchard and adjacent vegetation when hearing Ruth and Ben approaching.

The blue house was encircled by a large lanai that wrapped the uphill exterior. Without using a key, Ben opened the front door and held it open. Ruth walked in, and the downhill view from the living room floor-to-ceiling windows caught her attention. She walked over to examine the view. Through the trees, in the distance, she saw the unmistakable dark blue waters of the Pacific and smiled. Ben walked up behind her.

"Nice view, isn't it?" Ben inquired.

Ruth nodded, "Darling, this is truly paradise."

Ben started towards Ruth's bedroom, down a short hallway off the living room. "I put your stuff in da master suite. If you need me, I live in the other end of the house." Ben pointed down a longer hallway.

Ruth placed the pet carrier on the wooden floor and opened its door to free Mrs. Wiggins, who darted heading down the shorter hallway where Ben had gone. Upon hearing Ben's unfamiliar sounds, she abruptly stopped and skidded as she made a U-turn and returned to the carrier.

A few moments later, Ben returned to the living room, where Ruth had focused her attention on the lanai and uphill scenery of the fog making its way towards the house. Ruth was so enamored with the view outside she started for the front door.

"You need Cutters," Ben told Ruth as she opened the door. She had not heard him and continued to go outside and view the orchard and the fauna; mango, orange, lime, lemon, and other fruit trees scattered around. Ginger, bird of paradise, and anthurium plants define the separation of house and orchard. She took a deep breath and smiled.

Through the living room window, Ben watched Ruth, who was experiencing great difficulty walking and maintaining her balance due to her high heel shoes sinking into the grass. Suddenly Ruth started swatting the air around her as though she was being attacked by something. She began to slap her exposed arms and legs. Ben headed to the kitchen as Ruth tried to maintain her balance as she returned to the house. When she entered the kitchen, Ben held out the can of Cutter's bug spray.

"Darling, you didn't tell me about the mosquitoes. What is the can for?"

"It rain a lot here. Da haole use Cutters."

Ruth cocked her head, mouthing the word haole.

"Haole," Ben explained, "dat mean white people or tourist."

* * *

Ruth was asleep wearing a silk eye night mask with Mrs. Wiggins curled against her. The tranquil sounds of Mrs. Wiggins snoring, the crickets chirping, and coqui frogs croaking had abruptly given way to muted sounds of popping, which remotely sounded like the backfire of a car, followed by loud grunting sounds, had awakened Ruth. She removed her night mask and looked at the clock, which revealed 4:31. She sat upright and listened to the popping and grunting sounds appearing to be coming from another room or outside. She grabbed Mrs. Wiggins and held her close, stroking her.

"Darling, at least they are not in our room. This is Hawaii, not New York! I'm sure we're going to be alright."

Ruth continued her watch for about a quarter of an hour when the grunting sounds decreased and again gave way to the gentle sounds of the crickets and frogs. Ruth was still seated upright in bed, holding and gently stroking a purring Mrs. Wiggins. She returned Mrs. Wiggins to her spot before replacing the silk night mask and lying down.

The peacefulness of night gave way to dawn, announced by a lone rooster crowing, startling Ruth and Mrs. Wiggins. Ruth removed her mask, looked around, and realized it was her first morning in the country of the Big Island. The rooster continued crowing, others joining in, welcoming the rising sun and a new day.

* * *

Ruth was seated at the kitchen table sipping coffee and reading *The Big Island,* one of the throw-away magazines. On the cover was a photograph of a black sand beach, with palm trees and a waterfall cutting its way down a large cliff in the background. Ben entered and poured himself a cup of coffee.

"How did you sleep?" Ben inquired.

Ruth put the magazine down.

"Sleep? Darling, most of the night, I heard you grunting. You need to keep it down when I'm here."

"Grunt? I no grunt."

"Then what was that sound if it wasn't you."

"It da pig!"

Ruth cocked her head and gave Ben a curious look.

"Wild boar." Ben continued, "Dey come for the mac nut and mango. Not every night, some night, when dey get hungry."

"Darling, nothing can be that loud when eating."

"Look under tree, you see big dirt area dat done by pig. De laikem mac nut."

"Laikem what is laikem?"

"It Pidgin for like them. You know, laik-em! Pidgin easy to speak."

"Darling, you did a fantastic job unpacking and arranging my belongings before my arrival. The house looks like I've lived here for some time. Thank you."

"You're welcome. I thought you would like it."

Ruth nodded and returned her attention to the magazine and then to Ben.

"Darling, I want to go shopping and see the island."

"I drive you."

"I want to do it myself. Darling, I want a car."

"You take truck."

Ruth shook her head. "I do not drive trucks. I can barely drive cars."

"You need four-wheel drive. Truck mo betta."

"Darling, I said I don't do trucks. You have to find me a car."

THE NEIGHBORS

Ruth was in the living room watering plants when the front door burst open without a knock as Auntie, a jubilant robust mid-sixty-year-old Hawaiian-Asian dressed in a muumuu and wearing zoris, entered. Ruth was so startled by Auntie's abrupt entrance she dropped the glass Tiffany pitcher, which shattered across the living room tile floor.

"Oh! You clumsy lady," Auntie exclaimed in singsong Hawaiian pidgin. "Where Ben? He kokua you, klinim mess, den he kam my place. Da keiki's need him. Where he?"

"Darling, who are you?"

"Me? Auntie."

"Who ... what gives you the right to burst into my house without knocking?"

"Ben wok fo me."

"Darling, he works for me!"

"Oh, dat oh-kay."

"No, it's not okay."

"When you see Ben, tell him, come plenny wikiwiki," Auntie commanded.

A moment later, Ben came running into the living room from the back of the house.

"Oh, der you are!" Auntie exclaimed, addressing Ben, "Da keiki's need you. You klinim here first." Pointing to the broken Tiffany pitcher. "Den kam wikiwiki." She turned for the door and abruptly disappeared.

"Darling, what was that all about?" Ruth asked.

"What?" Ben inquired.

"That lady, what is with her?"

"Dat Auntie. I work for her, too."

"I don't like the way she just burst into my house. I want to be left alone."

"I talk to her."

* * *

Ben entered the interior of a large opaque plastic greenhouse Quonset hut. The aroma of a freshly mowed lawn with a hint of a skunk permeated the building. An elaborate watering system hung from the metal frame of the greenhouse. Auntie was trimming one of several hundred marijuana plants; most had reached maturity.

"A-lo-ha," Ben said as he entered.

"A-lo-ha, she plenny tight!"

"Oh, she oh-kay. She no like Luka, she like Ruth." Ben picked up a pair of trimming shears and started to trim one of the plants near Auntie.

"Luka, Hawaiian name. Ruth, haole name. She plenny haole. Ruth, mo betta." Auntie stroked one of the plants, adding, "Da keiki, dey nidim our kokua nau."

* * *

Wearing a sundress with house slippers, Ruth was seated on one of the Adirondack chairs on her lanai, typing on her laptop. A can of Cutter's bug spray was on the table. The sun beamed on a curled-up Mrs. Wiggins, who was on the grass at the foot of the steps. The brightness of the sun yielded to a darkness Ruth had never experienced. It started to rain lightly, followed almost immediately by a downpour. Mrs. Wiggins' tail twitched as she looked up at Ruth and let out a long sorrowful meow drowned out by the sound of the rain hitting the metal roof. Ruth jumped up and ran for the cat, reaching her in moments. As Ruth bent down and grabbed the cat, she heard a loud roaring, rumbling sound coming down the hill towards her. She looked toward the sound to see a foot-high torrent of water, mud, and branches flowing in her direction. Ruth could not maintain her balance and fell backward, landing on her derrière. The deluge was so powerful that Ruth and the cat started sliding down the hill.

Ruth continued to slide, holding the caterwauling cat up in the air. They were carried down the hill plowing through a thicket of bushes, and her mud-covered sundress moved up to her thighs. She saw she was about to hit a house and braced her legs for impact, holding the mud-covered cat close to her. They slammed into the side of the house, which shook as though a boulder hit it.

The downpour continued as Nalani and Meka, the middle-aged Hawaiian-Filipino house owners downhill from Ruth, ran to the uphill side of their house to see what caused the considerable thump, only to find Ruth and the cat covered with mud. Ruth looked up.

Nalani looked at Ruth, "Rain stop soon."

Meka reached down and helped Ruth up.

"Eh, wha? Ohhh!" Ruth exclaimed.

"We wait on lanai for rain to stop. Then you can go."
Nalani suggested as they walked to their lanai. The rain was so
heavy it washed the mud off both Ruth and Mrs. Wiggins.

Nalani escorted them to four rickety chairs surrounding a
table on the lanai. "You sit."

"I'm Meka," Meka said before pointing to Nalani. "Dis
Nalani, da misses."

"Darlings, it is nice to meet you. I'm Ruth Newcomb. I
live next door, up the hill. Does it always rain like this?"

"Dis sometimes happens when da rains are in da right
place on Mauna Kea. Da good ding is, it doesn't last too long."
Meka answered.

Nalani looked at Ruth's slippers, then up at Ruth. "No
won-da you fall. House slippahs no good in Hawaii; too
slippery. You need zori."

"Zori?"

"Haole, call dem flip-flops."

NOVEL

I NEED A CAR!

The bright Hawaiian sun filtered through the floor-to-ceiling kitchen nook windows where Ruth and Ben had their morning coffee.

"Darling, have you found a car yet?" Ruth inquired.

"Yes."

"Where is it?"

"It not ready."

"Why not?"

"No windows."

"Darling, what good is a car without windows?"

"Dat is all I could find. You take truck?"

"Ben, I don't want to use your truck. I want to own my own car. Where do we go to get a car? One with windows?"

"Hilo, it closer than Kona."

"Fine, we go to Hilo and buy a car."

"Auntie need me."

"She can wait. I need a car, now!"

* * *

The car dealership was small compared to those found on the mainland, with one or two of each vehicle model. Ruth was still dressed more like a Mainlander, wore a designer dress and high heels, and was with Ben and a car salesman looking at the small selection of cars.

"Not many cars have four-wheel drive," the salesman said, "you need a truck or SUV."

"I don't want a truck. What is an SUV?" Ruth inquired.

"Sports Utility Vehicle. Dey like a truck, but look like a cross between a van and a car, and a lot more comfortable." The salesman took Ruth and Ben over to a couple of SUVs. "Dis one will get you from Hilo to Kona on Saddle Road, like riding in first class. No bouncing, smooth ride. It's great when you get caught in a downpour. You can go almost anywhere on the island."

"Darling, what about Waipio Valley?"

The salesman shook his head. "These are All Wheel Drive SUVs, they may not make it. You need a four-wheel drive SUV. Let's go over here."

The salesman took Ruth and Ben to a four-wheel drive black SUV. "Dis da best four-wheel drive SUV. You won't slide off the road like other SUVs and trucks do when you go down to Waipio."

"Okay, I'll buy it." Astonished, Ben and the salesman look at Ruth, "On one condition, you show me how to operate it."

"It's easy. But first, you must always take off your high heels when you engage da four-wheel drive. Safety first."

Ruth got into the driver's seat and took off her high heels as the salesman got into the passenger's seat and gave instructions on operating the gears and pedals. Ben stood nearby, watching the training session unfold. Before long, the sound of the SUV started, followed by the wrenching sound of grinding gears. This was repeated several times before the grinding sound was followed by the SUV lurching forward and coming to an abrupt stop. Ben looked on, shaking his head, wondering if Ruth could ever handle the SUV. After an hour of training, Ruth could drive the vehicle around the lot with little trepidation and parked in front of Ben.

* * *

A pleasant breeze blew down Mauna Kea rustling through the macadamia orchard with a variety of chickens, turkeys, and néné's pecking the grass. Occasionally the sound was interrupted by a crowing cock. Mrs. Wiggins curled up on one of the Adirondack chairs on the lanai. Ruth was typing away on the laptop. "If you ever saw *The Trouble with Angels* with Haley Mills and June Harding, that would typify my schooling at St. Francis Academy. I was more the Haley character, whereas Sarah Martin was June's. As in the movie, we had fun devising schemes to be defiant. Even today, I don't like rulers; they remind me of the nuns using the back of our hands for target practice."

As Ruth continued to type, she heard pecking near the bottom of the lanai steps. She looked up and saw a couple of wild turkeys had made their way to Mrs. Wiggins' cat food dish, eating its contents. The chickens and néné followed the turkey's lead and went to the dish and water. Ruth bolted from her chair, frantically waving her arms. "Shoo, shoo!" The birds scurried into the orchard. Mrs. Wiggins disinterestedly looked up at the commotion and returned to her nap.

HONOKA'A

Honoka'a Town was the closest village with a post office. Almost every sign in town had an accent between the two a's. Locals and tourists alike left the pronunciation of the second "a" off saying Honokaa in lieu of Honoka'a. This was quite acceptable to most; however, those true to the old Hawaiian ways would always pronounce the second a.

In the center of Honoka'a, the paint had peeled on most of the wooden buildings. The aged elevated wooden sidewalk had an occasional missing board that made it hard to walk on, while the newer sections were concrete. The dilapidated sugar mill wasn't far from town. When the mill was in operation, the workers and townspeople hung out at Mr. Woo's, the only market for miles around. There was no doubt Honoka'a had seen better days. However, the town was going through a Renaissance. The government recently built a modern brick post office down the street from Mr. Woo's.

A breeze blew through the open-aired post office box collection area. Wearing a designer dress and high-heeled shoes, Ruth was collecting mail from her post office box. The only other person in the post office box collection area was Danny Mauka, the local television station manager. Danny knew everyone and what was happening on the island's north end. He smiled at Ruth as she walked past him, "What a wonderful dress you are wearing. Where's the wedding?"

"Wedding?" Ruth inquisitively replied. "Darling, why would I be going to a wedding? I am picking up my mail."

"Sorry, I thought there was a wedding I wasn't aware of. People always tell me when there is a wedding or other big event."

"Darling, sorry to disappoint you," Ruth responded and continued to walk down the street to Mr. Woo's Market, which was not much larger than a mainland convenience store. Inside were a variety of items, primarily small single-use or sample-size items, one of almost everything. Ruth walked through the aisles, looking for peanut butter. Finally, she spotted a small jar. She picked it up and looked at it. She frowned and shook her head, thinking one would be lucky to get a few peanut butter and jelly sandwiches from such a small jar. Ruth went to the front of the store to the sole cash register. Nearby, Mr. Woo, an older Asian man, wore a white apron stocking shelves. As Ruth approached him, he bowed, "How may I help you?"

"Darling, do you have a big jar of peanut butter?" Ruth asked.

"Have only small. Big ones at da supermarket in Waimea."

* * *

Waimea was about fifteen miles up the main road from Mr. Woo's. Ruth pulled her SUV into a parking space at the large Waimea supermarket. When she exited the SUV, she was beaming and proud that she had made the half-hour journey herself without incident.

Mr. Woo was right, and the supermarket was enormous. Locals and tourists alike pushed their carts through the large well-stocked aisles. The tourists could be readily identified because they were tanner than the locals and had crackers, nuts, and other fattening snacks and liquor in their carts. Ruth roamed the aisles, looking at all the unfamiliar local items and the mainland brand-name items she was familiar with. When she reached the peanut butter and jelly aisle, she was amazed by the large variety of local fruits and vegetables made into jams, jellies, and preserves next to the peanut butter.

Charlene, a lightly tanned copper-haired woman in a missionary dress with kitschy Hello Kitty zoris, was visually sorting through the variety of peanut butter jars. Ruth saw only one jumbo jar of peanut butter left on the shelf. Ruth and Charlene reached for that sole jumbo jar at that exact moment. However, Ruth was the first to grab it.

"I was reaching for that jar," Charlene exclaimed.

"Darling, it's *my* peanut butter." Ruth selfishly responded.

Charlene examined the overdressed Ruth from head to toe.

"Your first time on the island, isn't it?"

"Darling, I live here!"

Without maintaining eye contact, Charlene scanned the shelves and found and took a smaller peanut butter container. Looking back at Ruth, Charlene decided to defuse the conflict stating, "A long time ago, I was like you."

"Darling, I *am* the only one like me," Ruth exclaimed.

Charlene shook her head and extended her hand. "I'm Charlene Strong, Honokaa's high school counselor." Ruth refused to shake hands. "When I first arrived from the mainland, I used to be uptight like you. We are now on the Big

Island, not the mainland. Life is different here. In time, you, too, will change, become more relaxed, and enjoy our Big Island ways."

Without wanting or needing to respond to Charlene, Ruth turned and left her, who said, "Have a great day, A-lo-ha!"

NOVEL

DOESN'T ANYBODY KNOCK?

While Ruth was shopping in Waimea, William Ayala, the teenage son of Nalani and Meka, Ruth's neighbors, was carrying a Hawaiian floral arrangement of anthuriums and birds of paradise in a glass vase, opened Ruth's unlocked front door. After William placed the arrangement on the living room coffee table, he looked around the room and noticed changes Ruth had made to the Martin's former home. In the bookcase, he saw the photographs of Ruth with the Clinton's and Donald Trump, Jackie Onassis, Princess Dianna and Prince Charles. He spotted the Emmy placed in the center of the bookcase. Having only seen one on television, he went to the shelf and studied it up close. William remembered that many of the actors said how heavy the Emmy was, so he decided to pick it up and almost dropped it because it was heavy. He examined the gold statuette and the plaque that read "Outstanding Informational Series - 2001, Ruth Newcomb - Host, *From the Big Apple*" and then returned it to its resting place, turning his attention to the collection of hardback books, which include *The Adventures of Tom Sawyer, The Adventures of Huckleberry*

Finn, Catcher in the Rye, Uncle Tom's Cabin amongst Dante, Dickens, and other classics.

William looked at the flowers, "Des no gut here." He picked up the flower arrangement and headed for the kitchen, placing it on the island's center, ensuring everything looked perfect. He returned to the living room to leave when Ruth entered through the front door with her paper bag of groceries. Ruth screamed and dropped her bag.

"What are you doing here?"

William innocently replied, "Noth-thing."

"You are stealing something, aren't you?"

William shook his head no.

Ben came running in from the front door and noticed William, "William, what are you doing here?"

"Noth-thing."

"You go home."

William started to leave.

"No!" Ruth proclaimed, "I want to know what he is doing here."

"I do noth-thing."

"You are here. That's enough."

"I do noth-thing. I just leaving."

Ben did not want to escalate the situation further and commanded, "William, you go."

As William headed for the door, Ruth scolded him, "Darling, where I come from, people don't wander into other peoples' homes. It's a violation."

When William reached the door, Auntie burst into the room, addressing Ben and William, "You come, wikiwiki! Da keiki's no wait!"

"I go," William responded as he left.

Auntie observed the bag on the floor, "You fo'ever drop dings."

Ruth gave Auntie a look of disdain.

"I no like yu stink-eye. I go."

Auntie turned and left the house, leaving Ben and Ruth alone in the living room.

"Talk about violations! People enjoy popping in around here, don't they?"

"Uh-huh."

"Darling, what are those keiki things that lady always talks about? Why are they so important?"

"Keiki, it Hawaiian for little ones or children. If everything oh-kay, I go Auntie's."

Ruth watched Ben leave and head up the hill to Auntie's. After picking up the grocery bag, Ruth went to the kitchen and placed the bag next to the flower arrangement on the kitchen island. She reached for the yellow rotary wall phone, picked up the receiver, and then hung up. Opening a cabinet door, she pulled out a worn AT&T telephone book, placed it on the island, and then noticed the flower arrangement. She smiled, thinking Ben had put the arrangement on the island. Ruth returned her attention to the telephone book and saw that it had the original AT&T logo of years past. She shook her head, opened the book, looked inside the cover, picked up the phone, and dialed the number, "Police?"

* * *

Later that same day, Ruth was reading Dante's *Purgatory* in the living room. She heard footsteps coming from the lanai before the front door burst open. Two police officers entered. Ruth was startled. "What the heck! Doesn't anyone knock around here?" Hearing no answer, "I'm glad you are here."

"You want to report a break-in?" The first officer queried.

"Darling, why else would I have called you?"

The second officer tried to be funny, lighten the tension, and asked, "What was broken?"

Ruth saw no humor in the question, "I want to report a break-in. I even know who he is and where he lives. He's the neighbor boy next door."

The officers looked at each other and smiled.

"Oh, William ... William Ayala, he's harmless. He won't cause you no harm. He's a curious kid."

"I don't like it that he was in *my* house. In New York, this isn't done."

"Dis is Hawaii, not New York." The first officer countered.

"Did you lock da door before you left?"

"Yes, and Ben, my caretaker, also lives here."

"So maybe Ben didn't lock da door?"

"I don't know."

"No harm done. Nothing taken. Is der anything else you need?"

"Darling, I want something done."

"There isn't anything for us to do if nothing was taken."

Ruth shook her head.

The first officer looked to the second officer, "We're here. We check on Auntie."

* * *

Ruth was seated in her white Adirondack chair on the lanai, reading *The New Yorker* magazine. Ben was coming down the hill from Auntie's. As he approached the lanai, Ruth asked, "Ben, come here, please."

Ben walked over to Ruth and sat on the other Adirondack chair.

"Darling, I don't want to be disturbed. I want to be left alone."

Ben started to rise. "You want me to leave?"

"No, Ben, sit."

Ben sat back down.

"What I don't like," Ruth continued, "is everyone keeps bursting into my house, not knocking, from Auntie, to the police, to William. So, I want you to install a security system." Ruth laid down *The New Yorker* displaying an elaborate security system advertisement, and showed it to Ben. "Like this one."

"Door has lock."

"No, Ben, I want a security system."

"Dis not New York, dis Hawaii. No one has security system."

"Darling, I don't care if we are in Timbuktu. When can you install it?"

Ben scratched his head, "I don't know where to get security system."

Ruth pointed to the phone number in the advertisement, "Here's the number. I want it done. Do you understand?"

Ben nodded.

WAIPIO VALLEY

The aroma of coffee filled the kitchen as Ruth and Ben finished their morning brew.   She looked at the flower arrangement.

"Ben, I forgot to thank you for the nice flowers."

"Flowers? I thought you put them there."

"I wonder how they got here."

Ruth and Ben inquisitively look at each other when Ben realizes what happened.

"Dat what he do here!"

"Who?"

"William."

Ruth looked at the flowers and smiled.

"Darling, why didn't he tell us?"

"You scare him."

"He scared me! That was very kind of him."

Ruth looked down at *The Big Island* throw-away magazine, which had a photograph of the Waipio Valley on the cover.

"Darling, is Waipio Valley as breathtaking as these photographs?"

"Uh-huh."

"How long does it take to get there?"

"Too dangerous to drive, you hike."

"Hike from where?"

"You park at top, hike down to beach. Da hike takes half an hour to get down and over an hour to go up."

"I have an SUV. I can drive."

"Some people don't make it."

"The salesman told me I could do it!"

"Oh-kay, use only first gear and drive very slowly. Going down is hard; going up easy. You need carrots with stalk attached."

Ruth gave Ben a curious look. "Carrots?"

"You need carrots when you get to bottom." Ben got up. "I go to Auntie's."

* * *

Ruth, dressed in a designer outfit and high heel shoes, double-checked the front door, ensuring it was locked. She nodded and smiled.

Later she exited Mr. Woo's holding a bunch of carrots by the stalk heading for her SUV, and drove to the entrance at the top of Waipio Valley. The sun was shining brightly, not a cloud to be seen. The parking lot was filled with cars. The road ahead of her had barriers on both sides, narrowing down from the two-lane, well-paved road to a one-lane paved road that had seen better days. A large sign on one side of the road stated *STOP, Restricted Road, Only 4-wheel Drive Vehicles Permitted, One lane road, Downhill traffic must yield to uphill traffic.* On the other side was another sign, *WARNING, proceed at your own risk, Steep Grade, Engage all wheels, Engage first gear, Falling rock.* Ruth studied the signs,

NOVEL

deciding to go ahead with her plan and traverse the half-mile road down to the valley floor.

Ruth reached down and took off her high heel shoes, looked at the gears, and shifted the SUV into first gear. She pulled gently away and drove exceptionally slowly down the steep, one-lane road. Ruth was so intent on driving and staying on the road, avoiding the tourists hiking single file down the steep, narrow road, she overlooked the beautiful fertile valley and beach below. She was happy no one was driving up the one-lane road without a guardrail, as she wasn't sure how much room the two vehicles would have without one of them going off the steep cliff into the valley below.

Ten arduous minutes later, Ruth finally reached the bottom of the precipice, where there was a small area wide enough for two vehicles before the road made an abrupt hairpin U-turn towards the beach. She stopped and took a long deep breath, happy she had made it without falling off the road into the valley.

Regaining her composure, Ruth started driving again, following the road into the darkness of thick overgrowth of tropical foliage. It took a few moments for her eyes to adjust to going from the brightness into the deep darkness of the dense tropical jungle before her. The road had also changed; it was no longer paved but unpaved, muddy, and potholed. As she continued driving, occasionally, light streamed through the thickness of towering trees, helping to illuminate the road before her.

Still in first gear, Ruth made her way down the road, trying to avoid the water-filled potholes the size of Volkswagen Beetles and the occasional tourist walking in the same direction she was going. She reached a somewhat dry flat area and took a few moments to rest and check out the jungle surrounding her. To her right, a stream of light filtering through the trees illuminated the hull of a rusted car smashed against a tree. Ruth noticed a tree between the car and the road. Furthermore, the car was on its side with the wheels facing the road. Then Ruth realized that the car had come from the road above her, the same route she had traversed not minutes before.

While gazing upward into the trees, Ruth saw a rusted carcass of a pickup truck perched in one tree. Looking around, she spotted a car and another and another. The trees were adorned with rusted cars and trucks that didn't make it.

After a few moments, Ruth regained her composure and started driving again, following the muddy pothole-infused road, which eventually opened up to a sandy path leading through the pine and palm trees where other SUVs and trucks were parked. Wondering amongst the palms and trees were a dozen wild horses. She found a grassy part between two palm trees and parked. She reached down to put on her high heel shoes.

Five horses started to meander towards the SUV, unnoticed by Ruth. She got out and reached into the SUV, grabbed the carrots, and closed the door. As Ruth turned, she found herself encircled by the horses. She then understood why Ben told her to take carrots with stalks. Ruth took a carrot, held it by the stalk, and cautiously extended it towards one of the horses, who gently took it from her. She was jubilant, smiling to the point of almost laughing. She took another carrot, holding it by the stalk; another horse took it. The five horses had her pinned against the SUV, whinnying and nuzzling Ruth as she continued to feed them. She quickly ran out of carrots and held both hands up showing the horses she didn't have anymore.

"All gone."

At this point, the horses turned, leaving the SUV. A few moments later, more horses approached. Again, she held her hands up.

"My little darlings, I have no more, all gone."

The horses whinnied and meandered away, searching for their next victim.

Ruth started to walk down to the gray/black beach. The moment she stepped off the grassy area, her shoes sank deeply into the sand. Ruth was trapped, unable to move. It took some effort to slide out of the heels and go barefoot. She carried her shoes and headed to the beach to watch the waves crashing along the shoreline.

The secluded bay was perfect for surfing, and a few locals enjoyed the surf. The occasional tourist who had hiked down to the beach cooled off in the refreshing water. Before all the big resort hotels and people came to the islands, Ruth thought this was what Hawaii was like. The gentle trade winds rustled the palm trees causing Ruth to turn her attention to the land behind her. To her right, a river flowed into the ocean. To her left, a waterfall cascaded some fifteen hundred feet into the Pacific. It looked oddly familiar, and then she remembered Kevin Costner telling her and her television audience about the shooting of the last scene of *Waterworld* in Waipio Valley. She took a deep breath, sighed, and smiled at all the peacefulness and tropical beauty.

* * *

Ruth was driving back into the jungle, navigating the potholes and occasional tourist walking along the muddy road. In front of her, she saw the bright light shining through the trees, indicating the journey through the jungle's darkness was ending. She made it into the sunlight and the last flat area before she had to make the sharp hairpin U-turn to traverse the steep one-lane road back to civilization. Ruth took a moment to gather her wits before attempting to make the return trip up to the top of the cliff. She took a deep breath, looked at the clutch, put it into first gear, and pressed the gas pedal. As she released the clutch with her left foot, the gears ground slightly, and the SUV moved slowly forward. There was a loud thud.

Ruth realized the SUV had struck something and slammed on the brakes. She was sure there wasn't anything in front of the SUV before she started studying the gears. She looked up to see the body of a young man on the hood of the SUV and put the SUV into park, got out, and went to the man, his face still facing the hood of the SUV.

"Darling, are you okay? I'm so sorry."

The man looked up at Ruth. It was William.

"I am oh-kay, Mrs. Newcomb."

"Darling, I didn't see you there. I'm so sorry. You aren't going to sue me, are you?"

"Huh?"

"Are you going to sue me?"

"Why would I sue you?"

"I'm from New York, and everybody sues."

"I won't sue you. Can you give me a lift to da top?"

"Yes..."

Ruth started to get into the driver's seat.

"Darling, are you *sure* you're not hurt?"

"I am alright."

William got into the passenger seat. Ruth slowly drove the SUV up the Waipio Valley cliff road, intent on not becoming its next victim, as they both bounced all over the place.

* * *

NOVEL

The SUV successfully made it to the top of the cliff.

"Darling, do you need a ride home?"

"No, Mrs. Newcomb, Honokaa would be fine. Thank you for the offer."

They were back on a well-paved two-lane road going through sugarcane fields where the sweet aroma did not go unnoticed by Ruth. The sugarcane fields were interspersed with an occasional house or two off to the side of the road. William looked out the open window at the cane fields.

"Darling, about yesterday." Ruth paused, "Thank you for the flowers."

"You're welcome."

"You know you shouldn't go uninvited into other people's homes, right?"

"Uh-huh."

"Darling, it's not right, intruding like that."

"I'm sorry, Mrs. Newcomb."

More houses were coming into view as they approached Honoka'a. William slinked down into the seat. He was almost on the floor. They were approaching Honoka'a High School.

Mrs. Charlene Strong, the school counselor, stood at the curb, arms folded, looking down the street as the SUV approached. Ruth looked down at William, "There's no need for you to be down there."

After the SUV passed the school, William returned to his seat.

"William, aren't you still in high school?"

"Uh-huh."

"Then why aren't you in class?"

"I don't like English. I go to beach instead."

"Darling, you need English. School is important."

"Dat what Mrs. Strong, my counselor, says."

The SUV makes an abrupt U-turn, heading back toward the school.

"What are you doing?" William franticly exclaimed.

"Darling, I am taking you to school."

"I don't want to go!"

The SUV pulled up to the school. William got out, looking at the ground as he approached Mrs. Strong.

"Hello, Mrs. Strong."

Ruth listened to the conversation through the open window.

"William, you're early today. How was the beach?"

"It oh-kay."

"William, you get to Dr. Tilton's class. He's expecting you."

Mrs. Strong leaned down, looking into the passenger window. Both Ruth and Mrs. Strong instantly recognized each other.

"It's you!" Mrs. Strong exclaims. "Thank you for bringing William. At least he'll be able to catch part of his English class. I forgot to tell you the other day at the market. This may be The Big Island. However, we are a tight little island where everyone knows everyone else and what goes on. Thank you for bringing him to school; you performed an excellent service."

DA GHOST OF AN OLD KAHUNA

A heavy fog engulfed the area as Ruth typed away on her laptop on her lanai. Ruth heard a noise and looked up to see who it was. However, the fog was so thick that she started to pick up the laptop to go inside when she recognized it was William and put it back down.

"Aaa-loooo-haa, Mrs. Newcomb. What are you doing?"

"I am writing my memoirs."

"Why?"

"Darling, I had a wonderful life; people will love reading it. How did it go in school today?"

"Oh-kay. I got to help Auntie with her keiki's." William started to walk up to Auntie's, looking over his shoulder, saying, "Aaa-loooo-haa!"

* * *

As Ruth walked through the macadamia orchard, her slippers sank into the thick grass. Beneath the trees, mac nuts covered the ground. She frowned and shook her head. She turned to head towards the house when she saw Ben had started up the hill towards Auntie's, "Ben!"

He does not hear Ruth.

Ruth yelled louder, "Ben!" He turned. "I need to talk to you." When he reached Ruth, she continued, "Darling, how is it going with the security system?"

"Ah, I still look for one."

"It shouldn't take this long to locate a system."

"Dis Hawaii, take long time to get stuff."

"You've been spending too much time with Auntie."

Ashamed, Ben looked towards the ground.

"No, I haven't."

"Look at this place." Ruth made a sweeping motion with her hand. "The grass needs mowing."

Ben looked around at the overly long uncut grass, "Uh-huh."

"Look at all the nuts under the trees. They need to be collected and sold."

"Uh-huh."

"For years, the Martins raved about how good of a caretaker you are. Darling, I just haven't seen it, Ben."

"I sorry, da keiki's need attention. Dey no wait."

"Darling, I know children, I mean the keiki's, need attention, and so do my macadamia nut trees and the lawn. Please take care of it this week."

"Oh-kay."

Auntie came down the hill towards Ruth and Ben. She went up to Ben, "Oh, der you are!" Then turned her attention to Ruth, "How you?"

"I'm fine. I need Ben to spend more time with me."

"No, he need to spend time wit me and da keiki's. Dey important right now."

"Darling, my lawn and macadamia nuts are important too."

"Da mac nut wait. Keiki's no wait. Ben, you come."

Auntie started up the hill, followed by Ben.

"This week, Ben!"

Ben looked over his shoulder, "Uh-huh."

* * *

In her designer dress and high heels, Ruth drove down the two-lane road towards Honoka'a Town. A lone hitchhiker came into view; it was William. She pulled over, "Get in."

"Aaa-looo-haaa, Mrs. Newcomb."

William got into the car.

"Going to school, William?"

"No, Waipio."

"Why don't you want to go to school?"

"Dr. Tilton makes us read aloud. It embarrasses me."

"There is nothing to be embarrassed about. Public speaking is easy."

"Dr. Tilton is not human! People say he is da ghost of an old kahuna."

"Darling, Dr. Tilton cannot be all that bad."

"He is!" William exclaimed, "He makes us read da big words."

The SUV approached the school.

"When I lived in New York, I volunteered to help people learn to read. I can do the same for you, darling."

William looked at Ruth and smiled.

"I want you to go to Dr. Tilton's class." William frowned as Ruth continued, "Try your best. Then, after school, I want you to come to my place, and we will work on your reading."

William smiled, "Sometimes, Auntie helps me, too."

Ruth stopped the SUV at the front of the school.

William got out and went to the front walkway of the school. He looked over his shoulder.

Ruth was watching.

William continued walking and opened the front door. He looked over his shoulder again.

Ruth was watching.

William entered, and the door closed. Through the front door window, William looked out. The door opened as Mrs. Strong stepped out, mouthed thank you, and waved at Ruth.

READING IS AN ADVENTURE

The light streamed onto the lanai as Ruth typed away on her laptop. On the table next to her was *Time Magazine* with a publicity photo of her on the cover, the headline in red lettering read *From The Big Apple No More, A Tradition Dies*.

William walked through the orchard and approached Ruth. "Aaa-looo-haaa, Mrs. Newcomb."

"Hello, William."

William noticed Ruth's photograph on the cover of *Time Magazine*.

"That's you, isn't it?"

"Yes, darling."

"Why is your picture on da magazine?"

Ruth picked up the magazine and pointed at the headline.

"Darling, the headline says it all."

"I don't understand."

"It's simple."

Ruth opened the magazine to the page with a full picture of her on the set of *From The Big Apple* along with the article about her. She handed the magazine to William. He took it, looked at it, and then looked at Ruth. She looked back at

NOVEL

William. "Sit down. Why don't you read the article aloud to me? I will help you with the words you don't understand."

William sat down and started to read.

"Ruth Newcomb, former host of the syn-d—" William paused, turning his head sideways as he tried to pronounce the word.

"Syndicated," Ruth finished.

"--syn-di-cated television show *From the Big Apple* was born in East Hampton, New York. The so—" William paused again.

"Socialite," again Ruth finished the word for William.

Ruth and William were so involved Ruth overlooked the wild turkey, chickens, and néné had made their way to the porch and started eating Mrs. Wiggins' food.

"The so-cial-ite attended St. Francis Academy for girls and graduated mag-na co-me la-" William paused.

"That's magna cum laude, it's Latin meaning ..."

The sound of the birds pecking drew Ruth's attention. She looked at the birds, got up, and chased them away. "Shoo, shoo!"

William started to laugh.

"Darling, what's so funny? Every day they come, every day the same thing."

"Why don't you give dem food, too?"

"That's Mrs. Wiggins' food. I don't want to feed the entire island!"

"Da birds, dey eat bugs. Dey good for you."

"I'm not going to feed them, and that's final!"

* * *

Ruth collected her mail from her post office box while Danny, the local television producer, was collecting his.

"Excuse me. You're Ruth Newcomb, aren't you?"

"Yes, Darling, who else would I be?"

"Aaa-loooo-haa! I'm Danny Makua, KBI, Big Island TV station manager, channel 32."

Ruth acknowledged Danny. "Nice to meet you."

"I'm sure you have made quite a few adjustments to life here on da Big Island."

"Darling, more than you would ever want to know."

"Da first few months are hard, but you'll adjust."

Ruth closed her mailbox as Danny continued, "Would you be interested in doing a broadcast or two?"

"Darling, I am not interested in doing television, radio, or anything. I want to be left alone."

Danny reached into his pocket, pulled out a business card, and handed it to Ruth.

"Here's my card. If you change your mind, call me."

* * *

Ruth wore slacks for the first time, along with a large hat covering her face from the sun, was kneeling in the garden clipping flowers, and placed them in a Tiffany ceramic basin at her side. Mrs. Wiggins curled up next to her. William was seated in an Adirondack chair reading an article from *The New Yorker*. He placed the magazine on the table and looked at Ruth, "I finished, Mrs. Newcomb."

Ruth put the clipping sheers down, got up, and sat in the Adirondack chair beside William.

"Excellent, William." William smiled. "You have made a significant improvement in your reading."

"It's coming a lot easier, thanks to you and Auntie."

A paperback edition of The Adventures of Huckleberry Finn was on the table. Ruth reached for the paperback.

"I think reading is an adventure, and it's about time you start reading a novel. We'll start with an easy and fun one, *The Adventures of Huckleberry Finn*." Ruth handed the paper back to William, and he flipped through the book.

"What type of name is Huckleberry? Is he related to Huckleberry Hound, that cartoon dog?"

"No, but that's not important. What is important is that you enjoy Huck's adventures."

"Huck?"

"Darling, that's short for Huckleberry. You will get into the story and won't be able to put the book down."

"Ma-ha-lo, Mrs. Newcomb."

William opened the book, flipped to chapter one, and started to read. After a moment, he looked up, "It says he was in another book called *The Adventures of Tom Sawyer*. Shouldn't I read that book first?"

"Darling, I think this book is better."

"Oh-kay, but he sure writes funny."

"That's known as colloquial writing." Ruth noticed William cocked his head and continued, "Colloquial is like Auntie, when she speaks, that is known as Hawaiian Pidgin. In the case of the book, that is how Huck speaks. It will take you no time to pick it up. Continue reading, William."

William started reading. His lips moved slightly with each word as though he was reading aloud. Ruth watched William.

* * *

Ruth was watching television. Mrs. Wiggins curled up on her lap. Ben entered through the front door.

"Good evening, Mrs. Newcomb."

"Good evening."   After a brief moment, she asked, "Darling, have you found a security system yet?"

"No."

"I want you to check on it in the morning, okay?"

"Oh-kay."

* * *

The night was still. Ruth was sleeping, wearing her silk night mask. The grunting and popping sounds were so loud they awakened Ruth. She removed her night mask and sat on the edge of the bed. Mrs. Wiggins waddled into the bedroom, meowing. Ruth reached into the nightstand, took out a large flashlight, and turned it on as she headed outside.

Ruth used the flashlight to guide her, making her way toward the grunting and popping sounds. She turned the flashlight toward the sounds, which illuminated a giant one-hundred-and-fifty-pound feral pig, grunting and scratching the ground near the base of a macadamia tree, eating the nuts. The macadamia shells were so hard that they sounded like gunfire when the pig bit down and broke the shell. Distracted by the light, the pig looked at Ruth, grunted, snorted, and waddled into darkness.

NO MORE KEIKI'S

Bright sunlight filtered through the mango and other fruit trees that border the macadamia orchard. Ruth checked the mango fruit to see if it was ready to eat before she continued walking through the orchard. She looked down at the ankle-high grass, frowned, and shook her head in disgust as she saw a plethora of macadamia nuts on the ground. Under a few trees were large-sized holes where the night visitors had dug up the grass. Ruth was getting mad. She looked around for Ben. Not seeing him nearby, she called, "Ben!" After a few moments, she called, "Ben!" Ruth walked faster, past her house, and headed up to Auntie's, shouting, "Ben!" She passed through the trees and shrubs that separated her property from Auntie's. She found the greenhouse and headed for it. She called, "Ben! Are you in there, Ben?"

"Uh-huh!" Ben replied.

Ruth opened the door to the greenhouse and was greeted with the aroma of skunk and grass. She entered and found Ben and Auntie clipping marijuana buds from mature plants. They both looked up at Ruth.

"You, kokua?" Auntie inquired.

NOVEL

"No, I came for Ben."

Ruth took a moment and looked around the greenhouse. Her jaw dropped as she realized the keiki's were not at all kids or little ones but marijuana plants.

"That's marijuana!" She exclaimed.

"Haole call it marijuana. We call it pakalolo. You kokua?" Auntie responded.

Ruth did not like the current arrangement one bit. "What you are doing here is wrong. Ben, I want you down at my place now!"

Ben put his head down as if caught in the act of doing something wrong, "Oh-kay."

Ruth turned to leave.

"No!" Auntie commanded, "Ben, stay. Keiki's need kokua, now!"

"No! Darling, Ben will come with me to my place. I pay him to take care of my place."

"I pay Ben, too. Da pakalolo help people and make more money den mac nuts, Kona coffee, and orchids."

"What you all are doing is wrong; growing marijuana is illegal."

"Dis is medicinal marijuana." Auntie clarified.

"I don't care." Ruth said, then looked at Ben, "Ben, come!"

Ben shook his head.

"Ben," Ruth continued, "you have been hired to take care of my place. You haven't mowed the lawn in over a month. The nuts need attention and the security system. Well, what about the security system?"

"I work it."

"Enough of this, Ben. I have had all I can take of you and your lack of work. If you like it so much here, Ben, get your stuff out of my place and move up here with Auntie."

Auntie glared at Ruth, "He no live wit me."

"I want Ben out of my place tomorrow. You understand?"

* * *

On the lanai, Ruth typed on her laptop. Mrs. Wiggins was curled up in her usual sunny spot. William approached carrying *The Adventures of Huckleberry Finn*. Smiling as he reached Ruth, "Aaa-loooo-haa, Mrs. Newcomb... Am I disturbing you?"

"No, Darling. Have a seat." William took his seat in the other Adirondack chair.

"You were right, Mrs. Newcomb. I couldn't put *Huck Finn* down. It is a great book! I could identify with Huck cause we have a lot in common. I like how he uses pigs' blood to fake his death."

"It was a great story, wasn't it?"

"Yes, Mrs. Newcomb. Ma-ha-lo!"

William returned the book to Ruth, who placed it on the table next to *Catcher in the Rye*, which she handed to William, commenting, "You know, William, *Catcher in the Rye* is a great book. You will like it too."

"Ma-ha-lo!"

"Darling, I need help around the house, mowing the lawn, collecting the nuts, and doing odd jobs. Do you know of anyone?"

"Ben, he da bomb. There is no one betta than Ben."

"So you don't know of anyone?" Ruth asked.

William shook his head no.

"Darling, would you help me?"

"I am not Ben. I do not have tools or experience like him." William responded as he started to get up. "I need to help Auntie."

"Why are you helping her with *that* stuff? You shouldn't engage in such activities."

William sat back down, "That stuff? Such activities?"

"You know what I mean, William."

"No, I don't, Mrs. Newcomb!"

"What you are doing is wrong."

"There is nothing wrong with helping Auntie."

"William, I agree with you to a point. However, helping someone tend marijuana is not."

"Helping ohana is da Hawaiian way."

"If you go up there and help her, I don't want you around here anymore."

William got up and said, "What-ever..." as he started up the hill, still holding *Catcher in the Rye*.

BE CAREFUL WHAT YOU WISH FOR

It was a peaceful night until the sounds of the crickets and frogs were abruptly interrupted by Mrs. Wiggins outside in a cat fight, along with grunting sounds awakened Ruth. She removed the night mask and got out of bed, calling, "Mrs. Wiggins! Mrs. Wiggins!"

With flashlight in hand, Ruth ran frantically into the orchard toward the sounds of Mrs. Wiggins hissing and the pig grunting. Ruth reached the scene, shining her flashlight on the pig, watching it meander away, leaving Mrs. Wiggins sprawled on the grass.

"Mrs. Wiggins!" Ruth stopped dead in her tracks, not believing the carnage before her. "Oh, no, Mrs. Wiggins!"

* * *

A light rain fell as Ruth finished digging a hole in the soft red volcanic soil to bury her beloved cat. Ruth reached down, taking Mrs. Wiggins, wrapped in Ruth's New York red woolen scarf, looking like a mummy. She ceremoniously placed the

NOVEL

cat in the hole, filled it with soil, placed a handmade wooden cross at the end of the makeshift grave, and said a silent prayer. Ruth stood and shook her head in disbelief. She looked towards the house, the orchard, and the ocean realizing the vastness and loneliness of the island, and started to cry.

* * *

Later, Ruth sat on her lanai with the open laptop, staring pensively at the screen, and shook her head. She closed the laptop, got up, walked down the steps of the lanai to the garden area where Mrs. Wiggins was buried, looked at the barren burial site, and sorrowfully shook her head.

Unnoticed by Ruth, Auntie quietly walked up, placed her hands together in front of her, and bowed her head. After a few moments, Auntie started to speak. However, this time in perfect American scholastic English with no accent.

"It's hard when we lose loved ones, isn't it?"

Startled, Ruth turned and looked at her.

"It will take time," Auntie continued, "and you will get over it. You need a hug..." Auntie opened her arms to Ruth. "Come to Auntie."

Ruth hesitated.

"It's oh-kay," encouraged Auntie, "I am here for you."

Ruth hesitantly raised her hands to hug Auntie.

"You need someone right now. Auntie is here."

Ruth finally could not resist. The two of them embraced in a hug. Ruth started to cry.

"There, there." Auntie patted Ruth as though she were consoling a frightened child. "Everything is going to be alright."

Ruth sobbed, "Mrs. Wiggins was the last thing I had. I wanted to have solitude but not be alone like this."

After a few moments, Ruth and Auntie broke their embrace. Auntie looked at Ruth, "Sometimes, what we want is not what we truly need. Often, what we are looking for is right before us, and we don't see it. We look elsewhere because we believe it is there and not where it truly is. You came from the fast-paced, wikiwiki world of the Big Apple to the more relaxed laid back life of the Big Island. The two cannot coexist. You are here now, but for how long?"

Ruth shrugged her shoulders. "I sold everything and am here for good."

"You're a multi-millionaire. You can move back to the Big Apple anytime you want."

"There's nothing left for me there anymore."

"Then you must adjust to the Big Island life. Here, we help each other. We are all one big family; it's the Hawaiian way. The Hawaiians call it ohana. Ohana is the Hawaiian word for family. It doesn't only mean our blood family, but also our extended family, who are there for us in the here and now. William is not my son, but I treat him like he is. That's ohana. Hawaii was built on ohana; it is the magic of the Hawaiian people."

Ruth thought for a moment or two, "I think I understand. My needs and wants are out of whack; they are not set for the Hawaiian way. They are currently set for the Big Apple. That's in the past. I need to move on. As Mrs. Strong said when she arrived from the mainland, she used to be uptight, and that life is different here, and she changed; she said, in time, I too would change and become more relaxed and enjoy da Big Island ways."

Auntie looked towards her house and back at Ruth.

"Would you like to have a punch?"

"I'd love to."

Ruth and Auntie walked through the orchard toward Auntie's house.

"You are speaking perfect English now. So why do you speak pidgin?"

"It's expected!" Auntie smiled, "I have my Ph.D. in horticulture from Purdue, and if I were to speak proper English, things would be completely different. Besides, I enjoy speaking pidgin. Very few people know I have my doctorate. I keep that and speak perfect English to a select group who have at least a master's degree, like the Baccio's, Charlene Strong, and Dr. Tilton; other than them, people think I'm that sweet crazy Auntie born and raised on Oahu. In due time, you'll be speaking pidgin too."

* * *

Ruth was still overdressed, wearing a designer outfit, while Auntie a missionary dress as they walked into Macy's. Auntie spoke perfect English with Ruth, "We need to change your mainland attire to that of a kama'aina."

"A what?" Ruth asked.

"Kama'aina is the Hawaiian for a child of the land or better known as a local person. Haole used to mean white person, but now, to be politically correct, it means foreigner. This is all part of what I have been talking about, changing your mindset to be a part of da Big Island." Auntie lowered her voice and continued, "We have a secret."

Ruth leaned into Auntie so as not to miss a word.

"As I told you earlier, you know something few other people do."

"Darling, what could I possibly know that no one else knows?"

"My education and use of pidgin! It's between us girls. From now on, I will only speak pidgin. And it would help if you cut that darling stuff. Using darling may work in the Big Apple, but not here on da Big Island. We do things differently here." Auntie leaned even closer to Ruth and winked. "You understand, sista?"

Ruth laughed as they entered Macy's.

* * *

Ruth exited Macy's wearing a muumuu and zoris for the first time, carrying a few bags. The next stop was Lowe's, where both were pushing their carts into the garden department. Ruth looked at an assortment of smaller potted plants and picked up the more vibrant flowers, smelling them, before placing them in her cart. When she was done, Ruth joined Auntie, who was putting two bags of fertilizer into her cart. As Ruth approached, Auntie patted the fertilizer, saying, "Dis kokua, da keiki's."

"I don't understand why you are growing that stuff."

Auntie leaned close to Ruth, whispering in perfect English, "It's one way I can afford to live here."

"So you see nothing wrong with what you are doing?"

"There is nothing wrong with it. It's not like I'm trafficking or selling to kids."

"So that makes it okay?"

"Yes, I'm registered with the feds on an experimental horticultural program researching growing medicinal marijuana which we hope sometime in the future will help many suffering people." Auntie continued, "Did you know cannabis cures specific types of cancer? The Chinese have been using it for thousands of years. Cannabis is in its infancy. With more research, it will be the wonder drug."

NOVEL

"So, why does Ben spend so much time with you?"

"He normally doesn't, it's harvest time, and I can use all the help I can get. You're welcome to help any time."

Auntie moved back from Ruth, continuing in pidgin. "It da Hawaiian way!"

Ruth spotted chicken feed, grabbed a twenty-five-pound bag, and added it to her cart.

A NEW LIFE BEGINS

After Ruth got home, she took the flowers to Mrs. Wiggins' grave site. She carefully planted them in a colorful arrangement around the burial mound to ensure they marked the exact location where Mrs. Wiggins was enjoying eternity.

Afterward, she admired her diligent work making a beautiful tropical memorial for Mrs. Wiggins. She reminisced about the first time she was introduced to Mrs. Wiggins when Carol Burnett and Tim Conway appeared on *From the Big Apple*. Carol presented the kitten to Ruth and named it after her *Carol Burnett Show* character Mrs. Wiggins, the secretary to Mr. Tudball, played by Tim Conway. Whenever Carol or Tim appeared on *From the Big Apple*, Ruth made sure Mrs. Wiggins appeared; she knew Carol, Tim, and her audience loved Mrs. Wiggins updates on her growth and antics.

When Ruth returned to the house, she saw many birds pecking the ground. She went up the stairs of the lanai into the kitchen to prepare the chicken feed, filled Mrs. Wiggins bowl with the remaining cat food, then chicken feed, mixing them before returning to the base of the lanai steps, placing the bowl on the first step. She decided the first step was best because the birds would not otherwise see the cat bowl due to the long thick grass that would obscure the bowl. Ruth turned to go back up the stairs into the house. When she reached the door, loud cackling was heard from the base of the lanai. She turned to see three chickens pecking the feed in the bowl. Nearby, a rooster started crowing, attracting other chickens and birds. In the distance, she heard the gobbling of the wild turkeys as they, too, heard the commotion and made their way to the foot of the lanai. Ruth was proud of her accomplishment of taking the first small step of being one with nature and more Hawaiian-like and smiled.

* * *

The following day, Ruth was wearing jeans T-shirt, and zoris was inside the shed which housed the lawn-mowing tractor. She climbed onto the tractor's seat and was able to locate the on/off switch and other switches, including the one that operated the mowing blades. She set the blades in the off position and started the tractor. The tractor sound was slightly louder than expected, but she felt she could quickly adjust. Ruth felt like she did in a rumble seat as a child, vibrating and shaking her even though she wasn't moving. She looked down at the floorboard and saw pedals. With a bit of trepidation, she pressed the gas pedal. The tractor lurched forward so abruptly that she almost fell off and barely missed taking out part of the shed as she did. Realizing the pedal was overly sensitive, Ruth gently pressed it and cautiously pulled out of the shed.

Ruth felt it best to head directly to the orchard to learn how to use the lawn tractor before doing the areas nearer her house. On the way to the orchard, she felt she could also learn how to cut the grass before getting to the orchard and engaged the mower. At first, she wasn't doing well and could not drive straight or control the mower. As she drove, the chickens, wild turkey, and néné scurried out of her way. Ruth knew she would master the mower with time and practice making turns in the open grassy area before reaching the orchard. With each turn, she did better at learning the nuances of mower. Before entering the orchard, she paused momentarily to look at her work to see the crooked lane of cut grass leading from the shed. The smell of fresh-cut grass permeated the air. The birds had returned to the freshly cut route, pecking and eating fresh grubs and bugs the mower had kicked up.

Looking at the macadamia trees in the orchard, she realized she would have to be careful not to hit her head and navigate around the lower-hanging branches. After a few hours, Ruth had finished cutting the grass in the orchard and around the house. The birds followed behind the mower, enjoying the fruits of her labor the entire time. Near the shed was a large mango tree with oversized hanging fruit too high to reach from the ground. There was no reason to mow around the tree since the grass wasn't growing there. Ruth thought the ripe mangos would make a great meal. With the mower disengaged, she drove the tractor to the edge of the tree, reached up, and picked two large ripe mangos before expertly navigating the tractor into the shed.

NOVEL

NEW YORK CANNOT BE ALL THAT BAD

On the lanai, Ruth typed on her laptop as William approached.

"Mrs. Newcomb, here's *Catcher in the Rye*."

William handed her the book and started to leave. Ruth placed the book on the table.

"William, please come back."

William returned, still standing.

"William, I want to apologize for my rudeness the other day. It was wrong of me."

"Dat oh-kay, Mrs. Newcomb. Ben's brother, Michael, lives in New York. He says New Yorkers can be very rude."

"We New Yorkers are not rude, William, but sometimes the customs and the way of life of other cultures, even our own here in the United States, are misunderstood and taken as being rude or unacceptable."

"I think I understand. Do you have another fun book?"

Ruth thought for a moment and then snapped her fingers. "Come with me, William."　　William followed Ruth to the

NOVEL

bookshelf in the living room. She scanned the bookshelf. "Ah, here it is."

Ruth reached for James Michener's *Hawaii* and handed the book to William. William looked at the thick book; his eyes widened in amazement.

"The book is soooo thick."

"William, it's a good read. You will enjoy it."

William took the book, "Thank you, Mrs. Newcomb. I am sure I will like it as I did the other books." William started to leave. "Auntie's keiki's need me."

"Mind if I tag along?"

William looked at Ruth and shook his head no. Ruth closed the laptop and placed it on the table beside the chair. Leaving the laptop out in the open for all to see is something she would never do in New York. She slipped on her zoris and got up.

Ruth and William walked together through the orchard, headed for Auntie's. William curiously asked, "I thought you didn't like what we are doing, and now you want to help?"

"William, let's say I need to adjust from my New York ways and customs to those here on the Big Island."

"That brings up a question. Is New York as wicked and phony as Holden Caulfield says it is?" William asked.

"From Holden's perspective, it is. From mine, New York isn't really that way."

"I didn't think so, because you aren't like the characters in the book."

"I don't know if I should take that as a compliment or not."

"Oh, a compliment, Mrs. Newcomb. I couldn't put da book down. Reading is fun, just like you, Auntie, Mrs. Strong, and Dr. Tilton told me. I discovered so much about New York."

"Just think about it, William. You were able to accomplish it without leaving the island. And now you will discover Hawaii. It's a fictional account of Hawaii, and it is reasonably accurate about what happened and how the islands became the way they are."

They reached Auntie's greenhouse. William entered, followed by Ruth. Auntie and Ben, harvesting buds, looked up. Ruth looked apologetically at Ben, whom she had not seen since she banished him.

"Ben, I want to apologize about my behavior the *da* other day."

This was the first time Ruth had used the word *da* for *the*. Both Ben and Auntie noticed the change and reacted by smiling. Ruth continued to address Ben, "You can come back."

"Mahalo," Ben pausing a moment before continuing, "I thought you didn't like what we are doing here."

"I've thought helping each other is da Hawaiian way, isn't it? I'm here to help." Ruth caught herself continuing, "Ah, I mean, I am here to kokua."

"You go, sista!" Auntie proclaimed.

Auntie saw William was carrying *Hawaii*. She looked at William, "Dat good book! It Hawaii to da max."

"It is a *big* book."

"You read. You like. Yes?"

William nodded. "Mrs. Newcomb said I would like it, too."

Ruth saw Auntie and Ben had buckets and shears.

"Where do I get a bucket?"

Ben leaned into Auntie, "She never done dis before."

"What can be so hard about trimming?" Ruth responded.

"There's a special way I'll show you." Ben offered.

"No," Auntie exclaimed, "she learn from da masta. I show her! Come."

Ruth walked towards Auntie. William placed *Hawaii* on the counter, picked up a small bucket and shears, and started harvesting buds while Auntie showed Ruth how to harvest and put the fresh cuttings in the bucket.

"See, it not hard. You try."

Ruth followed the same procedure shown to her by Auntie.

"You do plenny good. You get bucket."

* * *

Later that afternoon, Ruth was on her lanai typing on her laptop. Ben walked up the steps carrying a large UPS cardboard box. He had his tool belt on and asked, "Mrs. Newcomb, what do you want done first?"

Ruth stopped typing, looking up, "What are you talking about, Ben?"

"You asked for a security system. I got da system. It's here in da box. Do you want da front door or your bedroom done first?"

"Ben, I no longer need a security system."

"Since you got here, you wanted a security system; now you don't?" Ben confirmed.

"*Dis* is Hawaii. You said Hawaii is laid-back. No one has a security system. We don't need it. Please give it to me. I'll return it."

OH, DEM PIGS!

For almost a week, the sounds of the rain hitting the metal roof, followed by the chirping insects and frogs croaking, lulled Ruth to sleep; she no longer needed her silk night mask. However, one evening the enjoyable sounds of the rainforest were abruptly broken by the nearby grunting and popping sounds of a pig. Ruth reached into her nightstand, grabbed the flashlight, and headed out into the darkness to locate the pig. The sounds came from Mrs. Wiggins' gravesite and a nearby mango tree. Ruth pointed the flashlight towards the gravesite and saw the flowers were gone, apparently eaten by the pig. Hearing a loud thud followed by a grunt, she pointed the flashlight toward the mango tree and saw the pig ramming the trunk with its body as a ripe mango fell to the ground. The light attracted the pig's attention, who looked at her as it ate the mango and trotted into the darkness.

The following morning, Ruth and Auntie were on Auntie's lanai having coffee. It was just the two of them, so Auntie spoke perfect English.

"The pigs are a major issue on the island and need to be kept in check. It's tough to do where we live because our properties are near a state park where the pigs are protected. I believe the pigs figured out that they are safe and cavort there.

"Usually, fences do a great job of keeping the pigs out. I've been thinking that we have Ben put up fences around our properties once harvesting is over. My concern is they may get to the pakalolo. Can you imagine what would happen with a pig high on marijuana?"

Ruth nodded with laughter. "What do we do to keep them out?"

"Keeping the fences in check is our first line of defense. Right now, we have to have Ben trap and dispatch them."

"Dispatch them?" Ruth inquired.

"Kill them, donating their carcasses to needy families, a local luau, or someone who would love fresh pork. For the other undesirables, such as mongoose, Ben dispatches them to what we locals call another zip code, meaning a field a few miles from here so they don't return. Having Ben around is such a help for us women.

"Paul once shot a 200-pound pig. A few days later, the Martins had Ben prep and cook da pig in their Imu, the sizeable earthen barbecue pit near your shed, and had a luau for their friends and ohana before they returned to New York."

"I remember them telling us about that adventure. They said the pig was tender and succulent."

"The rifle should still be somewhere in your house."

"It's in my closet," Ruth added. "Are you suggesting I shoot the pig?"

"Oh, not at all. There may be a night when you must protect yourself from da pigs. They sometimes get aggressive and may charge you. When they charge you, you have two choices: climb a tree or shoot. When I hear them at night, I always take my rifle. Luckily the flashlight usually scares them, and they trot away like what happened to you last night."

"I have at least two mongoose running around my place. I thought they would be like the squirrels in Central Park looking for a handout. They run away from me when I approach them. They don't seem to be an issue. So why would Ben dispatch them?" Ruth queried.

"Mongoose aren't really an issue. They love to consume eggs. With all the chickens around, we have a plethora of fresh eggs. Wait here!"

Auntie left Ruth on the lanai and returned moments later carrying a bowl with two eggs, one slightly smaller. Auntie took both eggs out of the bowl and placed the bowl and both eggs next to their coffee mugs. She pointed to the smaller egg.

"This egg is from one of the feral chickens. See how it's slightly smaller than the store-bought egg." Auntie took the larger egg into her hand, cracked it open into the bowl, followed doing the same thing with the smaller egg, and handed it to Ruth to inspect.

"Notice the difference in the yokes?"

"The yoke from the smaller egg is much larger than the store-bought egg. Why is it?" Ruth asked.

"It means the egg is feral; on the mainland, they use phrases like organic or free-range eggs. You probably haven't seen any eggs because your mongoose are eating them before you know they are there. We'll have Ben dispatch the mongoose to another zip code. Most of all, the feral eggs are free and much tastier than the store-bought ones. Would you like scrambled eggs for breakfast?"

RUTH'S IDEA

Ruth drove down the road towards Waipio Valley past the Honoka'a Post Office and Mr. Woo's, where she saw three tall palm trees that formed the letters TV below, which was a modern yet rustic-looking wooden sign with green lettering identifying the metal Quonset hut as being KBI-TV, Big Island TV, Channel 32. Ruth parked and entered.

The austerity of the interior bore a strange resemblance to Captain Binghamton's office from the 1960s *McHale's Navy* television series. Behind the sole desk in the front reception area of the hut was a young twenties something Hawaiian woman, playing solitaire on the computer, who looked up at Ruth as she entered the building.

"May I help you?"

"Yes, I'm Ruth Newcomb, and here to see Danny."

"He's expecting you. He's back there. Second door to da right."

"Thank you."

Ruth entered Danny's office to find him typing on the computer. He looked up and stood as she entered. The office looked as though it was frozen in time with the television playing a re-run of *Gilligan's Island.*

"Come in. Aloha!" Danny pointed to one of the two chairs in front of his desk. "Have a seat. Good to finally officially meet you. May I call you Ruth?"

"Yes, of course, darling, ah, Danny."

"I was hoping you would call." Danny continued. "I like your thoughts about doing a monthly show about da Big Island."

"I do have one request," Ruth asked. "Alexander Mackendrick, director of *Sweet Smell of Success* and dean of California Institute of the Arts Film School, kept an egg timer on his desk. When students would pitch an idea, he told them, 'If you cannot finish your pitch by the time the egg timer runs out, don't come back until you can.' And turned the egg timer upside down. I thought we could utilize the same concept with our segments, keep them as short as possible while getting the true essence across."

"What an unusual yet creative idea. I don't see an issue with keeping the segments short." Danny hesitated momentarily before continuing, "Ruth, you realize we can't pay you what you got in New York."

"That's okay. This is Hawaii, and things are different here. I want da money to go to da Honokaa Library. They need it more than I do."

"What a wonderful thing to do for the island."

Ruth smiled. "Ma-ha-lo, Danny."

"If the show is anything like *From the Big Apple,* locals, and tourists will like it." Danny continued, "What do you think about calling da show *From the Big Island*?"

"Love it! However, *From **the** Big Island* doesn't sound just right." Ruth responded.

"I think it's perfect."

"Well, it is almost perfect. I thought we need to make a minor change," Danny cocked his head as Ruth continued, "making it more Hawaiian and changing the word *the* to *da*. It's da Hawaiian way, correct?"

Danny raised his eyebrows, smiled, and nodded, "I love it!"

"It will make all da difference. We'll call it *From da Big Island*. However, we need something else."

"Like what?" Danny inquired.

"When I did *From the Big Apple*, our logo was a large stylized apple behind da title. We need to do something similar, perhaps a palm tree?"

"Overdone."

"Hibiscus flower?"

"Overdone."

"A lotus flower."

"Overdone."

Danny stared into space for a moment and then snapped his fingers. "I got it!"

"What?"

"FBI!"

"FBI?" Ruth responded.

"Yes, *FBI - From da Big Island*. Get it?"

Ruth nodded.

Danny continued, "We have FBI in large yellow letters, with *From da Big Island* in a smaller font."

"Won't people get confused with *the* FBI?"

"I don't think so. This is Hawaii, not da mainland. We'll even put the da in small letters between the F and B. How could anyone misinterpret that logo between the Federal Bureau of Investigation and us?"

NOVEL

Ruth cracked a smile, "We still may have legal issues. And there are other big islands around the world. We must better identify our Big Island of Hawaii from other big islands.

"When we came up with da logo for *From the Big Apple*, we put the name of da show inside a line drawing of an apple. What if we did something similar, such as encapsulating da letters FBI inside an outline of the island? That way, we have something unique, thereby reducing any confusion."

"What a wonderful idea, Ruth." Danny exclaimed, nodding in agreement, and continued, "Have you given much thought as to what you would like to do for your first installment?"

"I was thinking of doing something on Waipio Valley."

"I don't think that would be a good idea. It's been overdone and on da tourist channel."

"Yes, but not my angle."

Ruth wore a missionary dress and a red hibiscus behind her left ear, looking directly into the television camera, "Many tourists and locals attempt to make the arduous journey down to

Waipio Valley, and some don't." She turned, looked up, and pointed towards a few rusted car carcasses in the trees. After a moment, "Okay, let's get the cutaway shots of da cars."

Mickey, the cameraman, swung the video camera upwards, pointing it toward the cars in the trees.

"Mickey," Danny added, "don't forget to include the ones where the trees have grown around and through the cars." Mickey took the camera and walked into the brush to get cutaway shots of the rusted cars in the trees.

Danny walked up to Ruth, "This is a great idea of yours, Ruth. It's unique."

"Thank you, Danny. Everyone knows about da cars, but no one talks about them."

"Yeah, I remember a year ago when a couple of drunk tourist kids thought they would take their rental car down here to party on da beach. They almost made it. Da only thing that saved them from being killed was da tree. They were so drunk they didn't feel a thing. When they awoke the next morning, they realized how lucky they were."

"Do you know where their car is?"

Danny looked up in the trees, searching for the car. "It's here somewhere." Danny continued searching the trees. "I really can't remember exactly where it is. You can tell which one it is because the car isn't as rusted as da others, and it was a convertible."

* * *

Ruth, Ben, and Auntie were all drinking red punch and eating brownies watching Ruth's television which was Ruth ending her Waipio car segment. "That's it from the Waipio Valley graveyard of cars in the trees. Until next time, this is

Ruth Newcomb, *From da Big Island.* Aaa-looo-haaa!" The credits rolled by.

"Dat gut!" Auntie exclaimed as she looked at Ruth.

"It funny, too," Ben added.

Ruth is beaming. "Mahalo!"

"Der you go. You become mo Hawaiian." Auntie told Ruth as she took a bite from a brownie.

"Auntie, the punch and brownies are fabulous!" Ruth exclaimed, "Whatever do you put in them?"

"Coconut water make da punch," Auntie responded.

"Da brownies are from an old Hawaiian family recipe," Ben added.

NOVEL

TIME FLIES

Ruth drove down Alii Drive towards the Royal Kona Hotel, which looked like a stylized volcano across Kailua Bay. She was excited because she was picking up her first visitor since she moved to the island. She drove into the hotel's front entrance, where Gloria La Fong was waiting for her. She stopped and got out.

"Gloria, Aaa-looo-haa!" Ruth said as they embraced.

"Aloha! You look fantastic. I can't wait to hear about what is going on."

"I'll tell you all about it, Gloria. I thought we'd have lunch at a little restaurant I know that has the best seafood on the island. The only thing is, it doesn't have a waterfront view. Would that be okay?"

"You know the island best, Ruth. You always go to the best places."

* * *

They entered the Big Island Grill, which looked like a converted fast-food restaurant. On a wall inside was a poster displaying a plethora of fish with both their Hawaiian and mainland names, and next to it, a chalkboard written with *Fresh Fish Today – Opah and Hapu'upu'u*. Ruth and Gloria were not sure what Hapu'upu'u or Opah was. They studied the chart finding that Hapu'upu'u was grouper and Opah was moonfish.

Seated and eating their lunch, "Gloria, what do you think about the fish?" Ruth asked.

"When you told me this is the best place on the island for seafood, and the only downside was it doesn't have a waterfront view, I thought you were joking," Gloria responded. "Have you been to a hukilau yet?"

"Not yet. I think it's a wonderful idea to shoot a real hukilau from throwing out the hukilau nets to the beach festival and dance that follows."

"I'm sure you could integrate the hukilau song in the segment."

"Gloria, you are filled with ideas."

"Ruth, you've been avoiding telling me how you are adjusting. How are you really doing?"

"Gloria, remember how a wreck I was after Zach's death?" Gloria nodded as Ruth continued. "I thought his death was brutal, but worse was how I lost Mrs. Wiggins to that damned pig. What a way for her to go. It still makes me mad when I think about it. The pigs are becoming a significant issue here on the island. We did a segment on *From da Big Island* about the pig issue. It was well received, but we can do nothing to reduce the population explosion. Ben has been making extra money dispatching pigs."

"Dispatching? I don't understand." Gloria inquired.

"Killing and selling them for luau's or donating them to needy families."

"What a great thing for him to do: care for those in need. Do the pigs taste any different than what we get in the States?"

"Gloria, Hawaii IS a state. It's best to say mainland. However, to answer your question, I haven't had any yet. I understand nothing is better than a pig cooked the Hawaiian way in an Imu, a Hawaiian underground oven, for the entire day. I have one by the shed and hope to use it."

"You still are avoiding answering my question about how you are doing."

"Gloria, I prefer to spend our time together not as your patient, but as a friend. In that respect, things are going great, and I am keeping busy with *From da Big Island*, writing my memoirs, and helping a local high school senior with his reading."

* * *

Ruth and Danny sat at his office desk, reviewing legal papers. "Ruth, I think I have everything in order. Da two of us are da executive producers. Partial funding comes from da visitors bureau and our head offices in New York."

"Danny, did they put it in writing?"

"Ruth, it's right here." Danny took the contract and handed it to Ruth with his finger resting on the middle of the page. "See? *From **da** Big Island*."

Ruth looked at the contract. "I was afraid with da show going into syndication New York would want to change da name to *From* the *Big Island*."

"They loved it and agreed to partner with da visitors bureau to develop an advertising campaign. Da logo will go on T-shirts, coffee mugs, and the like. They're going all out." Ruth smiled as Danny continued, "Since you did a great job conveying so much information about da Big Island in so little time, everyone agreed to keep to the original short format. Da visitors bureau can utilize our segments as public service announcements worldwide."

"That is terrific news, Danny. We've come a long way in a short time. Our segments have been viral, from our first one with cars in da trees segment to da one we did on da sports fishers throwing chum into the water, drawing da sharks that were attacking da swimmers.

"And we cannot forget da pigs!" Danny added, "The way you set everyone up with da pig issue. Dat scene where da pigs were eating da ears of corn, then cutting to da pig at da luau with da ears of corn strategically placed around da pig, was precious." They both laughed.

"Danny, I was so busy filming that pig segment I didn't have a chance to enjoy the event. One of these days, I will."

* * *

Joe and Eileen Baccio decided to make a layover in the Hawaiian Islands on their return trip from Southeast Asia. They visited the Martin's numerous times over the years, know their neighbors, and loved the Big Island. Joe's idea was to invite Ruth and Auntie to the Mauna Kea Hotel Clam Bake Saturday evening.

The four of them sat beachside, where an elaborate buffet feast of fresh island lobster, fish, sushi, sashimi, prime rib, and other excellent food.

Auntie spoke perfect English, as she generally did with the Martins, Baccios, and Ruth. Auntie brought Joe up to date with the advancements she was making with her medicinal marijuana project and how she was developing a much more potent strain that she knew would help the millions in need.

"What we need to see happen, Joe," Auntie continued, "are changes in the law to make medicinal marijuana available nationwide. It's a shame to exclude something that can cure ailments like certain cancers and allow AIDS and HIV patients to eat where they couldn't before. I think we're heading in the right direction."

"I couldn't agree with you more." Joe concurred. "Hopefully, the government will approve medicinal use one day, and people won't have to go underground to get their medications. Thank you for what you are doing, and keep up the good work."

"To change the subject," Eileen said, "Joe and I are considering buying vacation property here."

"Buy here? It's so far from New York." Ruth replied.

"The Caribbean is just too crowded for us," Eileen continued, "as is Oahu. We prefer the more open and relaxed atmosphere of the Big Island. We don't like the rainforest side of the island where you both live. We prefer the dry side and are leaning towards the Waikoloa Beach Resort area, which has everything we need. Do you have any suggestions?"

"I haven't been here long enough to know what would work or not work for you, Joe," Ruth responded.

"Waikoloa Beach would be perfect for the both of you," Auntie adds. "As you said, it has everything you need and doesn't get the rain like we do."

"When are you thinking of buying?" Ruth asked.

"Within the year," Joe responded.

"Ruth," Eileen interjected. "I've noticed this is the first time we've been out, and we haven't been interrupted by your fans. I thought the show was very popular here."

"Eileen, the show is very popular. We're on the islands, and people are different here. They respect my privacy. Occasionally, some fans from the mainland will recognize and approach me for an autograph. What's nice is it doesn't happen all that frequently."

"We were watching TV last night and saw your segment on Queen Lili someone."

"You're talking about Queen Liliuokalani, the last Hawaiian monarch overthrown by the narrow-minded missionaries."

"It was a tremendously informative segment."

"Eileen and I," Joe interrupted, "liked that she wanted to tax prostitution, the lottery, and opium because people would do it anyway, and it was a revenue stream. I hope our government will also change its mind and tax medicinal marijuana as it did with the lottery. Only time will tell."

* * *

Ruth, Auntie, Ben, and William are all harvesting keiki's in Auntie's greenhouse. Their buckets were filled with buds. Auntie looked at Ruth, "You do plenny good, Luka."

"Luka, what's that?"

William could not resist, "Dat Hawaiian for Ruth."

Ruth remembered Ben's Luka Newcomb sign at the airport when she arrived.

The door to the greenhouse opened as two police officers nonchalantly entered, greeting everyone with "Aaa-loooo-haa!" Ruth's eyes widened as she looked toward Auntie.

"Aaa-looo-haaa!" Auntie, Ben, and William responded in unison.

Ruth was relieved, smiled, and added, "Aaa-loooo-haa!"

"Oh, Mrs. Newcomb," one of the officers addressed Ruth, "we congratulate you on your Emmy nomination."

"What are you talking about?" Ruth responded.

"It came over the radio that *From da Big Island* was nominated for an Emmy."

Everyone looked at Ruth and clapped.

"It was nominated for an Emmy!" Ruth exclaimed in astonishment. She had never thought *From da Big Island* was being considered for an Emmy.

"You go New York?" Auntie asked.

William looked at Ruth, asking, "New York! Can I go with you?"

"With me, where?" Ruth responded.

"To New York!" William exclaimed.

"Dat's were da Emmy's are, aren't they?" Auntie added.

Ruth nodded, "Yes, they are in New York City." After a brief pause, Ruth continued, "I really don't want to return to New York."

"It is important, isn't it?" Ben asked.

"Oh, Luka, you must go." Auntie pleaded, "Dis is important to you, to us, and most of all, da island."

NOVEL

DA BIG APPLE

Even though it was evening in New York City, the bright lights of the city illuminated the entrance of the Times Square Marriott Marquis Hotel as though it was still daylight. A black limo pulled into the valet area. The valet opened the limo door while a porter took the luggage out of the trunk. Danny stepped out, turned around, reached into the limo, and helped Ruth and Auntie out; all wore Aloha wear. Ruth, Auntie, and Danny stood and looked into the opened limo door. Moments later, Ruth leaned into the limo and said, "It's oh-kay. Come."

William stuck his head out the door, looked at the valet, and then focused on the people briskly walking by. "There are too many people!" William exclaimed, "Ben say he doesn't like all da people in New York. Dat's why he didn't come."

Ruth reassured William, saying, "Remember Holden Caulfield in *Catcher in the Rye*. It's okay!"

Slowly William stepped out of the limo. A few people stared at the foursome next to the limo, which was quite common in New York City, but what was uncommon was they wore Aloha wear.

"Are you from the tropics?" a porter asked as he continued placing the luggage on the baggage cart.

"Yes, we're from Hawaii," Ruth responded before addressing her entourage. "We've had a very long flight. Let's check in and get some rest."

"Can we see Times Square? Can we? Can we now, Mrs. Newcomb?"

"We'll explore tomorrow."

"Please?" William pleaded.

Auntie came to Williams' defense, "Da boy need to see Time Square at night. It unforgettable."

Ruth thought for a moment, then nodded, "Auntie's right. We'll go now." Ruth then addressed the porter, "Take these upstairs. We'll be back in a bit." The porter nodded. Ruth turned to the group, "Let's go." William, Auntie, and Danny followed Ruth out of the Marquis entrance area into Times Square, busy with cars and people rushing about. The lights of Times Square illuminated the group's awed faces.

"Here it is. This is Time Square."

William looked around the square, then up. "Da buildings are so tall! Higher than the waterfall in Waipio."

"Have you seen the New Year's ball dropping?" Ruth asked the group; all nodded. "It happens over there." Ruth pointed towards the One Times Square building.

People walked briskly by the foursome as they absorbed the Times Square commotion. Danny shook his head, "Too many people!"

Auntie added, "Dey too busy to enjoy life. Too, wikiwiki!"

"I don't think I like it here." William proclaimed.

"William, you just arrived. We are in the busiest area of New York. Central Park is not far from here and isn't anything like this." Ruth exclaimed to quell William's first impression of New York.

"I'm tired. Can we go to our room?" William responded.

* * *

The bellhop held the door for Ruth, Auntie, William, and Danny as they entered the enormous Presidential Suite.

Danny exclaimed, "I've never seen a hotel suite this big before."

"Dis is bigger than my house," William added.

Auntie spotted the grand piano. "Oh, a piano!"

"Where do I sleep? Da sofa?" Asked William. Ruth went to another door and opened it. "William, this is your room."

"I get my own room?"

"This is the presidential suite. We each have our own room."

* * *

The sunlight streamed through the trees on the *Tavern on the Green* patio dining area where Ruth was wearing a muumuu and Jim, Ruth's former television station owner, sat eating lunch.

"Ruth, the Emmys are this evening. No matter the outcome, I would like to offer you a contract."

"Jim, I don't want to accept your contract. Danny and I have a perfect one with Al."

"The one I am offering you is better."

"Jim, how do you know what I have with Al?"

"It's better. Trust me. The contract is for a show that is much more incredible than *From the Big Apple* or *From da Big Island* could be." Jim retorted as he took a sip from his

Manhattan. "It's an international travelogue-type show. I think you'll like the idea. You go to different places throughout the country and the world, showing us the out-of-the-way places to see. It's never been done before."

"It's an exciting idea, and I like my semiretired life in Hawaii."

"You like New York, too, don't you?"

Ruth gave a slight but noticeable nod.

"And you like Hawaii, don't you?"

"Of course, I do, Jim."

"It's the best of both worlds, Ruth. You can still live in Hawaii, come here, and do the show."

"The eleven-hour flights are too much for me, Jim."

"Eleven hours isn't that bad when you're traveling first class."

"I lose a day each way! Perhaps most of all, all those new post-9/11 restrictions are taking the fun out of air travel; like air travel was ever fun." Ruth quipped as they both laughed.

"It's an opportunity for you to reinvent yourself and make more money. Think about it, Ruth."

* * *

Auntie and William, both in Aloha wear and zoris, strolled through Central Park, walking by a pond loaded with ducks.

"William, you remember da duck pond in *Catcher in the Rye*?" William nodded as Auntie continued. "Dis is da duck pond."

"Der plenty of duck here." William retorted.

"What dat? It look like mongoose, but they climb trees!" William asked as he pointed towards a few small animals he had never seen before. They looked somewhat like a mongoose, but were darker and had bushy tails.

"Dey squirrel, dey all over da mainland."

Auntie and William continued their stroll through Central Park, absorbing the scenery around them, the ducks, the squirrels, the trees, and the people strolling. As they approached the *Alice in Wonderland* statue, they heard the familiar sounds of a ukulele strumming to an old Hawaiian song. A small crowd surrounded a Hawaiian man wearing an Aloha shirt and Rayban sunglasses. As Auntie and William approached the man, they recognized Michael, Ben's brother. Upon seeing Auntie and William, Michael stopped singing and strumming, "Auntie! William! Aaa-loooo-haa!"

"Aaa-loooo-haa!" they reply.

The crowd realized the music would not begin for a while and dropped a few coins and dollar bills into the ukulele case and continued their stroll through Central Park.

"What you do here?" Michael exclaimed.

"We here to see you, Michael," Auntie answered.

"You come all the way from da Big Island to see me?"

"Yups. We miss you. Ben and I need your kokua, Michael. It time you return to da island."

"I do okay here. I make plenny money." Michael tried to convince Auntie, who quickly realized he wasn't telling the truth.

"You make plenny money wid me on da island. You be mo happy."

"Ben misses you, and we need you in Hawaii," William added.

"Come back wid us." Auntie urged.

"Please." William pleaded.

* * *

That evening, the door to the Presidential Suite swung open by Danny holding an Emmy in one hand, the door in the other. Ruth entered carrying an Emmy. She was followed by Linda and Pauline, her sister and niece. Behind them followed Auntie and William, all wearing formalwear. Danny closed the door behind him. The group moved into the suite sitting on the sofa and in the chairs surrounding the coffee table.

"We knew you would win," Pauline exclaimed.

"Yeah, *From da Big Island* is da bomb," William added.

Ruth placed her Emmy on the coffee table. Danny put his next to hers.

"Don't they look great together?" exclaimed Danny. "I never knew they were as heavy as they are."

"That reminds me of the first time I won one. I almost dropped it on the stage."

"Aunt Ruth, Mother, and I remember our going to Sardi's after the ceremony. Are we going this evening?"

Linda added, "Darling, Sardi's is a great place to celebrate."

"It never entered my mind to celebrate at Sardi's," Ruth responded.

Linda and Pauline both made pouting faces. Linda attempted to convince Ruth, "Sis, you've been away too long. We always celebrated at Sardi's. Don't you miss it here, Darling?"

"I used to, but not anymore."

"Darling, Pauline said Jim was going to make you an offer. Did he?" Asked Linda.

"Yes, Linda, he did."

"Why don't you take it and move back here? You can stay with us until you find a place."

Pauline perked up. "Oh, Aunt Ruth, that would be simply fabulous. Did Jim tell you I'd be the producer of your show?"

"We discussed it."

William looked concerned, "Are you thinking of leaving us?"

"Oh, Luka, you can't." Exclaimed Auntie, "Think about us. Da island."

"What would dat do to *From da Big Island*?" Danny asked.

"I never said I accepted Jim's offer. Jim made an offer. I turned it down."

Linda was always against her younger sister moving to the Big Island, thinking it was foolish and Ruth's way to escape Zach's untimely death. Linda couldn't take it anymore, blurting, "Ruth, I've told you many times Hawaii is no better than a third-world country."

"It not bad!" Auntie proclaimed.

"Darling, the people are ill-educated."

"I'm almost educated." William added, "I graduate next month."

"All night, all I've been hearing is fragmented talk." Linda looked at Auntie, Danny, and William. "It's hard to understand you."

"It come wit time," retorted Auntie.

Linda looked at Ruth, "Darling, you see what I mean? And you are willing to put up with it?" Ruth nodded. "Come back here to civilized New York."

"I'm civilized." William exclaimed.

"Hawaii civilized." Auntie added.

"Darling, you call *that* language civilized?" Linda asked Auntie.

"What you say, sista?" Auntie quipped.

"Darling," Linda addressing Ruth, "that's my point exactly. Come back here. Listen to that deplorable language."

"What wrong wit pidgin?" inquired Auntie.

Linda directed her attack towards Auntie, "Darling, listen how you speak. No one with a real education speaks like that."

"Wat you mean, sista?"

"Darling," Linda addressed Auntie, "you need to come to the United States and get a real education."

Ruth became agitated with how her elder sister treated her Hawaiian ohana, especially Linda's latest United States statement.

"Linda, Hawaii *is* a state!" Ruth reminded Linda. "How do you know where Auntie was educated?"

"You go, sista!" Auntie encouraged Ruth.

Linda looked confused, directing her next question to Ruth, "Darling, what's going on?"

"I'll tell you what's going on, *darling*," Ruth responded, emphasizing the word darling. "Auntie speaks pidgin because she wants to speak that way, *darling*. She enjoys it, *darling*, and most of all, it is expected, *darling*. You can stop using that damn *darling* stuff because you cannot remember people's names. This is Auntie, this is William, and he is Danny." Pointing to each person as she says their names. All three smiled and gave Linda a howdy wave.

"Ruth, darling," Linda retorted, "you surround yourself with people like them. What kind of life is that?"

"It's the kind of life I need and want. I enjoy my life on da Big Island. I chose to live there, not because I have to because I like it there. I didn't know how much I liked it until this trip. New York no longer does it for me, all the rushing around and superficial people." Ruth motions and sweeps her hand toward Auntie, William, and Danny, continuing, "These people are my new family; the Hawaiians call it ohana. To put it succinctly, I have more friends on da Big Island than I ever had here in the Big Apple!"

Ruth looked at Auntie, William, and Danny, then at Linda and Pauline. "We have a long flight tomorrow. I don't want to go to Sardi's. It's late, and we need to rest before our long flight." Ruth stood. "Now, Linda and Pauline, let's call it an evening."

Linda got up, followed by Pauline. As they approached the door, Pauline asked, "Aunt Ruth, what about the show?"

"I am not going to do the show. Jim will find someone else. Pauline, you will still be the producer."

Pauline ran over and hugged Ruth. "I love you, Aunt Ruth."

DA BATTLE

Back on the Big Island, Ruth slept comfortably without the silk night mask. The sounds of grunting and popping were so loud it awakened her. She sat on the edge of the bed, slipped on her zoris, reached into her nightstand, took out her flashlight, and went to the closet and took out the rifle.

Using her flashlight to guide her, Ruth went through the orchard toward the grunting and scratching sounds. The flashlight illuminated a sizeable wild boar scratching the ground under a macadamia tree. With the flashlight in one hand and the rifle in the other, she raised the rifle feebly, took aim, and fired. The recoil of the rifle caused Ruth to drop the flashlight. When it landed, it illuminated the pig, who looked at her, grunted, then turned its attention to eat more fallen nuts.

A few moments later, in the distance, from the direction of Auntie's house, Ruth saw a figure with a sole flashlight approaching her. It was Auntie also carrying a flashlight and rifle. As Auntie approached, she yelled, "Luka, what da heck are you doing?"

"I'm going to get that damned pig!"

Auntie saw Ruth's flashlight illuminating the pig and directed her flashlight in the same direction as she approached Ruth.

"Thank God! I thought it was da local boys trying to steal my keiki's."

Ruth and Auntie laughed as the pig started to trot towards Auntie's.

"Oh, no!" Auntie exclaimed, "I don't want him to get into da keiki's; he'll go lolo."

Ruth could more accurately aim the rifle toward the pig using the light from Auntie's flashlight, which was following the pig. Carefully, she pulled the trigger.

* * *

Ruth, Auntie, and Ben were seated in lounge chairs on Auntie's lanai, each sipping red punch and enjoying brownies.

"We tell no one that Luka kill pig," stated Auntie.

"Luka, you in plenny trouble," Ben added.

"Trouble?"

"We next to state park. You can only kill pig with bow and arrow. We need to get rid of da evidence."

"Evidence?" Ruth inquired.

"Da pig!" Auntie and Ben exclaimed.

After a moment, Auntie smiled and proclaimed, "We have luau!"

DA GRADUATION

A large green and white *Congratulations* *Graduates* sign hung from the Honoka'a Gymnasium rafters. The bleachers filled with family members. Among them seated together were Ruth, Ben, Auntie, Danny, Nalani, and Meka. Mickey and another cameraman, wearing black *From da Big Island* T-shirts, filmed the graduation.

On the court facing the bleachers were forty empty seats and a podium. Michael, Ben's brother, holds his ukulele off to one side, maintaining a close watch behind the bleachers. He got the signal and started strumming and singing Queen Liliuokalani's *Aloha Oe*. Everyone stood as the students dressed in green graduation regalia and gold tassels hanging from their green mortarboard graduation caps walked from behind the stands to the seating area. William was amongst the proud students who waved at their families and friends.

* * *

The school's valedictorian had finished her speech and was returning to her seat from the podium. Mrs. Strong, wearing a green and white muumuu, returned to the podium and announced, "And now for our most improved graduate, William Ayala. Please approach the podium." The audience clapped as William proudly rose and walked to the podium. "Not only is he the most improved student," Mrs. Strong continued, "he is the first member of his family to graduate from high school." The crowd clapped and whistled as he made his way to the podium.

When William approached the podium, Mrs. Strong extended her right hand. William shook it. In her left hand was a plaque. The *From da Big Island* video crew captured the event as the high school and news photographers snapped Mrs. Strong's award presentation to William. Mrs. Strong moved back to the podium. "William, would you like to say a few words?"

"Yes, Mrs. Strong." William faced the crowd, specifically addressing his parents and Ruth in the stands. "I want to thank my mother and father. They had to put up with a lot from me." There was laughter throughout the crowd. "But most of all, I want to thank Mrs. Strong, Dr. Tilton, Auntie, and Mrs. Newcomb for helping me get here." William winked at Ruth and Auntie. "Ma-ha-lo."

William started to turn to leave the podium but quickly returned. "Oh, I almost forgot. Da pig for tonight's luau is from Mrs. Newcomb. Ma-ha-lo."

* * *

Later that evening, Mickey and the *From da Big Island* video crew were shooting the graduation luau festivities in Honoka'a Park, picnic tables filled with graduates, ohana, and friends. Tiki torches illuminated the *Congratulations Graduates* sign, which hung between two palms. Michael was among a group of performers who provided Hawaiian music for the graduation celebration.

Folding tables were filled with all the trimmings of a luau; one had chicken, the partially eaten pig, hamburger buns, and an assortment of utensils to cut and pull the pork off the pig.   Another table had poi, brownies, other desserts, plates, glasses, and giant five gallon jugs filled with red punch.

One picnic table had William, his parents, Nalani, and Meka on one side, the other his ohana and friends, Ruth, Auntie, Ben, and Danny, and all were enjoying the pig and all the trimmings.

"Ben, I still don't understand where da pig come from." Meka probed.

"Meka, I told you da pig kill Luka's cat. I use crossbow and kill da pig." Ben responded.

"You never use crossbow for pig before."

Ruth interjected, "There is always a first time for anything, isn't there?" She then used her spoon to eat what looked like purple pudding. This was the first time Ruth had poi. Upon tasting it, she grimaced. "This pudding is funny tasking. What is this purple stuff?"

"It poi." Nalani answered, "No use spooooon! Use finger like this." She brought her fore and middle fingers together and showed Ruth how to scoop up and suck the poi off her fingers.

"It called two-finger poi!" Added William.

At that moment, Mickey arrived at the table, motioning to Danny that he was set up for the closing. Danny looked at Ruth, "Luka, they are ready for you to shoot da closing."

Ruth looked at Mickey, "Bring the camera over here. I want to shoot my poi lesson before we do da closing."

"Luka, I'm already set up for da closing. Can we shoot that first, then shoot the poi sequence?" Mickey retorted.

"That will work for me."

Ruth and Danny got up, heading to where Mickey had set up the camera. He handed Ruth a wireless Lavaliere microphone which she put on her muumuu. As she did, she tells Mickey and Danny, "I don't want to do a run-through. Let's shoot it."

Mickey pointed the camera at Ruth, who was standing looking into the camera. Mickey gave Ruth the signal to start.

Ruth smiled, "We learned a lot in this episode, including how to eat poi. I want to dedicate this episode to William Ayala. I know he has a great future ahead of him. Until next time, this is Luka Newcomb, *From da Big Island*. Aaa-loooo-haa!"

NOVEL

EPILOGUE

In the years that followed my high school graduation, Luka, Auntie, and the Baccios provided for my college education in English Literature here on the islands and then my journalism master's at USC in California. Between my studies, I was always able to find time to surf. I documented my adventures in my surfing blog, which *Surfer* magazine liked and later contracted me to write surfing articles. I posted short surfing videos on YouTube. Luka loved my videos and arranged to have me do a few surfing segments for *From da Big Island.* This gave me public speaking confidence and on-camera experience, opening doors for me. The surfing videos quickly morphed into *Da Wave with William* television show produced by Pauline, Luka's niece. I still travel around the world doing the things I love. None of this would have happened without the help of my ohana, Luka, Auntie, Charlene Strong, Dr. Tilton, and my folks.

Due to the escalation of the pig issue following my high school graduation, Ben and Michael built fences around Luka's, Auntie's, and my folk's property. Sometimes, when a sounder of pigs breach one of our fences, Ben will dispatch them and fix the damage. Ben continues to help Luka and Auntie. In addition to helping Ben with his projects, Michael has a regular gig playing at luaus and hukilaus, and he is happy to have returned to the Big Island.

Joe and Eileen Baccio return to the Big Island a few times a year, primarily during the winter, and stay for a month or two at their Waikoloa Beach vacation home. Unlike Michael Corleone of *The Godfather* fame, Joe got out of the mob, went legit, and became a proponent for legalizing medicinal marijuana.

Auntie's medicinal marijuana research continued as she developed hybrid cannabis strains that increased potency and helped patients deal with pain without the psychotropic effects associated with marijuana. Many states have legalized medicinal marijuana, while others have legalized its recreational use.

The call of the island was also felt by Gloria La Fong, who regularly returned over the years before retiring in Kona.

Luka was happy with her decision years ago to move out of her comfort zone and do something she had never done before; having the courage to take that chance and not be afraid of the unknown made her move to the Big Island of Hawaii.

Luka eventually fully retired from show business, enjoying her retirement at Hale Newcomb. Once a month, she had *Girl's Day Out,* when Luka, Auntie, Gloria, and Charlene would get together and have lunch at an old favorite or new restaurant, discussing books they had read and updating each other on what was happening.

Luka became a well-known figure at the local libraries on the islands with her *Reading with Luka* program, where she would read a chapter from a book or have a visiting author

NOVEL

read, but most of all encouraged everyone to read. She always ended her reading program like her television shows, "Reading is an adventure. Until next time. This is Luka Newcomb, Aaa-loooo-haa!"

NOVEL

Glossary

The words below are utilized within this book and are intended to provide a basic reference. As with translations of any language, these words may have a more complex or multiple meanings. Not all pidgin words will be listed, especially when the English word can be readily recognizable, such as da for the, den for then, dey for they, dis for this, and the like.

Aloha shirt: A man's Hawaiian shirt
Aloha: Hello or farewell
CEO: Chief Executive Officer
Da Boss: God
Da Bomb: The best
Gut: Good
Hale: House
Haole: White people or tourist
Hukilau: A beach celebration involving catching and cooking fish and other foods with live music and dance
Hula: Hawaiian dance
Imu: Hawaiian underground oven
Kahuna: An expert in a field or a Wiseman
Kam: Come
Kama'aina: A local person
Keiki: Child or little one
Kiawe: Mesquite tree
Klinim: Clean
Kokua: Help
Laikem: Like them
Lanai: Porch or veranda
Lei: A necklace of Hawaiian flowers

Lolo: Crazy or Loko

Luau: A large outdoor party with live music and dance generally with pig cooked in an Imu

Luka: Ruth in Hawaiian

Mahalo: Thank you

Mauka: Mountain or uphill side

Missionary dress: A long loose fitting dress with long sleeves and a high neck

Mo betta: More better

Mongoose: A long slender mammal that looks somewhat like a squirrel with short legs and a faintly bushy tail

Muumuu: Cut-off also a Missionary dress with short or no sleeves and an exposed neck

Nau: Now

Néné: Hawaiian geese

Nidim: Need them

Nui: Great, big, grand, much

Ohana: Extended Hawaiian Family

Pakalolo: Marijuana

Paniolo: Cowboy

Plenny: Plenty

Poi: A purple edible paste made from mashed, fermented taro root

Shi-shi: Urinate or use the bathroom

Slippahs: Slippers, zoris, flip-flops, sandals, or other slip-on footwear

To da max: To go all out

Ukulele: A small four-stringed Hawaii guitar

Wikiwiki: Super-fast

Wok: Work

Zoris: Flip-flops, slippahs, go-aheads

NOTES

NOVEL

NOTES

NOVEL